DON'T
EVEN
BREATHE

DON'T EVEN BREATHE

KEITH HOUGHTON

Text copyright © 2019 by Keith Houghton
All rights reserved.

Published by Thomas & Mercer, Seattle

www.apub.com

Amazon, the Amazon logo, and Thomas & Mercer are trademarks of Amazon.com, Inc., or its affiliates.

ISBN-13: 9781503900912
ISBN-10: 1503900916

Cover design by Ghost Design

Printed in the United States of America

For Lynn
My beautiful wife
For giving me wings and for keeping me grounded

Chapter One

LINDY MUNSON MUST DIE

Long before she'd agreed to go on a date with him, Tyler had known he would kill Lindy Munson.

One day. Somehow. Preferably slowly.

For years, whenever Tyler had thought of the girl with the sallow complexion and the snow-white hair, he'd fantasized about doing something bad to her—probably from as far back as the sixth grade and the very first time she'd caught him studying her from across the school cafeteria.

Long-legged Lindy, with her teasing personality and her annoying popularity. A throat that was ripe for strangling.

Back then, Tyler had meant nothing to her. Not even an irritation. Something less than human. He'd been invisible, her gaze penetrating right through him, as though he didn't exist. It was a look of absolute indifference that had gobbled up every bit of his universe, until all that had remained was Lindy the Langolier eating into his brain.

Tyler couldn't recall the exact moment he'd decided to kill the most popular girl in school. The cafeteria incident had been the first of many, with Lindy's continued aloofness consuming him through the years.

What would it take to make her notice him?

Tyler had asked himself this question countless times during the past four years of high school, usually when he was lying awake at night and visualizing all the ways he could make Lindy *see* him. He'd lost track of how many abduction scenarios he'd planned out in fine detail, and what he'd do to her once they were finally alone together.

Tyler's stomach clenched as he glanced at the girl sitting next to him in the passenger seat of his Dodge Charger, her hands tapping along to the song on the radio. Her long smooth legs seemed to bend in the middle without any hint of knees, and her elbows seemed equally inconspicuous. Lindy Munson was a living, breathing Barbie doll, and although her curves were subtle, she knew how to make boys notice them. But as with most things made of cheap plastic, they could snap easily.

"Is this your first time?" she asked him as he parked the car so that it faced an area of undeveloped land opposite the high school, its headlights stirring up ghoulish shadows in the trees.

Far too loudly and far too quickly, Tyler laughed a "No!" as though her question was totally insane and without merit, because *of course* he did this kind of thing with a different girl every night of the week. *Duh!*

"It's okay if it is," she said, unbuckling her seat belt and smiling at him through her sticky red lip gloss. "I'll make it memorable."

Tyler had to suppress the urge to rip the self-serving grin off her face.

Even though they had been in the car for some time now, negotiating the evening traffic and making light chitchat, Tyler was still slightly disbelieving that the girl of his bad dreams was here in the flesh, and a blaze of unexpected nerves still burned in his belly.

She'd texted him:

Meet me outside Family Dollar @ 7

And he'd picked her up, teeth brushed, deodorized, his nerves through the roof as Lindy had gotten into his car.

Nobody had seen them leave the strip mall parking lot on Pine Hills Road—the most popular girl in school driving away with *him*. Everything was still a blur.

To avoid traffic cameras, Tyler had deliberately taken a circuitous route, keeping to the speed limits all the way. He'd kept their date a secret, and he doubted Lindy had shared their Saturday night rendezvous with any of her judgmental BFFs.

As far as everybody was concerned, Tyler was the last person in the world whom Lindy would be hanging out with on Halloween.

It couldn't have worked out better.

"I know this cool place in the woods," Lindy said, her long fingers curling around the door handle while her other hand pushed the door fully open. "It'll be perfect." She climbed out, fingertips sliding along the passenger window and leaving tracks.

He'd have to wipe away her grease. Wipe her off the face of the earth while he was at it.

Lindy continued around to the grass in front of the car. Tyler watched, a low rumble in the back of his throat as she raised her arms, dancing in the mote-filled headlights, her pointy breasts gyrating against her red tank top, her whole elasticated body swaying and twisting.

Lindy the temptress.

She looked like a girl in a James Bond title sequence, the one who ended up dead in the first act.

Tyler had fire in his belly.

Working on the problem of how to dispose of Lindy Munson's body had tested him, forcing adjustments in his plan, until he was confident he had it right.

In any populated area, completely disposing of a corpse in such a way that it would remain forever undiscovered was likely impossible. There was always the chance that some incriminating part of it would turn up unexpectedly and point an accusing finger at him. Bury it in a shallow grave, and there would always be that pesky one-in-a-million dog that would come snuffling along and dig up a bone. Submerge it in water, and gaseous decomposition would break it apart, bits of it bubbling to the surface, where it could become snagged on fishing hooks. Even feeding it into a wood chipper would spray a ton of blood evidence all over the place. Besides which, the mainstream media had introduced the world to the power of police forensics, and Tyler knew for a fact that if he wanted to get away with Lindy's murder, he'd have to make her disappear in a puff of smoke.

Then, at some point, he'd realized he didn't need to dispose of the body at all, just burn it. Toast marshmallows while Lindy fried. And that was why he'd also stashed a can of gasoline in the trunk, because fire was the only guaranteed way to destroy DNA evidence. Every last bit of it.

Lindy summoned him with a wave of her hand. "Come on," she called. She turned, skipping along a sandy trail that snaked downslope across the grass.

Tyler killed the engine and the headlights died.

Then, beneath the dusk-bruised sky, he followed her toward the woods, his legs a little wobbly at first, but strengthening with each stride. Becoming purposeful. He'd waited years for this moment. This could be *as alone* as the two of them might ever come to be. It was now, or maybe never.

The sandy trail headed downhill sharply before disappearing into the trees. He fumbled his way through clawing branches and around prickly undergrowth.

"Right this way," he heard her say from a dozen yards ahead.

Stoked by the anticipation of what was to come, Tyler picked up the pace, closing in on her, the fire in his belly spreading into his chest, fueling him, igniting him, propelling him.

No more humiliation.

No more Mr. Invisible.

No more Lindy Munson.

Hurrah!

All he could think about was wrapping his hands around Lindy's scrawny neck and squeezing the life out of her. The feel of her flesh under his hands. The quickening of her pulse. The sheer terror in her widening eyes as she realized what was happening to her. The heaving of her breasts as she struggled to breathe. Her nipples hard and erect. Strangling her slowly, maybe not even ending it right away, but rather letting her revive, over and over, each time with her knowing that the next throttling could be her last.

Making her *see* him.

Adrenalized, Tyler crashed through the undergrowth after her, his breath hastening and his senses sharpening.

"Hold up!" he shouted.

She did, and in just a few seconds he caught up.

She faced him on the path, nibbling her lower lip, giggling as she reached out and placed her hand on the hardening bulge in his pants. "Patience," she tittered, her smile growing into a whorish grin. "Don't jump the gun, little boy. We're almost there. I promise it'll be worth the wait."

But Tyler couldn't contain himself anymore.

His vision pulsated.

His ears rang.

He was about to *burst*!

Before she could lead on, he brought up his fist and cuffed her on the chin, hard enough to send her staggering backward. Even in the poor light, he saw confusion twist her face.

Was she beginning to see the real him for the first time?

With hooked fingers, he reached out for her again.

This time, Lindy turned and ran.

And Tyler gave chase.

Chapter Two

THE SWEET SPOT

Maggie Novak stood her ground as a youth wearing a *Scream* mask and brandishing a chef's knife hustled toward her on the street. She curled her fingers around the broomstick in her hands and glowered from under the brim of her witch hat, refusing to budge. Had this been any other night, and had Maggie been better armed, she would have drawn her police-issue .45-caliber Glock 21 and instructed him to lay down his weapon and remove his mask. As it was, she decided her aversion to Halloween had never been more justified than right here, right now.

"The least you can do is try and *look* like you're enjoying yourself."

The remark came from Maggie's sister, Nora, as they watched Whitney, Nora's five-year-old daughter, scamper from door to door, collecting candy in a jack-o'-lantern bucket. All across the twilit neighborhood, homeowners had transformed their front yards into illuminated scenes of horror, in which hordes of costume-clad children scurried from one hellish haven to the next.

"It's not like Halloween comes around every weekend," Nora continued.

Maggie thought that once a year was once too much, but she knew better than to say it out loud. There were many things that she and

Nora disagreed on, but now wasn't the time to get into another fruit-less debate.

Instead, Maggie pointed the tip of the broomstick at her sister's blue gingham dress, saying, "Remind me again why I have to be the wicked witch while you get to be Dorothy?"

"Because you hate *The Wizard of Oz*."

"I hate Halloween even more."

Nora gave Maggie a weary half smile, the same expression their mother had made whenever Maggie had disappointed her, which had been often. "Anyway, sis," Nora said, "you look hot in all that lace."

Maggie ran a finger around the neck of the costume. "That's because I'm overheating. It must be ninety degrees out here." Even in late October, Florida evenings could be hot and muggy, and tonight seemed to be prov-ing the point. Couple the lingering heat with the cheap polyester, and she pictured herself spontaneously combusting at any second.

Nora sighed. "It'll be over soon enough. Then you can be wherever it is you've got to be."

"I'm here because I want to be here."

Maggie's phone rang.

Nora shook her head. "We'll see about that."

Frowning, Maggie unclipped her phone from the elastic armband she wore over her dress sleeve. "I need to take this," she said, squinting at the caller ID.

"Then I guess I'll see you later, sis."

"Don't be like that. I'll catch up."

Nora looked doubtful. "We both know that's not going to happen. When duty calls, my big sister always comes running." She leaned over and kissed Maggie on the cheek. "Just do what you need to do. I'll try and let Whitney down gently."

Maggie watched her walk away, feeling torn. She put the phone to her ear. "Novak."

The call was from Detective Sergeant Lenny Smits, Maggie's immediate superior at the Orange County Sheriff's Office, otherwise known as OCSO.

"Detective Novak," he said, mispronouncing her name as *Nofack*, in the way that he always did. "You stealing children's candy again?"

Smits had been her Major Case Section superior since she'd joined Homicide Squad five years ago. For the most part, Smits was a cheerless bureaucrat, and although he did socialize with his underlings on occasion, she knew he hardly ever made social calls, and especially not on the weekend.

"Drop what you're doing," he continued. "I need you on a dead body at Lake Apopka. ASAP."

Maggie couldn't help smiling at Smits's phrasing. Even though his vocabulary was extensive, Smits wasn't known for his elaboration or his eloquence when using it. He spoke like a gangster from a B movie. And he had yet to figure out that this was the reason people smirked when he was being serious.

Maggie pulled off the witch hat. "Have you informed Loomis?"

"He's en route. Five minutes out. When can we expect you to join him?"

Maggie glanced at her car in Nora's driveway. The black Mustang convertible was less than two weeks old, and Maggie was still in that any-excuse-for-a-drive mode. "Well, let's see. I'm at my sister's place right now. I'll need to change. Give me twenty minutes?"

"Make it fifteen," he said and hung up.

Maggie hurried inside Nora's house, dumping the broom and the hat in the hallway, collecting her handgun and badge from Nora's designated safe place. It was her weekend on call, and she never went anywhere unprepared. She'd learned from that particular mistake the first week on the job, turning up at a crime scene unprepared, without so much as her police badge to make her attendance official. Smits, as cuddly as a cactus, had told her to get her act together or reconsider her career options. These days, Maggie never went anywhere without the full kit and caboodle.

She called Loomis on speakerphone while she changed, swapping out the dress for the black shirt and skinny jeans she'd worn earlier.

"Happy Halloween," Loomis said in his usual deadpan tone as he answered. "Remind me next year to electrify the doorbell."

"You wouldn't."

"Watch me. I will only be pushed so far to part with candy, Novak."

Maggie smiled as she pulled on her knee-high boots.

Ed Loomis had spent six years as an undercover narcotics cop in New York City before switching direction and relocating to Orlando to work Homicide four years ago. At first, Maggie had had reservations about their compatibility. She'd heard on the grapevine that Loomis was difficult to work with, hotheaded, but Maggie's fears had proved unfounded.

Loomis had turned out to be a gentle soul, on an even keel, and they'd gelled from the moment they met.

"This dead body," Maggie said as she zipped up the boots. "What are we looking at?"

"All I know is it's female and located on public land in back of Ocoee Parkway."

Maggie glanced at the holstered handgun on the arm of the chair next to her, a coolness forming in her belly. "Near the high school?"

"I guess. You familiar?"

"Kind of." She hung her badge on its necklace around her neck. "How'd we come to hear about it?"

"From a nine-one-one. Some local kid by the name of Pratt or Provitt, or something equally forgettable. You know what I'm like with names, Novak. At any rate, dispatch sent deputies, who have since confirmed the kid's story. There's a DB and we're the DB police."

Maggie scooped up the Glock and headed outside.

The swarms of costumed kids were way down the street, Nora and Whitney nowhere in sight.

"Listen, Novak," Loomis said as she got in the Mustang and fired it up, "I know it's our weekend to bail out the boat and all, but I'm mindful of your family commitments. If you want to get back to the party, I'm happy to go Han Solo on this. Let you pick up the slack in the morning."

Maggie recoiled at the idea. "Are you kidding me?" she said as she backed the car out of the driveway. "I would've gladly traded a kidney to get out of this gig."

There was a pause; then Loomis said, "Maggie Novak. You are one wicked aunt."

"You don't know the half of it. See you there in ten."

◆ ◆ ◆

Exactly nine minutes later, Maggie left the highway after the sign for Crown Pointe High School and followed Ocoee Parkway as it curved into darkness. She came to a small roundabout and went right, then hit the brakes, throwing herself forward against the seat belt, suddenly in no rush to reach her destination.

Less than one hundred yards ahead, flashing police lights projected red-and-blue specters on the curbside trees. Half a dozen EMS vehicles, including a big red Ocoee FD ambulance, were crowding the roadway leading to the school. Fifty yards away, where yellow-and-black police tape was strung across the full width of the road, a white sheriff's cruiser was parked at an angle across the lanes. Slightly closer still, a gray mini-van was parked against the curb.

Although Ocoee Parkway had been rerouted since the last time she'd been here, the sudden feeling of familiarity was striking, overwhelming even, and the coolness still lingering in her belly grew into a chill.

"Get a grip," she told herself. "It was a lifetime ago."

Even so, Maggie's sudden sense of dread was real, and it required focus to push down the memories trying to claw their way to the surface.

Not now.

A deputy sheriff spotted her car loitering at the roundabout and began to walk toward her, waving his flashlight. Maggie drove toward him, pulling up behind the minivan. The deputy looked to be thirtyish, with a crispness to his olive-green shirt that spoke more of his obsessiveness than it did his pride in wearing the uniform.

"Ma'am," he said as she climbed out, "I'm afraid you can't be here. We have a situation back there. You're going to have to get back in your vehicle and . . ." His words trailed off as his flashlight blinded her. "Detective Novak?"

She squinted from behind her hand. "It's me. Can you . . . ?"

He lowered the flashlight. "I apologize, ma'am. I didn't recognize you there for a second. Not with all the"—he rotated a finger—"Halloween stuff going on."

In her haste to ditch the dress, Maggie had completely forgotten to wipe away the gothic makeup that Nora had insisted on applying, as though the witch costume hadn't been torture enough. Added to the white forelock sprayed into her dark hair, and it was no wonder the deputy hadn't recognized her right away.

She blinked at the afterimages flashing in her vision. "It's Deputy Ramos, right?"

He seemed surprised that she remembered his name, and maybe even a little flattered. With more than one thousand active deputies spread across the county, her recognizing him by sight alone must have seemed impressive.

But Maggie had a *thing* for faces.

"How's your little boy?" she asked.

Now, his surprise was even more conspicuous.

"Doing great," he said, face brightening. "Thanks for asking. His doctors expect a full recovery."

"That's wonderful."

She'd first met Deputy Ramos about six months ago at a suicide by hanging in Azalea Park. At that point, he'd been on patrol less than a week, unlucky enough to be the first responder at the scene. She remembered his pallor that day being as green as his uniform, but not because of the young man's body hanging from the light fixture. That same week, Ramos's five-year-old son had been diagnosed with a critical illness, and things had been touch and go.

Maggie knotted her flyaway hair into a loose ponytail. "You're the responding officer on this one, too?"

"Yes, ma'am."

"Happy for me to take over as officer in charge?"

"Absolutely." It looked like a weight had lifted off his shoulders. "It's all yours." He gestured for her to take the lead, and they began to make their way toward the cordon.

Maggie stole a peek inside the minivan as they passed, noting the child seats in the back and the tiny overlapping handprints on the glass.

"When did you get here?"

"Approximately fifty minutes ago. I took brief statements, after which I secured the scene and contacted dispatch to notify Deathtectives."

Maggie smiled at his remark.

Deathtectives was the team name that Homicide Squad had adopted during an internal softball tournament a few years back, and it had stuck. There was even a trophy in the department cafeteria with the word *Deathtectives* engraved on its silver plaque. Some of her colleagues in Homicide Squad objected to the nickname, saying it diminished the department's stature, but Maggie thought the nickname gave the squad added gravitas.

Don't mess with the Deathtectives.

She clipped her holstered gun to her belt. "It was a local kid who called it in, right?"

"Yes, ma'am. His name's Tyler Pruitt."

"What do we know about this Tyler Pruitt?"

"Seventeen. Lives in Pine Hills. In his senior year, here at Crown Pointe."

Maggie switched her gaze to the dark outline of the high school across the street, partially obscured by foliage and the fading light. As with the roadway leading here, the school had been completely rebuilt from scratch in recent years, and then renamed. Its shapes and angles were strange to her, and yet the mere sight of it compounded the coolness in her belly.

"The girl's name is Lindy Munson."

Maggie swung her gaze back to the deputy. "She's the victim?"

For a second, the deputy looked confused. "No, ma'am. Munson is Pruitt's girlfriend. Also seventeen and also from Pine Hills. She's the one who found the body."

"But it was Tyler who raised the alarm?"

"Yes, ma'am."

Maggie made a mental note to listen to the 911 call. Valuable information could be gleaned from the words people chose to use in an emergency situation, and those they didn't.

"Did Lindy say how she came to find the body?" she asked as they ducked under the police tape.

"She's a mess. Not saying much. Aside from her details, I couldn't get anything else out of her."

They arrived at the sheriff's cruiser, its flashing lights dazzling.

"So what were they doing out here, Lindy and Tyler?"

The deputy opened the driver's door. "I couldn't get a straight answer on that one. But my guess is, they were being typical teenagers—if you catch my drift. Pruitt's car is parked near the head of the trail." He reached inside and reemerged holding a clipboard. "This road is one big loop, but it dead-ends at the school. Once the caretakers are done for the day, pretty much nobody comes down here after dark."

"Except for hormonal teenagers and murderers." Maggie saw his mouth open and close in response to her comment. She took the clipboard from his hand. "Where's the body located?"

"Down by the lake."

"The clearing?" The chill in Maggie's belly expanded into her chest.

"There's a trail," he said. "It leads through the woods to the water's edge. Even with a flashlight, it's a little tricky to navigate."

She knew it well, but didn't share the information. She wrote her name below Loomis's on the sign-in sheet, jotting down her time of arrival. "Did they say how often they come down here after school?"

"She says often. He says never."

"Okay." Maggie handed back the clipboard. "Let's speak with the kids."

Tyler Pruitt and Lindy Munson were sitting underneath the raised trunk of a white Ford Explorer with green Sheriff's Office decals. Two deputies stood at one side. The teenagers hadn't been separated, but there was a noticeable gap between them.

Maggie showed them her badge on the end of the chain necklace. "Detective Novak. Orange County Sheriff's Office. Everyone okay here?"

No response.

Maggie took out her phone and opened the camera app. "Okay. I know this has been a difficult evening for you guys, and I'm mindful of it. But your ongoing cooperation and patience is appreciated."

Again, neither of the teenagers responded to her introduction.

It looked like it would be one of those nights.

The girl was a leggy blonde with tear-swollen eyes and an angry graze on her chin. She had on a red tank top and a short denim skirt, and she was shivering despite the evening heat.

Maggie snapped a picture with her phone.

The boy was thick-set from the waist up, with an unruly mop of dark hair and a prominent chin that was probably the product of an underbite. He had on a navy-blue Crown Pointe sweatshirt and cream pants, his arms folded defensively across his chest.

"What's with the photo?" he asked.

"Reference material." Maggie checked the image quality before switching the camera app to video mode. "Plus, memory can be unreliable. It's the reason why I'm also going to record this."

"Isn't that a violation of our rights?" he said.

"Not at all. There's no expectation of privacy here."

The boy looked slightly disappointed, probably because his smart comment hadn't proven smart enough. Maggie saw his jaw muscles clench, and right away she had a handle on the kind of person Tyler Pruitt was: a kid with a box of matches and a fascination with fire.

Maggie positioned the phone so that both teenagers were in the frame. "Okay," she said, starting the video recorder. "Let's get down to business. The sooner we're done here, the sooner we can get you both home. First things first. Can you confirm your names for me?"

The boy scowled. "We did that already."

"I need for you to do it again." She saw his lips narrow into a defiant line. "But if it's too much trouble, Deputy Ramos here can give you a ride back to the Sheriff's Office. Get all your details on record. Could take the best part of the night, though."

"Tyler Pruitt," he snapped.

"What's your address, Tyler?"

Instead of vocalizing it, he dug a hand into a pocket and produced his driver's license, which he angled in front of Maggie's phone. "There. Now can we get out of here?"

"Soon." Maggie turned her attention to the girl. "It's Lindy, right? Lindy Munson?"

The girl glanced up again, her gaze snagging on the phone before finding its way to Maggie's face. She looked like she'd had the fright of her life and couldn't stop thinking about it.

Maggie hadn't forgotten the first time she'd seen a dead body, and the sight of it had disturbed her sleep for weeks. Even now, hundreds of dead bodies later, the memory of that first time still haunted her more than any other.

Maggie positioned her phone closer to the girl's face, focusing on the welt on her chin. "That's a nasty-looking scuff you've got there, Lindy. How'd you come by it?"

For the briefest moment, the girl glanced sidelong at Tyler, as though seeking his permission to answer, or looking at him to step in and save her.

"She fell," he said, his own gaze never moving from Maggie. "It was an accident. When we saw that *thing*, we just ran. Lindy caught her foot on a tree root."

"Is that right, Lindy? Did you fall?"

The girl seemed to think about it for a second; then she nodded stiffly. "Please," she said, her voice barely audible, her gaze imploring. "I just want to go home." Then she started to sob, her whole frame shaking.

Maggie stopped the recording. "Okay. Clearly, this isn't working. How about we continue with this tomorrow, after you guys have slept and things aren't quite so raw?"

This time, they both responded with a nod.

"But I will need you both to come down to the Sheriff's Office to provide separate statements. We'll also need you to provide exemplars while you're there."

"Exemplars?" the boy asked.

"Samples of your fingerprints, hair, footprints, that kind of thing."

"Why?"

"To rule you out of the crime scene evidence we collect. We'll also need the clothes you have on right now, tonight, before you leave."

The boy's scowl returned. The girl just sobbed some more.

"Don't worry," Maggie said. "We'll get you fixed up with throw-away coveralls. You can get changed one at a time in the ambulance." She handed them each a business card. "I'll expect to see you with your parents at the Sheriff's Office. The address is on the card. Let's say twelve noon. Any problems, you call the number right there. In the meantime, once you're both changed, we'll give you a ride home." She saw the boy's expression switch from aggravated to stressed.

"Thanks, but I'll drive myself," he said.

"I'm afraid we can't let you do that, Tyler."

"What?" Now he looked appalled.

Maggie thumbed over her shoulder. "See the police cordon on the way down here? It means your vehicle is technically inside a crime scene. Leave your keys with Deputy Ramos here, and we'll get your vehicle back to you tomorrow, just as soon as it's been cleared."

"No way!" He dropped to his feet. "How am I supposed to get around?"

"I'm sure you can use your imagination, or even the bus." Maggie turned to Ramos. "Can I borrow your flashlight?"

"Sure." He handed it over.

"Where's Detective Loomis?"

"Lakeside, as far as I know."

"Okay. These two are all yours."

The boy glared at Maggie as she walked away.

A dozen yards behind the EMS ensemble, a dusky-red Dodge Charger was parked half on the curb, at the head of a sandy trail that snaked down a steep grassy slope before disappearing into a densely wooded copse.

Maggie hesitated with one foot on the roadside grass, the other still rooted to the pavement, her heart suddenly thudding.

Twenty years ago, this whole area had been untamed brush, the trail winding through it like a maze. A decade later, the school's remodelers had scraped away the unsightly shrubbery, introducing the prettier Bahia grass. But the original path remained, like a stubborn scar, enticing teenagers into the woods.

Maggie followed it, her footfalls heavy, the chill in her chest reaching for her throat.

A spell of afternoon rain had left the ground soft, spongy, and each step was heavier than normal, as though gravity was stronger here. She could smell the stale dampness characteristic of swampland, and a trace of something else. Something like charcoal infused in the humid air.

At the entrance to the woods, more police tape was strung between the trees. Maggie hesitated again, her sense of dread on the rise.

"You're being ridiculous," she told herself quietly as she ducked under the tape. "Pull yourself together."

Easier said than done.

She had memories of this place that she couldn't fully dismiss. Memories that were bittersweet at best.

The flashlight chased shadows through the trees. Maggie followed the trail as it zigzagged between the prickly palmetto, trying to focus on the task ahead instead of what she'd left behind. Eventually she came across Loomis pacing back and forth at the edge of a clearing. When he heard her approaching, he blew out a sigh of relief.

"Thought you'd stood me up," he said, focusing his own flashlight on her. At six feet four and 180 pounds, Loomis was the definition of gangling. "Broomstick troubles?"

Maggie grimaced playfully. "Don't even go there. I was *this* close to being Dorothy."

"What stopped you?"

"A dress size and a baby sister. What monster were you tonight?"

"Myself." He raked his fingers through his dirty-blond hair. "Don't give me that look, Novak. The twins have just turned one. They can wait at least another year before I introduce them to devil worship." From his pocket, he handed her a pair of blue plastic overshoes and latex gloves.

"Your turn will come," Maggie said as she slipped them on.

"I am in no doubt. Until then, the candy is all mine." He hoisted up the police tape. "After you."

At first glance, the sandy clearing didn't appear to have changed much since Maggie had last been here. Maybe a little smaller than she remembered, a little more overgrown, but essentially the same hollow dome of hooked trees and tangled vines with a circular opening on the far side, where a mud beach gave way to black water. Even twenty years ago, no one had known whether the clearing that everybody knew as *Devil's Landing* was man made or a natural formation. Back then, she and her fellow high school seniors had hung out here, smoking pot and playing hooky. Judging from the empty beer bottles and fast-food cartons scattered around its periphery, the clearing was still as popular as ever.

"Welcome to the love nest"—Loomis aimed his flashlight at the center of the clearing—"where there's nothing like a dead body to dull the mood."

Working homicide for the last five years had desensitized Maggie to the sight of dead bodies. It was inevitable. Corpses came with the job. On any given week, Homicide Squad averaged a dozen new callouts, with at least one of those turning out to be a new murder case. On a regular basis, people turned up dead in a variety of ways—mangled, decapitated, mutilated, shot, crushed, exploded, decomposing, mostly due to natural causes, some through accidents, one or two in suspicious circumstances—but this was the one type that Maggie always felt hardest to stomach.

The body was on its back on the sand, its legs slightly spread apart, its arms positioned so that the hands completely covered the face.

And it had been burned—not cremated to ash and bone—but burned to a crisp, blackening all of the flesh not in contact with the sand.

She drew closer, curiosity outweighing her unease.

If it hadn't been for the stench of seared skin, the corpse could have been mistaken for a discarded store mannequin, torched by kids. The hair was completely gone, the scalp blistered to the bone, and most of the clothing had burned away, leaving black flakes on the sand. Bloodred fissures crisscrossed the torso where the deeper dermal layers had shrunken and split under the intense heat. Melted fat pooled like yellow candle wax in the concaves and cracks.

But it was definitely the remains of a woman; Maggie had seen enough burned bodies in her time to recognize the telltale signs. Even though the fire had made the sex indeterminable to an untrained eye, there were specific clues she knew to look for, including the ratio of flesh on the torso against the size of the abdomen, as well as the larger width of the pelvis. Both were present here, both dead giveaways.

"Prostitute?" Loomis said speculatively. "Some anonymous John had his wicked way with her, then brought her out here to die."

"We're a long way from the Trail." Maggie's comment referred to a particular stretch of Orange Blossom, notorious as one of Orlando's hottest red-light districts.

"Make the ride in fifteen minutes," he said with a shrug, as though he knew from experience.

"Running every red along the way."

"Even quicker on the turnpike. Doable, either way. Not that he'd have any rush. Look where we are. Isolated. This time of night, he could take his time. Wouldn't surprise me if they did the deed right here on the sand before he strangled her."

Maggie glanced at him. "Strangled?"

Loomis folded his arms. "Just putting it out there."

Maggie edged a little closer, dropping to her haunches. This close she could feel the heat still coming off the charred flesh. "The real question is, if she is a prostitute, why bring her all the way out here in the first place? There are plenty of other isolated areas closer to the Trail."

Loomis shrugged again. "Maybe he's local. Maybe he felt comfortable dumping her in his own backyard. Let's face it, Novak, unless you know this place is here, you wouldn't know it exists. I mean, come on, take a look around you. This spot is secluded, which is exactly what you need if you want to set fire to a body without anyone raising the alarm. No better place to burn off all the incriminating evidence without some hapless passerby stumbling right into it."

"Only, somebody did." She leaned closer, sniffing. "Do you smell that?"

"No good asking me. Everything here smells like toasted marshmallow. In fact, it's beginning to make my stomach rumble."

Maggie shook her head. "What is it with you and food? It smells like he used gasoline as an accelerant."

"Only way to get this kind of party started."

Maggie held a hand over the burned skull. "Still giving off quite a bit of heat. Can't be more than a couple of hours." She ran her flashlight along the part of the body in contact with the ground, where a three-inch ribbon of pink flesh and intact clothing separated the burned tissue from the sand. "Looks like he didn't use enough accelerant, though. Most of her back appears to be intact. Clothing as well."

"First timer?"

"Maybe."

"I guess you've got to start somewhere. There's no manual for murder."

Maggie took photos with her phone, the flash pulling out every bit of the macabre. There was something magnetic about the burned body. Something that seemed to warp the air, pulling down on the light and drawing everything closer, including her.

Hardly breathing, she took several close-ups of the hands fused to the face, and the gold band on the remains of the ring finger.

"Looks like she's married," Maggie said. "Might rule out your prostitute angle, Loomis. Plus, the presence of a ring goes toward ruling out a mugging."

"Maybe."

"No idea if she was alive when he set her on fire, though."

The thought was an uncomfortable one.

The truth was, until the medical examiner's autopsy report came back, it was impossible to say one way or the other. The positioning of her hands on her face was odd, Maggie thought, and she couldn't imagine the woman being able to keep her face protected in such a way while fire consumed the rest of her.

"Hey, Novak," Loomis said, pointing with his flashlight at the narrow beach. "Check out the fresh prints."

Maggie got to her feet.

A yard-wide strip of coffee-colored mud formed a clear division between the sand and the stained water. Several boot imprints were pressed into the mud, overlapping but distinct, noticeably deeper in the heel area.

"Could be size twelve," Loomis said as they edged closer. "Thirteen at a push. Definitely recent either way. The heel impressions are deep, but haven't completely filled with water yet."

Maggie took a photograph, then turned her attention to the lake itself. Now that every last bit of daylight was gone, the lake was all but invisible—just an expanse of darkness punctuated by a freckling of tiny house lights on what Maggie assumed was the opposite shore a few miles distant.

"Looks like he stood here facing out," she said. "The deeper heel impressions indicate someone leaning back, maybe as they threw something out into the water."

Maggie swept her flashlight across the black water. Almost immediately, the beam struck a small exposed mud mound about twenty feet offshore. An elongated hump about ten yards long, covered in tall green reeds. Her beam landed on a red angular object caught in the stems.

"Some kind of bag," Loomis said, aiming his own flashlight at it. "Could be a woman's purse. Maybe that's what the killer tossed?"

"Guess there's only one way to find out." Maggie pulled off the plastic overshoes and stepped into the water.

She heard Loomis fumble out his handgun behind her.

"What do you think you're doing, Novak?"

"My job."

"Are you crazy?"

"Possibly." She took another few steps, the lukewarm water climbing above her ankles. "Relax. It's much shallower than it looks."

"That's not what I'm worried about. It's the indigenous wildlife. Especially the ones with big pointy teeth."

Another few steps and the water was halfway up her boots. Disturbed mud swirling, clouding. One or two inquisitive mosquitos flickering in her flashlight.

"You do know alligators are bulletproof?" she said, pausing midway to glance back over her shoulder at him. "I'm serious, Loomis. A gator comes close, you need to hit it right between the eyes." She demonstrated by touching a fingertip to the slight hollow between her eyebrows. "Right here in the sweet spot. Or else it's game over for me. Think you can do that?"

As if on cue, something made a loud splashing noise out in the darkness, and she heard Loomis release an expletive, his flashlight sweeping left and right, as though its glare would ward off any approaching predators.

She snickered. "It's just mullet jumping."

"Just hurry it up, Novak. You're making me sweat here."

Maggie took a photo of the reed mound before continuing to slosh across the narrow. She clamped the flashlight in her mouth as she reached the mound, taking another photo of the object snagged up in the reeds.

"It's a purse all right," she said, retrieving it from its perch.

"You think it's the victim's?"

"I think it's too big a coincidence for it not to be." Maggie examined the handbag. Red leather with a faux crocodile texture. Metal clasps, glinting in the flashlight. "It seems fairly dry. Clean. We had rain earlier. Like those footprints, it hasn't been here long. I'll lay odds the killer tossed it out here."

"What brand?"

She glanced up, squinting. "Does it matter?"

23

"You know as well as I do, Novak. The brand of a woman's purse says more about the kind of woman she is than what's inside it."

Maggie pointed at a gold-colored bag charm dangling from the handle—the letters *M* and *K* set within a circle.

"Nice," Loomis said. "Those things aren't cheap."

"Which confirms she wasn't mugged, and completely rules out the prostitution angle."

"Thanks, Novak. Shoot my theory down in flames already."

Maggie popped the magnetic clasp and peered inside.

She located, amid the usual absolutely necessary clutter found in every woman's purse, a slim wallet, inside of which was a driver's license registered in Florida.

Maggie held it under her flashlight for a closer look.

The woman in the photograph appeared to be fortyish, with saggy jowls and mousy hair. She looked slightly sad, Maggie thought, in the way that people did when life had failed to pan out how they'd hoped it would, resulting in a lifetime of letdowns and unwinnable battles.

And something else.

Something that froze the air in Maggie's lungs.

"What's up, Novak?" Loomis called. "You look like you've seen a ghost."

But all at once Maggie couldn't speak, couldn't put into words or in context what her eyes were seeing. It was as though a disconnect had occurred between her visual and cerebral cortexes, causing her thoughts to crash into one another, hitting a mental wall and rebounding.

"Novak? Say something. You're beginning to scare the bejesus out of me here."

With her heart jackhammering in her chest, Maggie stared at the photo again, right into the adult eyes of her childhood friend. A friend whom she knew had burned to death twenty years earlier.

Chapter Three

ONE FOR THE TEAM

Earth calling Maggie Novak. Come in, Maggie Novak."

It took an effort of will for Maggie to drag her gaze from the driver's license, to break the spell that had her thoughts tripping over one another, none of them able to answer the one question burning a hole in her mind:

How was this possible?

Maggie blew out a cool breath as her initial shock began to wane, pushed aside by years of police work and her natural need to *understand*.

It was true: her friend had burned to death.

But not here. Not tonight.

She'd died in her sleep, in a house fire twenty years ago, along with her family.

At least, that's what Maggie and everybody else had been led to believe.

Now, she didn't know what to think.

This was definitely *her*.

Or was it?

The name on the license was different.

Had Halloween knocked her off-balance, and was her mind playing tricks on her?

Suddenly unsure, Maggie looked again at the photo, calling on her senses to be objective. As an investigator, she was trained to question everything, to trust the evidence no matter how unbelievable it might seem. Twenty years had passed since she'd last seen her friend. Plenty of time for memories to fade, or change. Yet even with the different name, she couldn't get past the fact that her gut was insisting this was her childhood friend.

"Talk to me, Novak," Loomis called as she stuffed the wallet and the license back in the purse. "On my own with the DB here. Feeling slightly freaked out."

"The victim," she said as she waded back to the beach, "I think I know her. Or at least I used to know her when we were teenagers. I haven't seen her for twenty years. What's strange is that the driver's license has her down as a Dana Cullen from Paradise Heights."

"It's just around the lake from here. Not that strange."

"It is when I tell you I knew her as Rita Grigoryan."

Loomis's flashlight tracked Maggie like a searchlight. "I don't follow. I thought you said she's Dana Cullen?"

"That's what her driver's license says. But I'm telling you her name used to be Rita Grigoryan." She climbed out onto the beach.

"And you're sure it's her?"

"Rita was like a sister to me. I'd recognize her anywhere. Here, hold this a sec." She handed him the purse.

"So how do you explain the different name?"

"I can't. Not yet, anyway." Maggie went over to the burned corpse again. Even with her newfound knowledge of the victim's likely identity, the body didn't look any less ghoulish the second time around. It was an image straight out of Maggie's nightmares.

She angled her flashlight so that it illuminated the charred fingers covering the face. Then she took a zoomed-in photograph with her phone. "Rita lost the end of her pinky when we were kids." She pointed at the victim's left hand. "See. The tip's missing."

"Okay. So why do I sense there's more to this than meets the eye? What aren't you telling me, Novak?"

Maggie looked up at him. "Because there's an even bigger problem with this picture than the name issue."

"Which is . . . ?"

"Rita Grigoryan died twenty years ago."

She saw confusion descend over his face.

"Died?" he said. "As in dead, died?"

"She burned to death in a house fire when we were teenagers. Rita and her whole family." She saw his confusion grow into disbelief. "I know. It makes no sense whatsoever."

"Unless you're mistaken."

"I'm not. It's her."

"But all you're going off is a thumbnail photograph."

"And the missing pinky."

"Which isn't unique, Novak."

"You're right." She stood straight, taking the purse back from him. "I can see exactly how this looks. But you have to trust me on this, Loomis. Rita and I spent the first eighteen years of our lives together. We were like sisters, virtually inseparable. I'd recognize her face even if I hadn't seen it in fifty years."

He seemed to think about it.

"I'm not mistaken."

"Okay," he said at last. "For argument's sake, let's say this is your childhood friend, who supposedly died twenty years ago. Aside from resurrection and cloning, how do you even begin to explain it?"

"I don't know. I'm still trying to wrap my own head around it. I'm all out of answers right now. But I will find out."

For several silent seconds, they both stared at the burned body.

Then Loomis said, "Come on. Let's go. This place is seriously creeping me out."

◆ ◆ ◆

Back on the street, and armed with a crime scene kit and a portable lamp, Maggie set about documenting the contents of the purse, examining each item in detail before photographing, bagging, labeling, attaching a chain-of-custody receipt, and then laying the item out on the protective plastic sheet she'd spread across the hood of the Sheriff's Explorer. Itemizing evidence wasn't something she found herself doing all that often, but according to Smits, Forensics Squad was busy processing an incident near Windermere, and the burned body at Lake Apopka had been downgraded to second priority. Faced with the possibility of a lengthy wait, Maggie had decided that being proactive was by far the best way to keep her thoughts from running away with her.

And so, while Loomis busied himself making small talk with the deputies, Maggie processed the contents of the purse.

For the most part, the items turned out to be unremarkable. Just the usual *can't-leave-home-withouts* that cause men to scratch their heads—including various store-brand makeup products, lip salves, pill bottles, purchase receipts, loose change, keys, and the obligatory smartphone. The only item that seemed unusual was an oval of curved wood with the glyph of a bear engraved into it and a small drilled hole off-center.

Why didn't you die in that house fire, Rita?

The cell phone was a $500 iPhone in a $5 clip-on cover. Maggie powered it up. The screen brightened instantly, presenting her with the picture of a desert landscape and a lock screen that was passable only with a fingerprint.

Rita's . . . No . . . *Dana's* fingerprint.

Dana . . . Rita . . . Maggie's head swam, trying to reconcile the two. Despite the missing finger, Loomis was still unconvinced that Dana was Rita. Maggie got it. But she was in no doubt about the victim's true identity. Maggie recognized that sullen face, knew that sad gaze that seemed to be able to look right inside her.

However, to avoid unnecessary confusion, she decided to refer to the victim as Dana, keeping Rita confined to her private thoughts, at least for now, where she had been the last twenty years.

Why did you change your name?

Maggie turned the phone over in her hands, wondering how likely it would be for the chief medical examiner to salvage a viable print from the burned fingertips. Not that he wouldn't give it his best shot, she was sure; Maury Elkin was nothing if not tenacious. Give him a challenge and he'd take it by the horns and run with it, sometimes to the detriment of everything else, including his life outside the ME's office.

Otherwise, it would be down to the Digital Forensics Unit to hack the phone, and Maggie knew such things were easier said than done.

Where have you been for all these years?

Experimentally, Maggie pressed her index finger against the sensor, but was denied access.

She heard Loomis emit a whooping laugh, and she looked around to see him sharing a joke with the deputies. In a job like theirs, some degree of gallows humor was permitted, if not essential, even if it had to be forced.

As crazy as it sounded, Ed Loomis had a hypersensitivity toward death.

For as long as she'd known him, it had always been the case that being in close proximity to a dead body for any length of time made Loomis nervous, even if that dead body wasn't in his direct line of sight. Just knowing that it was in his general vicinity was enough to make him on edge.

The first time it had happened in her company, Maggie had found it amusing—probably because a street-hardened undercover narcotics cop, and someone who had chosen to move into homicides, could get spooked so easily over a dead body—but then she'd learned sometime later that his parents had both been killed when he was a small child, and that he'd stayed with their corpses for two whole days until help had arrived. Now, whenever his anxiety surfaced, she'd let it run its course, knowing that the best way to combat it was with distraction.

She bagged the phone and turned her attention to the bunch of keys.

Except for a Chevrolet key fob with a Minnie Mouse sticker on it, the keys appeared to belong to regular house locks. Wishful, Maggie held the car key above her head and pressed the red panic button, listening for any distant chime of an alarm, but none sounded.

Why were you here tonight?

The absence of Dana's vehicle at the crime scene suggested that she hadn't made her own way to the lake. Even though Dana's home address was only a couple of miles away to the north, Maggie couldn't imagine her walking here. Not on Halloween. Either she'd arrived by taxi, which Maggie would check, or she'd been driven here, probably by her killer.

Maggie made a mental note to check the footage on any traffic cameras in the neighborhood—if any existed.

She checked the wallet again, this time extracting all of its contents, spreading them out on the plastic sheet: a bunch of credit and membership cards, all in Dana's name; a few local business cards; paper cash totaling forty-eight dollars; and a faded, dog-eared photograph.

Maggie held the photo under the glow of the portable lamp.

It appeared to have been taken with an instant camera—a square image with a white border. And it looked old. Time had leached the colors to a pinkish hue, as though it had been exposed to strong sunlight, and the white frame had yellowed. Despite several jagged crease marks, Maggie was able to make out the blurred subject matter, and her cool unease came rushing back.

"What's up, Novak?"

Startled, she looked around to see Loomis approaching.

"Just the usual suspects," she said, putting the photo facedown on the hood. "Credit cards, an inaccessible cell phone, and car keys but no car." She showed him the evidence bag with the wood carving in it. "What do you make of this?"

Loomis took it from her, his eyes narrowing as he peered through the clear plastic. "Where'd you find it?"

"Inside a zipped pocket."

"First impression—looks like a wooden Pringle."

"That's not what I was thinking."

"Okay. In that case, some kind of black magic voodoo thing. Maybe Dana's a witch. Let's be honest, it's the perfect night for it. Maybe that's how she cheated death the first time around."

"Your sarcasm is duly noted."

He handed it back. "You do know the only way to kill a witch is with fire, right?"

Maggie let him see her frown. "There's a gated community on the way in," she said. "Why don't you go canvass the neighborhood? I know the idea of hanging around here all night is freaking you out. There's no telling how long it's going to be before Forensics arrive. Maybe somebody saw something other than a couple of smooching teenagers."

Loomis seemed to brighten. "You're sure? I wouldn't want anyone thinking I abandoned you here."

She flapped a hand. "Will you just scram. It's not too late to bang on doors. Let's save ourselves some legwork tomorrow. Start with properties overlooking the lake. I'll call if I need you."

Loomis didn't need prompting twice. He rounded up a posse of deputies and headed out, and once they were gone, Maggie turned the Polaroid photo over again, the coolness heavy in her belly.

When they were barely eighteen, and as far as everybody knew, Rita had burned to death in a house blaze that the fire department marshal had later deemed accidental. According to the news at the time, both Mr. and Mrs. Grigoryan, Rita, and her two younger brothers had all suffocated in their sleep from smoke inhalation before burning into unrecognizable husks. The tragedy hadn't been tragic enough to make the national newspapers, but it had been solemnly announced on the local TV news, and Maggie still remembered it vividly, like a scald.

She remembered the images of crying students, some collapsing from shock, and the grim-faced teachers trying to contain their own upset, holding hands in solidarity while Principal Myerson gave his reaction to the terrible news.

She remembered rushing to the bathroom, where she'd gripped the sink for fear of fainting, tear-filled eyes staring at her from the bathroom mirror, her thoughts afire.

She remembered lying awake at night in the weeks that followed, restless, helpless, stupidly blaming herself even though it wasn't her fault.

Most of all, she remembered Rita's disappointed expression the last time she'd laid eyes on her.

Maggie's best friend had died that night, and Maggie had never quite gotten over it.

But you didn't die. You survived. How?

Maggie didn't have the answer. Not yet.

Somehow, Rita had survived the blaze that had killed the rest of her family, and the news of her death had been either a mistake or a lie.

Both outcomes were incredible.

How is something like that even possible?

Maggie's gaze fell to the Polaroid picture again, taking in the washed-out image of two seventeen-year-old girls sitting on the end of a bed, cuddling and grinning as the photo was taken.

If Dana wasn't Rita, why did she have Rita's photo in her wallet?

Chapter Four

THE GAP

Maggie couldn't sleep. Every time she closed her eyes, she saw the younger, flame-haired version of Rita standing in the middle of the clearing, barefoot on Devil's Landing, her gaze pleading with Maggie to *do something* as an inferno consumed her from the ground up.

A similar image had haunted Maggie for years.

Breathing hard, she rolled out of bed, grumbling as she clocked the lateness of the hour. It was a little after four a.m., and still dark out. Although Sunday had been slated as her day off, the lakeside murder had effectively rewritten her shift pattern for the week, and police reports didn't write themselves. At best, she had four hours' grace before she'd need to head into the office. Sooner, if sleep resisted.

Without switching on lights, Maggie pulled on her running gear.

Whenever she was this wired, she knew that trying to force sleep was like pushing water uphill with a rake. Her whole body had been vibrating like a tuning fork for hours, her thoughts ringing, and try as she might, she hadn't been able to stop her thoughts from charging down every mental dead end in an attempt to explain what was presently inexplicable.

How did Rita survive without anyone knowing?

She clipped her phone to her armband and then made her way outside, knowing that if she didn't burn off her excess energy, she'd be fried come morning.

In the dark, she limbered up at the foot of the driveway, forcing lactic acid from her muscles. Maggie had a policy: never run cold—always warm up first. She'd learned that lesson the hard way in her youth, experiencing crippling cramps that had floored her for long excruciating minutes, and miles from help. Nowadays, she never ran without stretching out the kinks first.

She had almost finished her warm-up when a light came on in the porch across the street. A second later, the front door opened and a dark-haired stringy man wearing plaid pajama pants and a baggy Ramones T-shirt came strolling out. He paused on the front walk to light a cigarette, sucking deeply before blowing a thick cloud of smoke into the night. He noticed Maggie and raised a hand in salutation. "Hey, neighbor."

Maggie waved back. "Hey, Nick. Since when do you like Ramones?"

"I don't. But the shirt was on sale, and I like the cut. For the record, I'm also the proud owner of a vintage Village People concert tee from seventy-nine."

Barefooted, he padded across the lawn toward her, a trail of smoke curling in his wake.

Nick Stavanger was the neighborhood night owl. He worked as a columnist at the *Orlando Chronicle*, where he regularly lambasted city commissioners about costly public policies and, on occasion, ran investigative pieces on crime and punishment. He and Maggie had been friends the last nine years, since he'd accidentally backed a U-Haul truck over her mailbox the day he'd moved in.

"You're up early, Maggie," he said, crossing the street toward her.

"Late," she answered.

"Ouch." He stopped at the foot of her driveway and began to mirror her warm-up routine.

Even in the poor light, Maggie could see a dried track of toothpaste on his T-shirt and two-day stubble coating his chin.

"So, Detective," he said, leaning to one side, vertebrae cracking, "what's the story here? Only time I see you up and around at this god-forsaken hour is when you have murder on your mind."

She reached over her head. "You can read all about it in Monday's paper."

He laughed. "Touché. Seriously, though, if you need to unload, I'm all ears. There's a bottle of twelve-year-old scotch on my coffee table right now, just crying out to be drunk. We could share sob stories and cheer each other up. Maybe watch *The Golden Girls*."

"You've got *The Golden Girls* on DVD?"

"I do. And while we're at it, let's not forget my *Friends* box sets."

"You certainly know how to sweet-talk a woman, Nick."

"I hope not." He blew out smoke. "Well, do I get a scoop?"

"Not right now."

He made a wounded face. "Tough crowd tonight."

As sincere as Nick was, Maggie knew that his offer to talk things through came with an ulterior motive. At heart, Nick was a journalist, and as such he never let a friendship get in the way of a good story. At some point, probably when they were well oiled and their inhibitions asleep, he'd start to press her for insider scoops—the journalist in him unable to resist—and what started out as a friendly chat would soon deteriorate into an awkward interrogation and then an uncomfortable silence.

"Got to run," she said, wrapping up her routine and jogging away. "Catch you later?"

"I wouldn't stake your career on it, Detective," he called after her. "Have a good one."

Maggie waved a hand, then turned her focus on her run.

Right away, her restless energy urged her to sprint, to burn it off as quickly as possible, but she resisted, keeping her stride steady as the road inclined out of the cul-de-sac. Elbows tucked in. Soft footfalls striking the cement.

As she turned right onto Hammocks Drive, she glanced back into the cul-de-sac, but all she could see of Nick in the dark was the glow from his cigarette.

It was all uphill from here to White Road. Maggie followed the snaking sidewalk, keeping her stride shallow to allow for the steepness of the slope.

Running wasn't just Maggie's way of keeping off the pounds. It helped her think, detach, and sometimes to zone out when too much thinking became unproductive. Health and work permitting, Maggie ran five miles every day without fail, her preferred route taking her east to the West Oaks Mall, where she would complete several circuits of the crumbling parking lot before retracing her steps home. The hypnotic metronome of pounding the pavement bringing order and occasionally enlightenment. It wasn't the most picturesque route—mostly the cream-colored featureless backs of mall buildings and the endless undulations of cracked asphalt—but it was quiet and deserted at six in the morning when she usually ran, and that was the draw.

But she didn't head that way this morning.

At the intersection with White Road, Maggie went left instead of right. And as her speed increased on the flatter level, her thoughts revisited the events of the last few hours.

An apologetic associate medical examiner and his assistant had arrived at the crime scene at around ten, and while they had busied themselves assessing the burned body, Maggie had studied the setup from a killer's perspective, reconstructing in her mind the various scenarios that might have led to the same grisly outcome: Dana's death.

First off, she'd wanted to know how Dana had come to be in the woods.

An absence of drag marks meant one of two things: Either Dana had walked to the clearing unassisted, or her killer had carried her there.

The former pointed to Dana still being alive at that point, while the latter indicated a killer with the physical strength to carry a dead weight some hundred or so yards from the roadway.

Were you still alive at Devil's Landing, or already dead?

Secondly, Maggie had wanted to know why the killer had chosen that particular spot as his dump site.

Although it wasn't located in the sticks per se, the clearing was isolated. It pointed to someone familiar with the lay of the land—a local man, as Loomis had said, or even somebody associated with the high school across the street.

Did you know your killer?

Shortly after eleven, weary-looking Forensics Squad technicians had arrived at the death scene, and a detailed inspection had ensued, including a videoed walk-through. Then, with the assistance of a dozen deputies, the entire cordoned-off area had been systematically searched. Evidentiary items had been photographed in situ and logged before being collected, and casts had been taken of the boot prints in the muddy beach.

Around midnight, Loomis had returned empty handed. All told, he and his posse had canvassed more than one hundred homeowners in the gated community hugging the lake. But none had reported seeing anything out of the ordinary—except, of course, for bunches of small ghouls scuttling from house to house—and nobody recalled seeing anyone suspicious on the parkway either.

Under the cover of dusk, and with most people who were outside at the time preoccupied with the Halloween festivities, the killer had come and gone seemingly unnoticed.

Maybe a traffic cam had picked something up?

Finally, the burned body had been carefully extracted from the woods, and, satisfied that all the death evaluation steps had been completed, the associate medical examiner had released the scene. One by one, the EMS vehicles had disappeared into the night, and everyone had gone their separate ways.

But Maggie hadn't called it a night, not right away. She'd made a detour, stopping by the address on the driver's license, curious to see if there was a husband waiting for his wife to come home. But the house had been dark, and her persistent knocking had gone unanswered, leaving her even more unsettled.

Maggie sidestepped a burst pumpkin lying in the middle of the sidewalk, its jack-o'-lantern face ripped wide open, gooey bits of it spattered down the street.

For the life of her, she didn't *get* Halloween.

Nora said it was because Maggie didn't have kids, and that being a parent changed everything. Parenthood transformed the mundane into the marvelous. Maggie had seen the change in Loomis when the twins had come along. His priorities had switched overnight, and now he thought twice about putting himself in harm's way.

Was that an evolutionary thing, or just part of growing up?

Maggie's foot slid on a chunk of pumpkin skin, and she corrected her balance, crossing the street and going north on Montgomery, her thoughts returning to the case.

Sometime Sunday, Maury Elkin would examine Dana Cullen's burned remains, and tests would be undertaken to determine the exact cause and time of death. A murder investigation would be officially opened, and a time line for Dana's last known movements would be established as quickly as possible. Friends, neighbors, and coworkers interviewed. Anyone with an ax to grind routed out and questioned.

The wedding band on Dana's finger pointed to her being married. It didn't account for her first name being changed, but it could account for the different last name.

Is your husband lying awake in bed right now, wondering where you are?

At the outset of every homicide investigation there were always dozens of questions in need of answering. Some answers would come quickly—the victim's place of work, their familial relationships, their lifestyle—while others would need painstaking care and attention to tease out into the open.

Who were their enemies? Who did they owe money or favors to? Who would benefit from their death?

Uncovering the truth about someone's life was like doing a jigsaw puzzle with the gray side up. All the pieces were there, but it was only when all of them were fit together that it could be turned over and the bigger picture revealed in all its glory.

Maggie spotted the corner with Oak Street in the distance, and slowed her pace as the pavement headed uphill again.

Although she was barely a mile from home, she hadn't been this far along Montgomery in years. Purposely, she avoided this part of the neighborhood. In total, she could count on one finger how many times she'd ventured here on official business in the last two decades.

She slowed to a fast walk, suddenly reticent about getting any nearer to the street that was home to so many of her childhood memories, good and bad.

Even in the dark, the street didn't appear to have changed much. The trees seemed a little taller, the houses a little smaller. Fences in need of painting and lawns in need of mowing. A picture-perfect postcard of sleepy suburbia, with no indication that anything bad could ever happen here.

But it had.

As Maggie reached the corner with Oak, she stopped altogether, a few yards short, unable to go any farther, her stomach knotting.

It was all in her head, she knew, but she could smell smoke lingering in the damp air. A distinct reek of smoldering wood that clawed at the back of her nose. And now that she listened, it was easy to confuse the rustle of leaves for the sound of flames licking wood and bubbling off paint.

Maggie held on to her cloying breath, her heart suddenly pumping wildly in her chest.

An empty lot lay between the first two houses on Oak Street. A large rectangle of darkness that, at first glance, could be mistaken as an innocent parcel of land waiting to be developed.

But it hadn't always been this way.

As a child, Maggie had spent many hours here, riding her bike up and down the street with her friends, or getting into mischief at the lake at the end of the block. Skipping ropes and Rollerblading and fighting for turns on someone's Nintendo. And as a young teenager, she'd hung out at number 1265 most weekends, doing girly stuff, daydreaming out loud, and boy-talking. But something bad had happened to bring a sudden and devastating end to all that, and things had never been the same again.

Maggie's lungs began to burn, but she held on to the fiery breath all the same, her wide-eyed gaze roving the empty lot across the street.

Time had grassed it over, and several trees had sprung up in the passing years, but Maggie had a sense of things still being askew here, running much deeper than what met the eye. Unless somebody pointed it out, no one would ever know that a house had once stood on this spot, that there used to be ten properties on this quiet lane instead of the nine still standing.

But Maggie knew that beneath the grassy surface lay a bed of ash and the charred remnants of the house where a loving family had all met a fiery death.

Or so she'd thought.

Her lungs continued to burn, imploring her to breathe. But Maggie clung to the superheated air, letting the fire spread through her chest until it forced tears from her eyes.

And only when her senses started to get fuzzy and spiral out of control did she let it out.

Chapter Five

EARLY BIRD

At this time of the morning, the Major Case office was all but deserted—just a janitor buffing the floor, and a dedicated civilian administrator catching up on paperwork.

Feeling frayed around the edges, Maggie got herself a coffee and sat down heavily at her desk.

Despite running off her nervous energy, sleep had still evaded her, the gap on Oak Street weighing heavy in her thoughts. She'd tossed and turned and finally given in, deciding that if she was fated to remain awake that she might as well put the time to good use. She'd showered, put on a gray pantsuit and white shirt, and then driven to the Orange County Sheriff's Office on West Colonial, arriving at five a.m., three hours ahead of the weekend shift.

Her intention was to find out everything she didn't know about Rita/Dana and her missing years.

But the first thing Maggie had gotten out of the way was her typed prelim report for Smits, knowing that it would be expected when he came in later. Smits wasn't just a stickler for procedure; he supported and endorsed old-fashioned policing. Although everything was digital and emailed internally these days, Smits preferred case updates on paper. His philosophy being, *If you can hold it in your hand, you're more inclined to absorb it.* The single sheet of copy now lying on the sergeant's desk contained a thousand words summarizing Maggie's observations of the lakeside crime scene, including discoveries, few as they were. It would have to do. Once the ME had examined the body and confirmed they were dealing with a homicide, a more comprehensive report would follow.

Maggie tapped her workstation out of sleep mode and entered her username and password. The screen presented her with a cluster of icons pinned to a spruce-green background bearing the five-point star of the Orange County Sheriff's Office.

She looked at it for a moment, sipping coffee.

Although Maggie excelled at it, she'd never wanted to be a cop, least of all a homicide detective, and after almost eighteen years of working in law enforcement, she still wasn't sure what made her take up the badge all those years ago.

Like her brother before her, she'd studied at the University of Central Florida with every intention of following in their parents' footsteps and going into teaching. After all, becoming an educator was the Novak family tradition. A career in teaching was expected, going back generations. Her brother, Bryan, had landed a teaching job right after graduation, and eleven years later, Nora had followed suit. But Maggie, the middle child, had left the College of Education and stalled, all at once not sure that teaching was her true calling.

For months she'd drifted, half-heartedly looking at one dreary career option after another, all the while her parents were encouraging her to do the right thing and *teach*. She'd contemplated taking a year off to travel the world, to separate herself from their daily indoctrination. Several of her college friends had taken off, backpacking across Asia, through Thailand, and down into Australia. Maggie had thought about joining them, about experiencing life on the road, and perhaps finding inspiration in her travels. Then fate had intervened, and her decision to join the Sheriff's Office had been divisive, causing a family wound that had never quite healed.

Maggie connected her phone to a USB hub and started uploading the crime scene photos she'd taken a few hours earlier to a folder labeled *NOVAK & LOOMIS—HALLOWEEN HOMICIDE* located in Major Case's secure cloud storage. Altogether, there were several dozen pictures and videos, and the onscreen dialogue box announced it would take approximately seven minutes to complete.

As the files transferred, Maggie accessed the Crime Information Center, running a person search through its database. She wanted to know if either Dana or Rita had been mentioned in any police reports during the past twenty years, anywhere in the continental United States.

Within milliseconds, the search reported *No results*.

Not even a mention of the Pine Hills house fire tragedy.

Maggie wasn't surprised. Twenty years ago, the electronic storing of crime reports was at its early stages, and computerized information from back then was sparse.

Experimenting, she opened an internet search page and typed *Rita Grigoryan* into the text box, not knowing what to expect, surprised when almost a quarter-million hits came back.

The first few pages advertised various social media profile links. Maggie clicked through a dozen or so before concluding that she was chasing a wild goose. And clicking *Images* only confirmed it. Not one of the portrait photos was similar to the image of her flame-haired friend, which was burned into her memory. Although the internet had been commonplace when tragedy had struck the Grigoryan family, social media had still been in its infancy, and in those days of dial-up and capped data limits, hardly anyone uploaded byte-heavy photographs of themselves.

Maggie leaned back and drank coffee.

Where have you been for all these years?

Of course, the obvious answer was *dead*.

But that wasn't what she was looking for.

Rita had survived the house fire on Oak Street. Maggie wanted to know how.

Why did you change your name to Dana?

A search for *Dana Cullen* came back with plenty of hits and no substance. More self-promoting images of women bearing absolutely no resemblance to the woman in Dana's driver's license photo.

How can someone go from being dead to being undead?

It was the right time of year for it, but Maggie didn't believe in the supernatural. There had to be a rational explanation behind Rita becoming Dana, one rooted in fact and not fiction. Examining the original reports from the time of the house fire would be a good place to start.

Maggie accessed the online records section of the District Nine Medical Examiner's Office and ran a search for the twenty-year-old autopsy reports pertaining to the deceased Grigoryan family. She knew the notes would make for grisly reading, but given no obvious explanation to account for Rita's miraculous resurrection into Dana, what choice did she have?

The search request returned no results.

Again, not that big a surprise. The original documents had probably never been digitized and were still sitting in a box in storage somewhere. All she had to do was file a request to see the paper reports.

A text box popped up in the middle of the screen, informing her that the upload was complete. Maggie clicked back to the virtual folder, expanding and examining each of the photos in turn.

The camera flash had cast a sterile light over each scene, leaching color and blanching faces, highlighting Lindy's mascara-streaked cheeks and flimsy demeanor, Tyler's spiteful glare and curled fists. The burned corpse covered in its cracked and crusty coating of crisped flesh and fat.

Who wanted you dead?

Equally important was the question of *why?*

It was clear to Maggie that Dana's murder was neither random nor spur of the moment. Her killing hadn't come about as the result of a mugging or an assault. She hadn't been killed in a drive-by shooting or in an act of random violence. The location and the accelerant were signatures of someone who had planned to kill Dana and then burn her body in the clearing. In cases of premeditated murder, it was extremely rare for the killer not to be driven by a motive. A purpose existed behind Dana's murder. Find that reason, that motivation, and Maggie knew she would be more than halfway to an arrest.

Who hated you enough to take your life?

Maggie played the brief video she'd taken of the teenagers, watching it with the sound muted as Tyler glowered and Lindy blubbered. On camera, the tension between the pair was obvious. If she'd tried, Lindy couldn't have positioned herself farther from Tyler, their combined body language saying more about what had happened between them than what they had found in the woods.

No love lost between these two.

Maggie replayed the clip, paying closer attention to their mannerisms and the way Lindy cringed each time Tyler opened his mouth. Then something caught her eye, and she expanded the video to full screen, rewinding it a fraction and then pausing the recording at the moment Tyler thrust his driver's license at the lens.

There was a big ugly ring on his middle finger and what looked like a dry smear of blood on his knuckles.

She hadn't noticed it in the low-light conditions last night. But here, backlit onscreen, it couldn't be missed.

Maggie took a screenshot, the taste of coffee bitter on her tongue. Then she grabbed her Glock and left the office.

45

Chapter Six

INGREDIENTS OF INTENT

A ghostly haze hung in the eastern sky as Maggie parked the motor pool sedan outside the wrecking yard on Wilmer Avenue. It was just after six a.m., and Orlando was beginning to stir.

She took a flashlight from the door pocket, then approached a service cabin situated next to a mechanized entrance gate. A yellowy light was on inside the hut, and a bleary-eyed youth looked up from his cell phone as Maggie tapped her badge against the window.

"We impounded a red Charger last night," she said as he slid aside the pane. "You brought it in earlier this morning."

"Aisle twelve." He pushed a clipboard toward her. "Sign and date."

Maggie logged her name and time and purpose for her visit onto the grubby record sheet, then waited for the youth to buzz her through a smaller side gate. The second she was inside the compound, he hung his head over his phone again.

Dawn light accentuated the rooftops of nearby buildings, but darkness still clung to the yard.

Maggie followed the beam of her flashlight across the cracked concrete, the hulks of impounded vehicles looming in its glow, the smells of engine oil and rubber thick in her nose. She passed row after row of vehicles, most showing signs of crash damage, but some lined up neatly like family cars waiting at the theme park admissions.

With no on-site impound lot of its own, the Orange County Sheriff's Office used the wrecker service as standard practice in the recovery of crime scene vehicles, and a corner of the wrecking yard was reserved for what OCSO labeled *vehicles of interest*. After being cleared by Forensics, Tyler Pruitt's bloodred Dodge Charger had been towed here as a matter of procedure. And there it was, gleaming in her flashlight.

Maggie took a photo of it with her phone, the flash briefly revealing the stacks of cars on either side.

The ticket stuck to the Charger's windshield confirmed it was the correct vehicle. A short checklist documented that its tires had been swabbed for trace evidence, but the bodywork hadn't been fingerprinted or the insides inspected. Maggie put on latex gloves from her pocket, and opened the driver's door.

Inside, the car smelled faintly of cheap perfume.

Maggie inspected the empty door pockets before opening the glove compartment and shining the flashlight on its contents.

What was she expecting to find?

She'd come down here on a hunch, following her gut instinct and the voice in the back of her mind that insisted something about the whole Tyler/Lindy setup felt a little hinky.

The blood on Tyler's knuckles, coupled with the fresh graze on Lindy's chin, had convinced Maggie that he had hit her.

But why?

Did they have a bust-up right before finding the dead body?

Inside the glove compartment, she found the usual paperwork: an owner's manual, a service history booklet, an insurance document. Nothing unexpected.

She swept the flashlight over the back seat and into the foot spaces. Again, nothing. If anything, the car was immaculate, spotless, which came as a surprise, given that its owner was a seventeen-year-old student.

Maggie popped the trunk and went around to the back of the car. She took a photo of the license plate before hoisting up the lid.

Apart from a solitary plastic storage box pushed right up to the back seat, the trunk was empty. Maggie dragged the box toward her, and right away she knew she'd made a discovery.

Tyler Pruitt had a kill kit in his car.

Chapter Seven

CATCH THE WORM

The sedan's tires crunched bits of loose asphalt as Maggie drove along Wolf Road in Pine Hills. Dawn light casting long shadows. The neighborhood looked fast asleep, a palpable end-of-the-world stillness on the street.

Maggie decided she'd watched one too many zombie movies.

She pulled up outside a single-story house half-hidden by hunched trees, and took a moment to assess the property.

From the little she could see beyond the threadbare front yard, the house looked tired and partly dilapidated. Naked wood siding in desperate need of a new coat. Window panes grayed with grime. A weathered American flag hanging limply from a pole that jutted out at an angle from the front wall.

Nearer, the corroded skeletons of several dismantled motorcycles were going to seed on the balding lawn.

Maggie wondered how Tyler could afford a high-spec car when he lived in a dump like this. No being cradled in the lap of luxury here. No transformational lottery win. No way he could even begin to make the monthly repayments working whatever weekend job he might have.

A sheriff's cruiser pulled up behind her sedan, and a green-uniformed deputy sheriff climbed out. Barrel-chested with a trim moustache. She recognized him, pinning the name Willits to his roundish face.

Maggie slipped into her suit jacket as she got out of the car. "Deputy Willits."

"Ma'am."

She nodded toward the house. "Male teen suspected of striking a female. I need you to provide backup, that's all."

"No problem." His expression was serious.

Maggie clipped her Glock to her belt, then made her way up the oil-mottled driveway, knowing that if the outside of the house was anything to go by, the inside would be much worse.

As an investigator, Maggie saw some sights that would make regular folk's toes curl. Homes seemingly plucked from third-world slums, complete with feces-infused carpets and rat-infested kitchens. Squalor that made the sewer system seem sterile. On occasion, she'd even had to resort to wearing a protective breathing mask when entering certain properties, hoping that her inoculations would safeguard her from any bacteria lurking inside. As a rule, she tried not to judge people by their lifestyle choices, but it was hard to understand why some people chose to exist in a continual state of uncleanliness, especially when a bar of soap cost pennies.

Near the front door, a mismatched pair of weathered lawn chairs stood on either side of a foam cooler with several inches of water going stale in the bottom. Crushed beer cans and empty food cartons lay where they'd fallen.

She rapped her knuckles against the discolored wood of the front door, waited ten seconds, then knocked again, this time harder, longer. When no one answered, she reached across to a small grubby window and banged the flat of her hand against the pane until her palm began to sting.

Finally, she heard movement coming from inside. Heavy footfalls, and a man's voice cussing and complaining as he approached the front door.

The door scraped open to reveal a stocky, shaved-headed man with a shaggy gray beard and a craze of tattoos on his arms. Fiery dragons chasing voluptuous nymphs onto his shoulders and up his neck. He had on stained sweatpants with holes in the knees, and a black tank top with the words *May Contain Alcohol* emblazoned in white across the chest. Suspicious blue eyes under the shadow of a heavy brow. Maggie estimated his age to be midsixties.

"Don't want any," he snapped before she could introduce herself. "Don't think I need any either. Got more than enough to go around and then some. And if you're selling redemption, lady, I ain't buying. Not today."

He tried to shut the door in her face, but Maggie put out a hand, stopping it halfway. He pushed, but Maggie resisted.

"Sheriff's Office," she said, holding her badge in the gap. "I'm looking for Tyler Pruitt."

He seemed to notice the deputy standing off to the side for the first time, and eased off the door. "What's the kid done now?"

"Are you his father?"

"Do I look like that cretin?" he said.

"I wouldn't . . ."

"Tyler's my grandson."

"Are his parents home?"

"Nope. His father skipped town the day he was born. And my daughter, she died from breast cancer, couple years back. Tyler lives with me now."

"I'm sorry."

"Why? You knew her?"

"No, but . . ."

"Then there's no need for your fake sympathy, is there?" He stared at her, eyes challenging.

Maggie put away her ID. "Sir, I need to speak with your grandson. Is he here?"

He nodded over his shoulder. "Far as I know, still in his room and sleeping like a baby. Kid hit the juice pretty hard last night. Both did." He worked up a belch, as though to confirm it. "You here about that body he found?"

"Yes. That's right. I know he was pretty shook up. I need for him to answer a few questions. Then I promise I'll leave you alone." She put her foot on the doorstep. "May we come in?"

"Not sure about that."

"You have my word, I'm not interested in anything else you might have going on here."

He looked offended. "As in, what?" He waited for her to answer, raking thick fingers through his straggly beard.

Maggie sighed. "You know, I think we got off on the wrong foot."

"I'll say."

"It's early and I'm pretty strung out. I don't mean any disrespect. It's been a long night. If I can just have a quick conversation with Tyler, we'll be on our way."

He seemed to think about it for a moment; then he stepped aside. "Okay. But I'm only giving you permission to speak with the kid. You hear? Not to go rooting through any of my private stuff. Unless you got a warrant, the rest of the house is out of bounds."

"I understand. Thank you."

He made an *uh-huh* sound.

Maggie motioned for the deputy to follow her inside.

It was dim in the house, almost murky, and what little Maggie could see of it immediately reminded her of a junkyard. Used auto parts crammed in every available space, the cloying odors of grease and motor oil layered on top of decades of neglect. It smelled like the wrecking yard.

"Room at the end of the hall," he said, gesturing.

"Sir, Tyler is a minor. I'll need you present."

"Soon as I hit the head, lady. I ain't holding back for nobody. Go ahead. I'll be two shakes." He turned and disappeared in the gloom.

With the deputy in tow, Maggie felt her way along the dark hallway, easing past a tower of motorbike wheels. She came to a partly closed door with a yellow metal road sign pinned to the peeling veneer: a stick man falling over the words **TRIPPING HAZARD**.

She went to knock, then changed her mind, gently pushing the door open instead and reaching for the light switch. Then she stood still for a moment, taking in the sight before her.

The first thing that struck Maggie about Tyler Pruitt's bedroom was the overpowering locker room stench. The air smelled bad, like something had crawled into a corner and died. Years of ingrained sweat and engine oil. Heaped clothes reaching for the ceiling.

The second thing that struck her was the colorful mosaic that covered every square inch of the walls and ceiling. Not an artistic collage by any means, rather a deviant's grotto created out of hundreds of pages torn from porn magazines. A multitude of lip-licking girls in every compromising position imaginable.

Maggie put the heel of her hand on the butt of her Glock.

As for the boy himself, he was sprawled on a discolored mattress on the floor, asleep. Naked, aside from a pair of faded boxer shorts. A ring of empty beer bottles holding an AA meeting on the filthy carpet next to him.

Maggie thought about clearing a jumble of clothes off a stool and sitting down. Changed her mind.

"Tyler," she said.

He didn't respond.

Maggie repeated his name, this time louder.

The boy stirred, groaned.

"Tyler. Wake up."

He rolled over to face her, eyes screwed shut. "Mom?"

"No, Tyler. It's Detective Novak. You need to wake up. Right now."

A bleary eye cracked open, followed by the other. For a moment he gazed up at her; then realization hit home, and he reacted as if stung, scrambling into a defensive position against the porn-papered wall.

"Your grandpa let us in," Maggie said before he could ask, or start to scream at her to get out of his room.

Tyler drew his knees up to his chest, glancing at the deputy standing inside the doorway. "Why are you here?"

"We need to have a conversation," Maggie said. "But only with your grandpa present. Right now he's busy emptying his bladder." Maggie gestured at the ceiling. "Interesting concept you've got going here. Very artistic. Did you come up with the idea all by yourself?" She looked back at him, noting the embarrassment glowing in his cheeks. "Must be a little disconcerting having a grown woman here in your bedroom, surrounded by all this vulgarity."

"Grandpa!" Tyler shouted.

Heavy footfalls sounded in the hall, and a second later the grandfather hustled past the deputy and into the room. "Cool your engines," he said.

"I don't want them here."

"Don't matter one iota what you want. How many times have I told you I don't want no cops knocking at my door?"

Tyler cowered as if struck. "I didn't do anything."

Maggie raised a hand. "Please, sir. Right now Tyler is just helping with my investigations. I just need you to bear witness, that's all. Can you do that for me?"

"Suppose." He folded his illustrated arms and leaned against the doorjamb. "So he doesn't need a lawyer or anything?"

"Tyler isn't under arrest. But it's his right to have an attorney present, if that's what he wants." She swung her gaze back to the boy for confirmation.

"I didn't do anything," he repeated. "Ask me anything. I've nothing to hide." A little show of bravado for his grandpa's sake.

"In that case, you won't mind showing me your hand."

"What?"

"Your hand, Tyler."

Glowering, Tyler stuck out his left hand, shook it at Maggie. "Satisfied?"

"Your right hand," she said.

The glower deepened.

"Just get done with it," the grandfather said.

The boy did as he was instructed, holding out his other hand in such a way that the palm faced Maggie.

"Show me your knuckles," she said.

"I didn't do anything," he repeated again, this time through his teeth.

"Cut the crap," said the grandfather. "Just do as the lady asks."

A low growl rumbled in the back of the boy's throat as, slowly, he turned his hand around.

In the glow from the overhead light, the dry blood smeared across his knuckles and crusted on his ring was unmistakable. It seemed, after the deputy had brought Tyler home, the boy had been too involved in drowning his sorrows in beer to wash it away.

The grandfather leaned up off the door. "You been fighting again, boy?"

The boy's jaw clenched. "No, sir. I swear. I don't know how it got there."

"I do," Maggie said. "And I'm willing to lay odds that if we analyze that blood, it comes back as being Lindy Munson's."

Now the boy glared at her, his body language that of a cornered animal desperate to escape.

"What's she talking about?" the grandfather said, coming over. "You hit a girl?"

"No!"

"Tyler was with her last night," Maggie said. "She had a cut on her chin. Your grandson has blood on his knuckles. Right now, I need to know where that blood came from." She took from her pocket a portable DNA collector that she'd stashed there before heading out. It consisted of a cotton swab in a sealed plastic tube. "I need to collect a sample, just in case it came from some other part of the crime scene."

"That dead body he found?"

"Yes." She popped the lid on the collector.

All at once the grandfather didn't look sure. "I don't know," he said, stroking his beard. "Maybe he needs that lawyer after all."

Maggie turned to him, her expression deadly serious. "And like I said, that's Tyler's right. But you need to know, sir, I'm on a deadline here, investigating a particularly vicious homicide that took place just a few hours ago. Every bit of evidence collected while it's still fresh can go a long way toward apprehending the killer." She saw the indecision twist his face. "Plus," she added, "you've got to know, the state attorney is a real ball-breaker. She regards the withholding of potential evidence as an obstruction of justice, prosecutable in a court of law."

"She'd do that to a kid?"

"As God is my witness, I've seen it with my own eyes."

The grandfather let out a frustrated breath. "So what do you expect me to do? It's not my hand."

"No, but Tyler is a minor and you are his legal guardian, which means you have the final say." She held up the swab. "Give me your consent to collect the evidence I need. Otherwise, you'll leave me with no choice but to take your grandson in. And then, well, the state attorney will get her say on what happens next."

Tyler scooted up against the wall, tucking his hands behind his back. "Don't let her do this, Grandpa."

But the grandfather had already made up his mind. He put one foot on the mattress, leaning down and grabbing the boy's wrist from behind his back, yanking Tyler's hand into plain view. The boy resisted, whimpering, but his grandfather was the stronger of the pair.

"Take your precious sample," he said to Maggie.

Maggie rubbed the swab into the dried blood on the ring, then clipped it back in its sealed tube. "Thanks."

He released the boy's wrist. "We done here?"

"Almost. One last thing." She swapped the DNA collector for her phone and opened up the picture album. "I just need Tyler to clear something up for me, real quick." She turned the screen toward the boy. "Is this your car?"

Tyler refused to look, massaging his wrist instead.

"Let me see," said the grandfather.

Maggie showed him the image she'd taken of the back of the Charger, the license plate lit up in the flash.

"Yep," he said. "It's his car all right. Tyler said you impounded it."

"We did. It was parked at a crime scene. We needed to check it externally for trace evidence. Earlier this morning it was towed to a secure compound. I've just come from there." She swiped to a picture of the storage box in the trunk, then held the phone so that both Tyler and his grandfather could see the screen.

She watched for the boy's reaction, knowing that any second now the penny would drop, and that when it did, so too would his jaw.

As predicted, the moment Tyler's eyes registered the nature of the image, his mouth fell wide open.

"Can you explain for me," she said, "why you have bleach, gasoline, zip ties, and a roll of duct tape in the trunk of your car?"

He shook his head, panic rising in his face.

"Well, you should know, this kind of combination is what we loosely refer to as a *kill kit*." She moved the phone into his personal space. "Take another look at these items, Tyler, and tell me, was it your intention to kill Lindy Munson in those woods last night?"

Her last question was like dropping a lit match on a keg of gunpowder. In a flash, Tyler reacted, lunging at her and whacking the phone out of her hand. It smashed into the wall as Tyler exploded to his feet, shooting for the door.

But he didn't get past Deputy Willits. The officer grabbed the boy, slamming him up against the porn-plastered wall.

"Don't you ever learn, boy?" the grandfather said. "Running never solves anything. Best you start talking, boy. And no bull, you hear? Either you answer the lady's question right now, or you answer to me later."

Tyler's eyes were wide, feral, racked with fear.

"It was her idea," he screeched. "She told me to bring those things. I was just following her orders."

Chapter Eight

IN SEPIA

Maggie burst through the swinging doors leading into the Major Case offices, almost causing a passing admin clerk to spill the case files she was carrying.

"Thought you'd run out on me, Novak," Loomis called as Maggie approached their back-to-back desks. He had on a dark-green suit, brown dress shirt, and red necktie, his feet perched on an open drawer. "Almost put out a BOLO on you," he said with a wink. "Be on the lookout for a tardy detective."

She shrugged out of her jacket and draped it over the back of her chair. "Who dressed you this morning? A leprechaun?"

He chuckled. "I see lack of sleep hasn't dented that world-famous charm of yours. Sunday best, Novak. Sunday best. Besides, I'm color blind, remember? It was still dark when I picked them out. I was aiming for all green." He dropped his feet to the floor. "Where've you been? It's after nine. I thought you'd be in here bright and early. I tried calling."

She slid her phone across the desk to him.

His smile dissolved when he saw the cracked screen and the broken bezel. "What the . . . You just got this."

"Well, now I need another." She said it loud enough to turn one or two heads.

In her absence, the weekend shift had moseyed in—two fellow detectives drinking coffee and chin wagging at the bulletin board, and several civilian administrators taking up the slack. Morning sunshine slanted in through the blinds, and the overhead fans whirred.

"Smits?" she said.

"In his office."

She glanced over. "We need to bring him up to speed."

"Smits can wait." He flapped a hand. "Sit, sit. Take the weight off your feet for a minute. Tell me what's going on. That look you're wearing says *harassed* to me."

Maggie stayed standing. "Tyler Pruitt is in Interview One."

"The kid with the snazzy car?" Loomis sat up, taking notice. "You brought him in, on your own?"

"No, with a deputy. Over an hour ago."

"Okay. What's the kid saying?"

She pointed at her face. "See the frustration? That's just it. He's saying nothing. He's pleading the Fifth and asking for a lawyer."

"Okay. And . . . ?"

"And it's the weekend. Best case scenario, a public defender can't be here until late afternoon at the soonest. Probably tomorrow."

Loomis rotated a finger. "Rewind a little here for me, Novak. You've had the kid sitting in an interview room for the last hour?"

"In stony silence."

"Can I ask why? Tempting as it may be, you can't book every nasty asshole for being a pain in the ass. We'd need prisons on every corner."

"I found gasoline in the trunk of his car."

"Well, no real surprise there . . . it's a car. Sometimes it's been known for people to carry spare gas in case of an emergency."

She made a face. "Are you deliberately being sarcastic?"

"Not deliberately. But I have been practicing more than usual lately. I'm hoping to have it perfected by the end of the week."

She managed a smile, some of the tension easing in her neck. With the assistance of his grandfather, bringing Tyler in had been a breeze. But trying to get him to talk had been like putting out a forest fire with a squirt gun. She'd tried every persuasive trick in the book, but the boy had remained tight lipped and uncooperative. Even threats of violence from his grandfather had fallen on deaf ears.

Loomis leaned his bony elbows on the desk. "So what gives with this kid? I know you didn't haul him in for a gasoline violation. Even on a bad day, you're not that persnickety. What else did you find?"

"Duct tape and bleach, for starters."

"Better. Now we're talking. You're thinking maybe this kid's our killer?"

Maggie felt her brow crinkle. After spotting the blood on Tyler's knuckles and then making the connection with the graze on Lindy's chin, she'd been too focused on establishing that his assault on the girl had taken place to take the leap that Loomis had intuitively taken without breaking a sweat.

"You know," she admitted, glancing over to Smits's office again, "that wasn't the path I was headed on."

"You thought he had plans for Lindy alone? Not like you to miss the bigger picture, Novak."

"No, you're right."

Maggie didn't say that when she'd noticed the blood on the boy's ring, all she had seen was red. Partly, it was an aftereffect caused by the shock of learning that Rita hadn't died twenty years ago. Mostly, however, it had reminded her of an incident from her own childhood. Something she wasn't proud of.

Loomis leaned back in his chair and laced his fingers. "Alternatively," he said, "it's coincidence, right? I mean, come on, Novak. What're the chances of this kid planning something sinister in the exact same spot that some other killer dumped a body just a couple of hours earlier? How likely is that?" He didn't wait for her to answer. "If you ask me,

I think we caught this kid right at the start of a killing spree. Nipped a serial killer in the bud. First, he torches Dana Cullen—don't ask me why—and secondly he lures Lindy there to do the same to her."

"Nice theory, Sherlock," Maggie said with a nod. "Except, Tyler was the one who called it in."

Loomis looked at her like she'd just told him that he'd been walking around all morning with his zipper down.

"I'm pretty sure Tyler hit Lindy. That's the real reason I brought him in. I spotted blood on his knuckles in one of the crime scene photos. Out of curiosity, I went down to the impound to check his car."

"And that's when you found the incriminating evidence."

"Only, now I don't know what to think. I found what could be construed as a kill kit in the trunk. But when they stumbled across Dana's body, Tyler was the one to call it in. It doesn't add up."

Loomis made a face. "Teenagers." He picked up a stack of 5 x 7 color prints from his desk and handed half of them to her.

Maggie recognized them as printouts of the crime scene pictures she'd uploaded earlier.

"Ammunition," he said. "Just in case Smits goes on the offensive and we need to defend ourselves." He pushed to his feet and brushed himself off. "Okay. Let's do this, I guess."

They made their way to the small, glass-walled Duty Sergeant office situated in the corner of Major Case.

For a number of reasons, Maggie had never warmed to Lenny Smits—not least because of his frostiness. Smits was one of those people who was bad at making friends and good at making enemies. Even before they reached the door, she could see him standing at the sunlit window at one side of his office, using tweezers to select live crickets from a Tupperware container before dropping them into a soil-filled terrarium. With his imposing frame and graying hair, the sergeant had always reminded Maggie of the movie actor Alec Baldwin from his *30 Rock* days.

She felt Loomis's hand on her shoulder. "Hold up, Novak," he said. "It's feeding time at the zoo."

But Maggie pushed open the door and went inside.

"Read the sign, people," Smits said without looking up. "I'm busy with Betsy. Come back in ten."

"We won't be here in ten," Maggie said. "We've a homicide to investigate." She pulled out a flimsy plastic chair and sat down at the desk. Immediately, its hard back rubbed against her spine. The chairs were a control mechanism, Maggie knew. Smits had had the crappiest ones possible installed so that he could keep his visitors uncomfortable and on the edge of their seats.

Maggie waved for Loomis to join her.

He shook his head.

Still with his back to them, Smits dropped a cricket in the glass tank, then swung his gaze around for the first time. "You know what fascinates me about tarantulas?"

Loomis closed the door. "They're great with kids?"

Smits frowned. "Their bark is worse than their bite."

Loomis frowned. "Bark?"

"Their bad reputation," Smits said. "Smart-ass." He put the tweezers aside and pressed the lid down on the container. "When the reality is, they never attack unless provoked." He turned to face them, showing a mirthless grin. "Okay, detectives, what do you want?"

"Case update," Loomis said.

Smits pointed at him. "You. Sit."

"Me?"

"Yes. You. Now."

Reluctantly, Loomis sat down next to Maggie. He crossed his legs one way and then the other. "We'll make it quick, Sarge," he said. "Then we're out of your hair for the rest of the weekend."

"Cross your heart and hope to die?" Still, Smits's smile had no friendliness in it.

Loomis nodded, not looking so sure.

Smits ambled over from the window and dropped into a big padded leather chair behind his desk. It raised his eye level six inches above theirs. He glanced at the gold watch dangling on his wrist. "Okay. You have two minutes. Shoot."

"Did you read my report?" Maggie said right away.

"I did. And I have to say, Detective, it's a little on the thin side. For instance, you mentioned you know the victim, but not in what capacity."

"Knew," Maggie corrected, causing Smits's eyes to narrow. "I haven't seen her in twenty years."

"Childhood friend," Loomis added.

Maggie glanced at him. "And before you suggest it," she said to Smits, "there's no conflict of interest here. We've been out of touch for the last twenty years."

Smits stuck out his lower lip. "Name?"

"Rita Grigoryan."

He sucked in his lip, then balanced a pair of reading glasses on the end of his nose, picking up a sheet of paper from a tray and briefly perusing it. "Not the same name you've stated here in your report."

Loomis placed one of the photos on Smits's desk. "That's because, in the present day, she's also known as Dana Cullen."

Maggie sensed Loomis glancing sidelong at her, but her own gaze was fixed on the picture. Even though it was upside down to her perspective, she could see it was an enlarged version of the driver's license photo she'd recovered at the lakeside crime scene. Maggie's stomach muscles tightened.

Smits didn't even look at the picture, which was atypical of him. Each of the six homicide detectives under his command knew that he was visually stimulated, and that the simplest way to keep him happy was to feed him something he could hold in his hands. Crime scene pictures were a particular delicacy that kept him sated for hours.

"Sounds like someone has their wires crossed," he said, looking over the top of his readers at each of them in turn. "So which is it, detectives—Rita or Dana?"

"Both," Maggie said.

He let out a tired breath, filing the report back in the tray. "Okay. Explain."

Maggie prodded a finger at the photo. "I'm not yet sure why she changed her name, but twenty years ago, when I knew her, Rita Grigoryan was her name."

Smits sat back a little. "Grigoryan? Why does the name sound familiar?"

"Her father owned a prominent accountancy firm back in the day. You probably heard of him. Big Bob Grigoryan. He had billboards up all over the city."

Smits nodded. "I do remember Big Bob. Now *that* takes me back some. How'd that slogan of his go? 'I got time for your dime.'" He looked at Loomis for confirmation.

Loomis shrugged. "Don't ask me, Sarge. Apparently, Big Bob's accountancy skills weren't as legendary in New York."

Maggie placed a photo from her stack next to the first. It was a zoomed-in shot of a gleaming gold ring wrapped around what looked like a burned twig. "The victim was wearing this wedding band. I'm thinking her being married accounts for the different last name."

"But you can't explain the first?"

"Like I said. Not yet."

She saw a look of skepticism descend like a mist over Smits.

"No disrespect, Detective," he said, "but I'm going to need more than your word to confirm an ID. Twenty years is a long time. It's a generation. Details blur. Heck, I can't even remember my first wife's face—not that I'm complaining."

Loomis laughed what was clearly faked laughter.

Smits didn't seem amused.

Loomis cleared his throat, shifted in his seat. "Let's not forget Novak has a photographic memory."

Smits rolled his gaze round to Maggie. "I never knew that."

"Well, it's not quite eidetic," she said. "I'm just good with faces."

Smits leaned all the way back in his big chair and rocked slightly. "Way I see it," he said, "the purse and its contents are good starting points in establishing who's who here. You state in your report that you recovered the purse from an island out on the lake?"

"Reed mound," Maggie said. "It's a small mud hump about the size of a tennis court, covered in reeds. And it wasn't even a stone's throw offshore." She slid a photo onto the desk. It showed Smits's *island* with the small chunk of bright red reflecting their flashlights in the reeds.

Smits shrugged. "Okay, so how do we know it belongs to the victim?"

"For three reasons." Maggie placed a photo of Dana's purse in front of him. "One, the purse was clean as a whistle." She pointed at the shiny red leather and the gleaming buckles. "It rained yesterday afternoon. The reeds were still damp, but the purse was bone dry. We also found fresh boot prints on the shoreline close to the body." She added a photo, tapping a fingernail against the picture. "You'll notice the deeper heel impressions and the position of the prints in relation to the water? Both indicate someone leaning back as they faced the lake."

"We think," Loomis said, "to toss said purse out in the water." He demonstrated, sinking an imaginary basketball in an imaginary net.

Smits didn't look impressed with Loomis's athleticism, or with what he no doubt was beginning to think were their strong-arm tactics. "And it was still daylight when he supposedly tossed the bag?"

"We think early dusk."

Smits nodded contemplatively. "In which case, and correct me if I'm wrong here, he would've been able to see he'd goofed up and the bag didn't go in the drink. Begs the question, detectives, why didn't he fix it?"

"The water looks deeper than it is," Maggie said. "And there are gators in the lake. It's possible he got cold feet."

"Okay. And your second point, Detective?"

Maggie placed another 5 x 7 on his desk.

Smits glanced at it through his readers, one eyebrow raised. "What's this supposed to be?"

"A copy of an old Polaroid picture. I found the original in the victim's wallet."

Smits picked up the photo for a closer look. "Kind of blurry. What exactly is it I'm looking at?"

"Rita," Maggie said, her voice quieter than intended, "when she was seventeen."

"That so? Well, excuse me if I'm having a hard time seeing it." He switched on his desk lamp, studying the photo under the light. "Where's she been keeping this, a sunny windowsill? I can barely make out there's two people in this shot, never mind recognize features. What makes you think one of these girls is your childhood friend?"

"Because the other girl in the photo is me, and I remember it being taken."

◆ ◆ ◆

Both Smits and Loomis stared at her, the only sound coming from the tarantula feeding on the live crickets.

"Rita got an instant camera for her seventeenth birthday," Maggie explained. "She went through a spell taking pictures of everything from sunsets to squirrels."

Smits waved the photo. "And the both of you, it seems. Were you aware she'd kept this?"

"In truth, I've never given it any thought."

She hadn't. Teenage years were an exploration of the emerging self. A one-way trip to adulthood, marked by detours. Sometimes, dead ends. Who studied the road map once the destination was reached?

Maggie sat back and let out her breath. "Like I said, it was a long time ago. We did a lot of things that last year. Most of it I've forgotten. But I do remember her dad taking this photo. It was the night of the senior prom. The fact I found it at the crime scene goes a long way to proving the purse belongs to her."

Smits pulled off his readers and rubbed the bridge of his nose. "Okay, what's your third reason?"

Maggie added another photo to the growing mosaic on Smits's desk. This time, it was a close-up of the victim's burned left hand.

"Rita was the victim of a stupid prank when we were little. She lost the end of her little finger. As you can see here, the same tip is missing. I believe it proves Dana and Rita are one and the same."

For a moment, Smits scanned the montage of images, his tongue making brief appearances as he studied each print. Then he leaned back in his chair again, looking dissatisfied. "What else you got?"

Loomis said, "That's it, as far as an ID goes."

Maggie said, "The killer used an accelerant. Possibly gasoline. The boy that called it in, he had a can of gasoline in the trunk of his car, as well as bleach and duct tape."

"And . . . ?" It was a similar cool reaction to the one she'd gotten from Loomis. "Where are you going with this? You think he's involved?"

Loomis was quick to say, "I do."

Smits's gaze hung on Maggie. "How about you, Detective? What do you think?"

"I think he assaulted the girl, right before they found the body. I know he went on their date with a kill kit in his car. I think he's definitely a person of interest. I don't know if he's the killer."

"Do we need to bring him in?"

"Novak has him in Interview One as we speak," Loomis said.

"Has he talked?"

"He's lawyered up," Maggie said.

"Has he even provided a statement covering last night?"

Maggie felt heat in her cheeks, knowing that apart from the verbal statement made to Deputy Ramos at the crime scene, they had nothing on paper regarding Tyler's story.

Smits leaned back, the air going out of him. "Well, it's Sunday. Unless he has a lawyer on retainer, which I doubt, no public defender is coming to his aid anytime soon. What about charges?"

"Not yet." Maggie thought about Tyler knocking the phone out of her hand and the possibility, should Lindy fail to incriminate him, of charging him with assault of a police officer. But then Smits would probably say it was her own fault for being in the kid's bedroom in the first place, and what did she expect anyway? "Before we head down the legal route," she said, "I'd like to speak with the girl first. Get her side of the story. She's due in at noon to give her statement. The last thing Tyler said before he pleaded the Fifth was she made him do it."

"Hit her?" Smits looked apprehensive.

"Tyler's comment was in relation to the stuff we found in the trunk of his car. He said he was told to bring them to the lake, and he was just following orders."

"Could they be working together on this, these kids?"

It was one of many scenarios Maggie had considered last night as she'd pored over the crime scene, and later as she'd tossed and turned in bed. Her gut had told her that everything wasn't as it seemed. When it came to premeditated murder, she knew never to underestimate anyone connected with the scene, no matter how initially remote they might have appeared.

"It's possible they're providing a mutual cover story," she said. "We only have their word they found the body when they say they did. Tyler seems to be the dominant party. But it's just as possible Lindy is the one in control, and all those tears were just an act designed to throw us off the scent."

"Sounds like you have your work cut out for you."

Maggie said, "I'm expecting that when we question the girl, we'll get a clearer picture of what happened last night."

Smits seemed to mull things over for a second or two; then he leaned forward. "Okay. Here's what I want the two of you to do. Right now, forget the petty assault. It's a misdemeanor. If the girl wants to press charges, we'll get someone else to fill out the paperwork. You have more pressing matters to attend to. Somebody murdered this woman. You need to concentrate your efforts on finding her killer. If it turns out these kids are involved in more ways than they're saying, we'll come down heavy and make them talk." He gathered the photos together and handed them back. "You have a couple of hours before noon. Check in with the ME. If you're confident on the victim's ID, then go speak with the husband. Bring me back something concrete I can get my chops into. In the meantime, until you can give me something stronger than suspicion, cut the kid loose."

Maggie went to object, but Smits raised both hands.

"You can always bring him back in," he said. "Now go. You're using up all the oxygen."

Chapter Nine

POINT BLANK

Had it not been for the lack of signage, the District Nine Medical Examiner's Office on Michigan Street might have passed as a strip of local businesses. Lawyers' offices, a veterinarian practice, a nail salon or two—maybe. The nondescript beige building sat within a wraparound parking lot edged in trees, its internal workings hidden behind tinted windows and a general outpouring of blandness.

Nothing to see here; keep moving.

"Sure you need me riding shotgun on this?" Loomis said as he parked the motor pool sedan in a space reserved for visiting police personnel. "You know Elkin hates overcrowding."

His sunglasses obscured it, but Maggie knew there was reservation in his eyes. Behind the facility's characterless facade were enough dead bodies to give her partner a major panic attack, and he knew it.

"We'll make it a smash and grab," she said as she unbuckled her seat belt.

"In and out?"

"Promise."

"Okay." He pushed open the door. "I'm trusting you here."

After their case update meeting with Smits, Maggie had called ahead and spoken with Maury Elkin, the county's chief medical examiner. Even though it was Sunday and the ME's office would be staffed at a minimum, she'd requested a rush to be put on the examination of the burned body recovered at Lake Apopka. As with all premeditated homicides, time was of the essence. What was learned or not learned within the first forty-eight hours could be crucial to catching the killer. But Elkin was already one step ahead of her. He'd prioritized the few weekend incomings, postponing those that bore all the hallmarks of natural deaths, shunting Maggie's homicide to the head of the list.

Maggie would owe him. Again.

Vegetation steamed as Maggie and Loomis crossed the parking lot in the morning sunshine. A cerulean sky hatched with vapor trails. Maggie pushed her sunglasses up her nose. Already, November was beginning to feel like a continuation of October, with the unrelenting heat seemingly in for the duration. Ten degrees warmer than usual, for the next week at least, according to the meteorologists. Unlike Loomis, who seemed to worship hot weather, Maggie had never been good with too much heat, and it exasperated him whenever she insisted on setting the car's air-conditioning to deep freeze. *For someone born and raised in a subtropical climate*, Loomis had said, *you're one atypical Floridian, Novak.*

When they were halfway to the main entrance, Loomis's phone rang. He fished it out, then offered the phone to Maggie when he realized who the caller was. "It's for you," he said. "The boyfriend."

For a second, Maggie didn't make the connection. Then realization hit her like a flamethrower and her stomach burned with guilt.

The boyfriend was Steve Kinsey, a part-time surfer and full-time psychiatrist whom Maggie had first met at a fund-raiser six months ago. They'd been dating ever since. Although they lived separately and things weren't too serious, recently it had become something of a custom on the weekend to stay over, either at his place or hers, and last night, after Whitney's neighborhood candy crawl, it had been Maggie's turn to sleep at his. But then the call had come through about the lakeside DB, and Maggie's plans had melted like Halloween candy left out on the sidewalk.

She told Loomis to go on ahead, that she'd catch up, then jammed the phone to her ear. "Steve?"

"Hello, stranger."

"Before you say anything, I owe you a humongous apology."

"No need."

"Seriously. Something came up last night and our date completely escaped my mind. I would've called, but my phone got trashed." It sounded like a bunch of excuses. Maybe because it was. "I'm guessing that's why you're calling on Loomis's phone?"

"Maggie," he said, "it's okay. Nora told me you were busy. That's why I left you alone till now."

"Nora . . . ?" Something like a hornet buzzed in her head. "Nora *called* you?"

"Apparently right after you left her standing in the street. She said work had beckoned and it was unlikely you'd be coming over."

"Nora called *you*?" The hornet bulleted around in her head, ricocheting off her skull.

She heard Steve laugh. "Now don't go getting all Rambo on her, Maggie," he said. "She meant no harm by it. Nora's goodhearted. She used her initiative, is all."

"It's not her place."

"Well, I guess she figured you'd be too wrapped up in what you were doing to remember our dinner plans. Looks like she was right." She heard him laugh again, and the buzzing in her head subsided.

"Steve, I . . ."

"Maggie. Listen to me. I came into this with my eyes wide open. I *understand*. You always say it's murder being a homicide detective, but I think it applies to partners, too. And this isn't me complaining. It's called being empathetic."

This was Steve to a tee—the unerring ability to lift her burden with a single well-placed pick-me-up.

Put under a spotlight, she felt bad about letting him down, especially because this was the second time this week that she'd pulled the plug on their plans. Not only that, now that she thought more about it, Steve had promised homemade lasagna and a movie of her choosing.

"Thanks," she said, "for not dragging me over hot coals. I know I get sidetracked with work, and I know I'm not always the best communicator when it comes to my personal life. I know I'm the opposite end of perfect. It's just that I don't want you thinking . . ." She paused, not wanting to use a weak phrase and give him the wrong idea.

Their relationship was still relatively new, still in the discovery stage where one insensitive sentence could blow up in their faces. Sometimes, keeping the peace meant avoiding verbal triggers.

The first words that immediately sprang to mind were *I don't want you thinking . . . I don't care*, but that wasn't right.

Although Maggie did care about Steve, she wasn't yet at the point where she wanted him to know she did, or how deeply.

Years ago, Maggie had torn herself out of a destructive relationship that had almost ruined her emotionally, and since then she'd vowed never again to enter into another on a whim, or get in too deep before she'd tested the waters.

Sometimes, she thought that each passing lover had paid the price for one man's faults, with her being too withdrawn, too cold, and too reluctant to commit. At times, being deliberately awkward in a bid to save herself from potential heartache. It had taken Maggie a while to realize that this kind of lifestyle had done more harm than good, damaging her more than the destructive relationship had, and turning her into someone she wasn't. And Maggie didn't want to live that way. She wanted to be herself in all relationships, more so in the one that mattered the most. So when Steve came along, she'd made a pledge to herself to be less closed, less inflexible, and less inconsiderate of her lover's feelings.

It was great in theory, but not always entirely practical.

The second words that came to mind were *I don't want you thinking . . . my work is more important*, because she couldn't deny that it was. Maggie had been a homicide detective long before Steve had entered the picture, and would no doubt remain in her role long after he'd gone. To diminish its importance would be akin to Steve saying that surfing didn't play an important role in his life, when they both knew that it did.

"I don't think anything," Steve said before she could make up her mind. "I knew all about your unusual working hours from the get-go. And I'm fine with it. Honestly. If we're being brutally honest here, I have to admit, your unwavering dedication to the badge is one of the things I admire about you."

Admire, not love—Maggie released a quiet sigh of relief.

"If it's any consolation," he said, "Spart enjoyed your half of the lasagna. He lapped up every morsel like it was his last meal on earth."

Maggie found herself smiling.

Spartacus was Steve's eight-year-old red-wheaten Rhodesian ridgeback, fond of chasing Frisbees and tripping Maggie up. During the last six months, Maggie had gotten close to the dog—animals hold no prejudices—and rarely passed on the chance to go for a run with him around the golf course near Steve's place.

"Maybe we can make up for lost time this evening?" Steve suggested. "If you like, we can grab takeout and catch a movie."

"Sounds great. But can we play it by ear? I'm not sure how this case will pan out yet."

"Absolutely. Just let me know either way. I've a few things lined up today myself that I need to take care of. It would be good to see you later, though."

"In that case, I'll make every effort."

They said their goodbyes, and Maggie drew a deep breath before heading into the ME's office.

"Thought I'd hang out here," Loomis said as she pushed through the glass doors and pulled off her sunglasses. He was loitering at the reception counter, his pallor as pale as the decor.

Off to one side, in one of the lobby's sitting areas, a family was patiently waiting to hear about the death of a loved one, each member wearing the same hard mask of shock painted in grief.

"Coward," she whispered to Loomis as she signed the visitor's book.

"You know the saying, Novak," he whispered back. "There are old cops and there are bold cops. But there are no old bold cops."

Maggie handed him back his phone. "Remind me. I need a new one."

"My spare is back at base," he said. "Use that until you get fixed up."

"You mean the one that cuts out all the time? So generous."

"It's in my nature."

The receptionist informed them that Dr. Elkin was in Building Three, and they headed along a curving corridor to the back of the office suite.

For odor control reasons, the District Nine Medical Examiner's Office was split into three buildings separated by courtyards. The first building housed the administration hub and the offices where associates could interact with families and law enforcement in everyday surroundings. The second building contained the autopsy suites that included three huge walk-in coolers and a main examination room large enough to house the deceased victims of a small-scale disaster. And Building Three—otherwise known as the *decomp morgue*—was a self-contained facility in back, in which bodies in advanced stages of decomposition could be examined in an environmentally controlled setting.

Compared with the administration building, the air inside the decomp morgue was frigid, and Maggie half expected to see her breath as they made their way to the examination room. On the ride over, a tension had begun to grip her at the thought of seeing Rita's burned body again, and now it had become a tight belt around her chest, affecting her breathing. Up to a point, the passing hours, combined with a lot of mental wrangling, had subdued her initial shock over the identity of the burned body. She'd accepted that her childhood friend had been murdered. But what she still found hard to come to terms with was that Rita had survived the house fire on Oak Street twenty years ago. She was determined to uncover exactly what had happened that fateful night.

The sooner she was through this, the better.

As they entered the last room, Maury Elkin put down the tablet computer he was working on, and waved them over.

Loomis once said that Elkin reminded him of Forest Whitaker. But apart from a droopy eyelid, Maggie couldn't see the resemblance. At first sight, the single most noticeable thing about the chief medical examiner was his coloring. Maury Elkin was two tone, his predominantly dark skin dappled with irregular lighter patches. When meeting new people, he shrugged off his patchwork appearance, saying that his mother tie dyed him when he was a baby. But the truth was, Elkin had a pigment-destroying skin condition known as *vitiligo*.

"Definitely homicide," he said, cutting right to the chase. "Just what you need on a sunny Sunday morning."

Elkin stood underneath a big surgical lamp suspended from the ceiling, dark ashy marks on his surgical scrubs. The charred corpse lay on a gurney next to him, the burned flesh appearing blacker and somehow scarier in the unflattering light. The limb positioning was different, too. During his examination, Elkin had laid the arms at the sides, and in so doing he had revealed a face, or what little there was left of it.

Maggie heard Loomis release a quiet expletive.

Her own belly flip-flopped.

Heat had fused skin to skin, then melted it away as the flames had begun to feed off fat. What remained were slivers of seared flesh draped over a sooty skull. Facial features reduced to mere bumps. No nose, no ears, no eyelids, no lips to speak of. Just big staring eyeballs, as opaque as frosted glass.

Maggie felt the breath catch in her throat.

"No doubt about it," Elkin said as they gathered around the corpse, "burning to death is just about the least glamorous way to go." He pointed with a gloved finger. "First, the skin fries and peels off. Then the deeper dermal layer shrinks and splits, allowing fat to exude. And that's when the real interesting chemistry starts. Clothing acts like a wick, pulling the soft fat into the flames and creating an exothermic reaction. With enough wick material, a human body can burn like a candle for hours. And given enough time, the muscles dry out, pulling up the limbs into what we call the pugilistic stance." He demonstrated by making fists and posing like a boxer.

"Thanks for the graphic breakdown, Doc," Loomis said, swallowing loudly. "No disrespect, but if you ever get to finish that horror novel you're writing, remind me not to read it."

Elkin relaxed his pose. "I'm in shock, Ed. I didn't think you could read."

"Exclusively short words. No more than three syllables. Preferably on pink paper. Yeah, it's been known to happen."

"Why didn't the whole body burn?" Maggie asked, finding her voice. It sounded slightly distant, scratchy.

"Insufficient wick material," Elkin said. "Even with the accelerant—"

"Gasoline?" Loomis interjected.

"Correct. The fire burned itself out before it grabbed hold. Not that it makes any difference to the death diagnosis." He handed Loomis the tablet computer from the end of the gurney. "Your victim died from a single GSW, resulting in traumatic aortic rupture."

Loomis blinked at the touch screen. "Gunshot wound?"

"What were you expecting, Ed—strangulation?" He winked at Maggie. Elkin jabbed his thumb into the plastic apron covering his belly. "The bullet entered her abdomen right about here," he said, "nicking her aorta on the way through. Cause of death—exsanguination."

"In other words, she bled out." Loomis offered Maggie the tablet. She shook her head. He handed it back to Elkin.

"Was she still alive when she was set on fire?" Maggie asked. The thought sent a cold tremor vibrating through her.

"It doesn't look like it," he said. "I found no presence of soot in the trachea or mixed with the mucus in the distal airways. To be certain, I've sent a blood sample to the lab for screening, but I'm not expecting it to come back showing an elevated carboxyhemoglobin level. In my opinion, the fire happened postmortem."

"To destroy the body and any evidence," Loomis said.

"How long did it take for her to bleed out?" Maggie said.

Elkin shrugged, his plastic apron rustling. "It's hard to say precisely. My professional guess is, probably less than a minute."

Long enough, Maggie thought, for Dana to realize she had been fatally wounded, to stare death in the face while her killer doused her in gasoline, knowing that her fiery end was imminent.

What did you think in those final moments?

"As you know," Elkin continued, dragging her thoughts back to the present, "the survival rate for most people shot once in the abdomen is fairly good. Providing the bullet doesn't hit a major organ, gunshot victims can usually live long enough to seek medical assistance. In this case, and for her sake, the bullet nicking the aorta was a stroke of luck."

Loomis tilted his head back slightly, regarding Elkin down the length of his nose. "What are you saying exactly, Doc?"

"That by shooting the victim once in the midriff, it's possible the killer intended to incapacitate her, not to kill her right away. Nicking the aorta was a mistake."

Loomis turned to Maggie, his jaw tight. "He wanted her alive when he set her on fire, Novak. Makes it personal. No way this killer didn't know Dana."

Otherwise, she knew, the killer would have shot Dana in the chest or the head, and multiple times. Emptying the revolver into Dana to ensure she was dead. But Elkin's observations told a different story. The killer had wanted Dana incapacitated but alive when he lit the match, wanted her to *suffer*. "Thankfully," Elkin said, "the exsanguination saved her from unbearable pain."

"We didn't find any pooled blood at the crime scene," Maggie said. "Or any trace on the trail leading there."

"Well, it's possible the exsanguination was confined internally. I found a significant amount of blood within the abdominal cavity, indicating a fast bleed. But that doesn't tell us where she was shot and died. Let me show you the x-rays."

All at once, Maggie was beginning to feel uncharacteristically nauseous.

"You okay?" Loomis whispered as Elkin wheeled a portable x-ray cart from its base in the corner.

Maggie flashed a cool smile. "I'm crashing, is all. Up all night and no breakfast. Need a sugar fix."

He nodded. "Soon as we're done here."

"We need to speak with the husband."

"And we will. Right after we've refueled."

Elkin powered up the portable unit. The large screen, positioned in portrait mode, lit up, showing an x-ray of a human torso, specifically the hollow area between the pelvis and the rib cage, the jagged spinal column running down the middle.

"Ed, you've been shot, right?"

Loomis touched a hand to his right side, just below his ribs. "A through-and-through. Bled like crazy. Didn't feel a thing at first. Hurt like hell afterward."

"That's because you're all skin and bone."

"You mean rock-hard muscle." Loomis punched his own belly as if to confirm it.

Elkin found Loomis's defensiveness amusing. "All I'm saying is, when you're on the slim side, unlike me, it's easier for projectiles to pass all the way through. But in enough quantity, belly fat can act like Kevlar. The thicker the fat layer, the more energy it can absorb. Brown fat especially slows down anything trying to penetrate it. A long time ago, when I worked in the ER, there was this gunshot victim that came through. A five-hundred-pound male with twenty-six bullet wounds in his gut."

Loomis made a *wow* sound.

"He was the victim of a machine-gun attack. We had to use three gurneys strapped together and six men to wheel him in. Quite a sight to behold. More than two dozen bullets and not one of them made it to any of his organs." Elkin gestured toward the blackened corpse. "In comparison, your victim's wafer thin. But I did measure approximately four inches of belly fat. Enough to catch and slow a bullet shot at distance." He pulled up another x-ray, this time a close-up of the bullet. "See how far the slug penetrated? It's gone almost the whole way through. Given the thickness of the belly fat, its penetration is consistent with a close-range shooting."

Maggie said, "How close?"

"My guess is, the killer had the muzzle pressed against the victim's abdomen when he shot her."

In other words, he'd looked Dana in the eye as he'd pulled the trigger. Maggie's shiver came back.

Loomis peered at the screen. "Looks like a nine mil," he said. "We didn't find a casing at the crime scene. Maybe he picked it up."

Sometimes, it happened. And more frequently these days. Shooters collected their spent cartridges to prevent forensic investigators from finding telltale clues. Salts in sweat left residue on casings, and heat from firing the cartridge etched the fingerprint into the metal. Modern forensics could pull those prints, and those involved in repeat gun crimes were aware of it.

"I've sent the slug to Firearms for analysis," Elkin said. "We've had a quiet few weeks, so I'm hopeful for a quick turnaround."

Maggie knew that if the gun had been used in a previous felony, the match would be flagged up. Any profile information already on record could help them narrow down potential suspects. She made a mental note to cash in a favor with her contact at the ballistics lab, see if she could hurry the report along.

"What about identifying features?" Maggie asked.

Although she was certain of the victim's identity, it never did any harm to verify it, especially in light of any legal disputes that might arise later in their investigation.

Elkin showed them an image on the tablet. It was a picture of a nude woman lying facedown on a metal plinth, her skin deeply pink and mottled with splashes of purple, her limbs burned black, and her torso outlined in a dark fringe—a ribbon of charred flesh running all around her, ending in the back of her blackened skull.

It was the reverse view of Dana Cullen.

"As you can see," he said, zooming in on the image, "the victim has no tattoos or significant scarring on the area of the body that survived the fire."

"What're the chances of pulling something out of the burned side?" Loomis asked.

"Less than zero."

"What about fingerprints?" Maggie said, thinking about accessing Dana's phone.

"Again, not possible. There's too little tissue left." Elkin touched a button on the x-ray unit, and the image on the screen switched to an array of a few dozen thumbnail images of x-rays. He sought one out and tapped it. The image expanded to fill the screen. It looked like five broken twigs. "This is the only internal identifying feature I was able to find. You're looking at the victim's left hand. As you can see, the little finger is missing its distal phalanx."

"She lost it when she was young," Maggie said. "Any other breaks?"

"Not that I've found. No previous fractures and no surgical implants. Some signs of early osteoarthritis, though, but nothing major. Judging from general plate degeneration and joint wear and tear, I'm placing the victim's age between late thirties and early forties." He tapped back to the thumbnail array and brought up an x-ray of the skull.

The imaginary belt around Maggie's chest tightened a little more. Although the image contained no skin or hair, or any other facial features for that matter, the skull's hollow stare was unsettling, as though it demanded attention.

"The teeth are a little hit or miss," Elkin said. "Some old amalgam fillings. Otherwise, not in particularly great shape. My guess is, the victim hadn't visited a dentist in a very long time." He looked at Maggie. "You said you already know the ID?"

Maggie answered without hesitation. "Yes."

"Well, if you need me to corroborate it, your best bet at this stage is to send me the victim's dental records, if they exist. Dental practices tend to destroy ex-patient records after a few years of nonactivity. And these teeth have been neglected awhile." He gestured for them to follow him over to a lab table in the corner. "I did find this, though."

A metal kidney bowl sat underneath a powerful magnifying lamp. Elkin switched on the light and angled the lens so that they both had a view of a gold ring in the bottom of the bowl.

"The victim's wedding band," Elkin said.

In processing the body, Elkin had removed it from Dana's hand and soaped away the soot. In so doing, he'd uncovered an engraving inside the ring:

DC + TJC FOREVER

Loomis took several photos of it with his phone and uploaded them to Major Case's cloud storage.

"I'll email you the autopsy report before end of day," Elkin said as he switched off the lamp. "Aside from that, we're done here."

Chapter Ten

RECHARGE THE BATTERIES

Y ou do know we're going to have to dredge that lake," Loomis said as he and Maggie sat down in a booth, two hot coffees and a box of colorful doughnuts between them.

They were at a fast-food restaurant near the turnoff for Crown Pointe High School, a couple of miles south of Paradise Heights, where an odd mix of Sunday morning patrons were reading the papers and stocking up on calories. The rich aroma of roasting coffee and the sweet scents of confectionaries.

Maggie slid her old SIM card into the new phone she'd picked up on their way to the doughnut shop. Respectfully, she'd declined to take Loomis up on his offer of her using his unreliable five-year-old spare. The new phone had a bigger screen than her other, which was easier to see in daylight, and boasted a better camera, too.

"We know the killer tossed her purse," Loomis said as he took a hearty sniff inside the box of doughnuts. "Stands to reason he tossed the gun as well. It's now a murder weapon. He'd be a fool to hold on to it." He picked out a blueberry doughnut and bit into it.

Maggie was still a little shaken after their visit to the morgue, the horrifying image of Dana's melted face branding itself into her mind's eye. Normally, a visit to the ME's office didn't faze her; she'd done it hundreds of times. Emotional detachment was the ticket. Out of the two of them, Loomis was the one who got itchy feet and needed a strong coffee afterward. But today was different. For the first time since becoming a homicide detective, Maggie had had a relationship with the person lying on the gurney, and her whole perspective had flipped on its head.

"This is so clichéd," she said as she checked that the phone was operational. "You do realize that just by being here we're conforming to every stereotypical preconceived idea about cops and doughnut shops."

Loomis raised an eyebrow. "We do this at least once each week. Don't act all put out and proper, Novak. You love it. Besides, where do you think those TV shows got their information? Single-handedly, the police keep the doughnut industry solvent." He nudged the box toward her. "Eat."

"I'm not hungry."

"You said so yourself, Novak. Your blood sugar has flatlined. I don't want you going all frail and flimsy on me. Eat, or Steve will skin me alive."

"Steve's harmless."

"I've seen the way he handles a knife and fork. That dude is a pro." His expression was serious.

Maggie checked that her phone contacts were accessible.

"How's he doing, by the way?"

"Steve? Fine. Why do you ask?"

"I don't know. He seemed a little pissed on the phone."

"He did?"

"Couldn't you tell?"

"No."

"Like you'd called his kid ugly."

"He doesn't have a child."

"As far as you know he doesn't." He saw her frown, and said, "Get outta here, Novak. I'm messing with you. Anyway, the thing is, what is he now—forty-three, forty-four?—and his worldly accomplishment to date is being a part-time surfer dude from the Outer Banks. That's got to be a worry."

"You're conveniently forgetting he's a full-time certified psycho-therapist with more than ten years' experience under his belt."

"Don't get picky. Anyone can get those certificates printed online." He gobbled up another chunk of doughnut. "The fact of the matter is, he claims you're his first serious girlfriend, ever. And this comes from some dude who's combed the beaches up and down the Atlantic coast, from Montauk to Miami."

Maggie placed the phone facedown on the table. "Okay. Spit it out."

"Hey, I don't want to rain on your parade. But if you ask me, something doesn't ring true here."

"Then it's lucky for me no one asked you." She picked up her coffee and leaned back in the booth.

"Hey, don't get all defensive on me, Novak. I'm just saying. You know I go for the jugular."

"I know you can be immensely insensitive without even trying. And wrong."

"But you love me nevertheless." He stuffed the remainder of the doughnut in his mouth. "Right?"

"If you say so."

He picked out another frosted doughnut. "So what did you do to him?"

"We had dinner plans, yesterday evening. I was supposed to go to his place after the Halloween crawl."

"You called to cancel, though."

"That's just it. I completely forgot. Nora called on my behalf."

"Ouch. That's got to hurt."

"Let's just say it smarts a little."

"Steve got secondhand news from the baby sister. No wonder he was pissed."

"I'm telling you he wasn't."

"Take it from a guy who knows guys. He was pissed." He nudged the box a little closer to her. "Come on. Eat. I don't want you fainting on me. We've a long day ahead. You need your energy."

Maggie rolled her eyes. She reached into the box, her hand passing over an orange-and-chocolate-chip doughnut before scooping up a regular glazed.

Loomis looked offended. "What's wrong with the pumpkin special? I chose it specially for you."

Maggie showed him a glimmer of a smile. "I'm allergic to Halloween." She took a bite, scooping crumbs back into her mouth. "Anyway," she said, "how is it you manage to eat as much junk as you do without piling on weight?"

"Genetics. Plus, my resting metabolic rate is through the roof. My doctor says I burn twice as many calories in my sleep than I do working out."

"You're weird."

"Can't argue with DNA, Novak."

They feasted awhile, washing the sweet and sticky doughnuts down with plenty of coffee.

Here in the doughnut shop, where people were enjoying breakfast and catching up on world events, it was hard to imagine that bad things could happen to regular folk. That people could be shot, point blank, and set on fire.

Did Dana ever eat here, maybe even sitting in this same booth?

Licking his fingers, Loomis said, "So how you holding up?"

"In what way?"

He leaned closer. "I know we touched on it briefly. But we didn't get a chance to bare our souls last night. Some may not agree, but I'm not a total invertebrate. I have eyes, senses. This murder has shaken you up, Novak. You're not yourself. It must have hit you hard, finding out this victim was your girl."

A bite of doughnut stuck to Maggie's throat on its way down. She helped it on its way with a gulp of coffee. "Let's just say, it was the last thing I expected."

"I know you said you hung out together. But were the two of you super close? Besties?"

"How did you get to be so nosy?"

"It's in my job description. The word *detective* kind of gives it away. If you'd prefer we didn't—"

"No," she said. "It's okay. Just give me a second."

Maggie leaned back in the booth, nursing her coffee. As a rule, she never withheld pertinent case information from Loomis, and she believed he did the same. To do so would be counterproductive, not just for them, but to the investigation as a whole. Two heads were always better than one. Their partnership was more than a case of simply working together. It was a union based on mutual respect and cast-iron trust. But in this instance, she found herself holding back, unwilling to completely bare all, because to do so would expose her past failings.

Nothing she could do about it.

"Rita and I grew up in the same neighborhood," she began slowly. "We went to the same schools. We hung out in the evenings and on the weekends. And you're right. For a while we were best friends."

"Like BFFs?"

She found her smile, even if it was weak. "We hadn't invented those acronyms back then."

"You know what I mean."

"I spent a lot of my early childhood playing at her house. I grew close to her family. So when the house fire happened . . ." A hot geyser plumed inside her. She closed her mouth, hoping that nothing would leak out.

"Any idea who might have wanted her dead?" Loomis said softly.

She shook her head. It didn't dissipate the heat.

"No weird neighbors or disgruntled boyfriends?"

"Loomis, it was twenty years ago."

"Just saying. We make enemies from the day we're introduced to other people. You run faster than another kid, they want to break your legs. You score higher on a test, some average Joe holds that grudge for the rest of his life. You steal some dude's girl . . ."

"Are we speaking from personal experience here?"

"Aren't we always?"

Loomis never failed to surprise her.

"The truth is," she said, sitting forward again, the heat subsiding, "we have no idea what's happened in her life over the past twenty years, especially when it comes to any unsavory characters she met along the way. We need to fill in the twenty-year blank. There's so much we don't know."

"Like how Rita managed to escape the house fire."

"Exactly. And why she became Dana. It's basic information we need to find out."

"Let's hope the husband has some answers."

They finished up and then made their way outside.

"Abby is cooking pot roast for dinner this evening," Loomis said as they walked to the car. "Why don't you come over? Fetch Steve."

"That way he can tell you all about his beach babe conquests?"

"Don't be bitter, Novak. Doesn't look good on you."

"Even if he has any," she said as they got in the car, "which I'm in no doubt he has, he won't share."

"How do you know?"

"Because he's a shrink. And shrinks are notorious for never taking their own advice. He talks less about himself than I do."

Loomis turned the ignition. "I'll take that as a yes, then."

"Pot roast."

"Trust me, you don't want to miss out. Abby nails it." He glanced at her as he buckled up. "This isn't a request, by the way. I'm worried about you, Novak. I don't think you're eating enough."

"You worry too much."

"Someone's got to. One thing's for certain—you're going to need much bigger fat reserves for the baby."

"What baby?"

"The one Steve has planned."

"And you know this how?"

"Because he's in love and you're a keeper."

Maggie smiled dismissively. "Never going to happen."

"We'll see."

He put the car in gear and drove out onto the highway, whistling like he didn't have a care in the world.

It had never occurred to Maggie that Steve might want to start a family at some point. The subject hadn't come up, and he'd never hinted at any kind of desire to join the ranks of fatherhood. But if it did turn out to be the case, that Steve wanted children, Maggie would be ready with her answer.

Chapter Eleven

IT'S ALWAYS THE HUSBAND

Someone should definitely do something to spruce this place up," Loomis said as they headed into Paradise Heights. "Starting with dynamite."

The name Paradise Heights conjured sunny images of multimillion-dollar palatial homes set within idyllic scenery. Grand water-fronted estates steeped in old money, with gleaming playboy yachts moored in a marina.

In reality, the small community located on the eastern edge of Lake Apopka was one of the poorest suburban neighborhoods in this part of the county, with a hodgepodge of rundown properties and family-run businesses that reflected their low-income households.

Maggie had always wondered if the name had been adopted with good intentions, or if it had been someone's idea of a joke. If Loomis's gloomy expression was any kind of barometer, there was her answer.

"Missing out on a little TLC around here," he commented as they turned into Summer Haven Lane. Another name bearing no resemblance to real life.

Maggie wasn't so quick to form a negative judgment. Foliage grew rapidly in the subtropical climate, and things could look overgrown and unkempt overnight. Plus, people lived where they could afford. The poverty line didn't breed bad folk; it just kept the lowest paid separated from those with enough wealth for it not to matter.

Dana's home address brought them to a small pink-painted wooden cottage sitting in the middle of a well-tended cactus garden. Tall trees draped in Spanish moss overhanging the property. Last night, when Maggie had stopped by, none of the details had been visible.

Loomis killed the engine, and they sat quietly for a moment, taking stock while Maggie used her new phone to take a test picture of the house. The image came out color saturated and crystal sharp.

"Okay?" Loomis asked.

"Perfect."

Before setting out to the ME's office, Maggie had logged into the Orange County Comptroller's computerized records system to determine the identities of those residents registered at this address. According to the voting register, Dana had lived here with her husband, Thomas Joseph Cullen, for a little over eighteen months now. Without running a wider search, it was anyone's guess where they lived before here.

A male rider in a red helmet roared by on a dirt bike, disturbing the Sunday morning peace, blue smoke trailing.

Loomis muttered something about unlicensed road use and that there were never any cops around when you needed one.

Maggie took a photo of the biker as he skipped the sidewalk, shooting between two houses farther down the street.

Then she zoomed the camera in on the white Subaru Baja pickup truck parked in the driveway of the Cullen residence. A decal on the driver's door advertised CULLEN LANDSCAPING underneath the image of a cartoon character wielding a chain saw. She snapped a picture.

Informing the next of kin that their loved one had died was part of the job that many people in law enforcement dreaded, and understandably so. This kind of meeting had to be played by ear, and gently. Right now they had no way of knowing if the husband was involved in the murder. Although statistics showed that most murders of married women were perpetrated by their husbands, the last thing Maggie wanted was to spook Cullen and give him an excuse to clam up. In instances of uxoricide—when a man killed his wife—Maggie had found a surprising number of husbands unable to hold it together when questioned. One wrong comment could sabotage a pending confession.

"How do you want to play this?" Loomis said as they got out of the car. "Good cop, bad cop?"

"Let's just be ourselves."

"It's what I said."

"Just remember we're the bearers of bad news."

"Relax, Novak. Everybody knows I'm a sensitive guy."

But Maggie knew it wasn't the whole of it. Although Loomis could be sensitive, when it came to dealing with certain men, he could be downright undiplomatic. She'd decided it was a *man thing*. An inherent refusal to wear another man's shoes.

Maggie glanced in the truck as they walked up the driveway. Although the outside looked recently washed, the inside was a different matter. A fine layer of white dust clung to the dash, and the seats were covered in a fine powdering of soil and grit. Larger grains, as well as bits of plant debris, were scattered on the carpeting.

Loomis jabbed a thumb against the doorbell. A resonant ding-dong sounded, and a few moments later the front door creaked opened to reveal a middle-aged redheaded man with a curly beard. He was a head shorter than Maggie, hefty looking rather than sculpted muscle. He had on a green polo shirt, khaki chinos, and slip-on boat shoes. Embroidered in yellow on the left chest of his shirt was a miniature copy of the Cullen Landscaping business decal.

"Mr. Cullen?" Maggie said, pulling back her jacket so that he could see the police badge dangling on its necklace. "Sheriff's Office. Detectives Novak and Loomis. Can we step in and talk?"

Thomas Cullen's eyes flicked from Maggie to Loomis—who presented his own police badge on cue—then back to Maggie again. She detected no hint of fear in his eyes, or the makings of any panic. If anything, his expression was impassive.

On the face of it, he didn't look like a man who had set his wife on fire the night before.

"Going somewhere?" Loomis said before Cullen could answer. He gestured at a piece of carry-on luggage standing in the hallway behind the man, a raincoat folded over the extended handle.

"Excuse me?" he said with the same blank expression.

"Planning a trip?" Loomis said.

While Cullen glanced behind him at the carry-on, Maggie gave Loomis a look that told him to let her handle things.

"It's my wife's," Cullen said.

"It's your wife we need to talk about," Maggie said.

Cullen's gaze came back to her. "Well, I can tell you categorically Dana's lying. She has an overactive imagination. Makes things up. Whatever she's saying I did, I didn't."

"We're with Homicide," Loomis said. "Your wife's dead, Mr. Cullen. Are you going to let us in or do I have to put you in bracelets right here on your doorstep?"

◆ ◆ ◆

He's faking it, Loomis mouthed to Maggie as they stood in the bathroom doorway, listening to Cullen throwing up.

Maggie made a cut-throat gesture. "You okay, Mr. Cullen?" she said without taking her eyes off of Loomis.

Faking it, Loomis mouthed again.

Cullen was hunched over the toilet, retching. He raised a wobbly hand above his head, then bent over and retched again.

When presented with such life-altering news, everyone reacted differently. In Cullen's case, the moment he had put two and two together, his face had turned a sickly shade of gray, and the seriousness of the moment had sent him rushing to the bathroom. Maggie and Loomis had followed him down the hall, partly to offer their support, but mostly to make sure that he didn't make a bolt for the back door.

Cullen flushed the toilet and then stooped over to the sink, splashing his face with water and rinsing his mouth before drying off on a towel.

"Let's go sit," Maggie said when he was done. She waggled her fingers, indicating he should come out of the bathroom.

Shoulders slumped, Cullen shuffled past them, one hand maintaining his balance against the wall as he headed for the living room. As they fell in behind, Loomis made a face at Maggie. She knew what he was thinking: that Cullen's behavior was too spontaneously theatrical to be genuine. From dispassionate to emotional wreck in the space of a second. Later, she knew, Loomis would confirm her suspicions by saying something along the lines of *Real men don't react that way*.

The living room looked like an explosion in a paint factory. Everything mismatching chintz and clashing colors. Handmade crocheted blankets draped over the furniture, and more accent cushions than a home decor center. Maggie wasn't sure if it was the overkill of good taste, or an attempt to brighten up an overcast life.

Cullen sank into a floral-print easy chair. "What happened? Was she in an accident?"

Maggie cleared a crumpled heap of blankets off a couch and sat down. "Mr. Cullen, before we go down that road, I need you to confirm a few things for me first. I appreciate this is difficult for you. Can you do that for me?"

He nodded, but didn't look sure. He looked like he wanted to shrink into himself and never come out again.

Maggie signed into Major Case's cloud storage on her phone and brought up the first of three close-up photographs. She showed him the first. "Mr. Cullen, is this your wife's purse?"

He looked at the screen. "Could be," he said, his voice sounding small and tight. "She has one just like it. Bought it from an outlet mall in the city a couple weeks ago."

"How'd she afford it?" Loomis said. He'd remained standing, fingers hooked loosely in his back pockets.

"She works hard. It was her birthday. She treated herself."

Maggie brought up another photo. "Mr. Cullen, does your wife drive a Chevy?"

He nodded.

"Is this hers?" She showed him the image of the electronic key fob with its Minnie Mouse sticker that she'd found in Dana's purse.

A tremor twitched his lips. "She puts those stickers on everything. It's her *thing*. Dana loves Disney." He looked up at Maggie, his gaze suddenly racked with concern. "Was she in a car crash?"

"No, Mr. Cullen. As yet, we haven't located your wife's car. Do you know where it might be at?"

He shook his head. "She left in it yesterday. That was the last I saw of it . . . and her."

Maggie brought up a photo of the wedding band that Loomis had taken at the coroner's office, specifically a close-up of the **DC + TJC FOREVER** inscription on the inside of the ring, confirming, at least in Maggie's mind, the victim's identity once and for all.

She saw Cullen gulp, his eyes filling with tears.

"Mr. Cullen," she said, "I know this is hard for you. But please try and stay strong. You're doing great." She held the phone closer to him. "For the record, is this your wife's wedding band?"

He made a single sharp nod. "Those are our initials. But this must be some kind of mistake."

"I'm afraid it's real. Your wife is dead, Mr. Cullen. The Sheriff's Office extends its sincerest condolences. We are very sorry for your loss."

Maggie hated saying those words. They sounded so clinical and scripted, cold. But it was always best to be direct, leaving no room for uncertainty, because when it came to news of a death, the best way to convey it was directly and to the point. Easing into it, or beating around the bush could lead to confusion, and confusion only led to doubt. And that was the last thing any police officer wanted the next of kin or other concerned party to feel, because doubt raised false hope and could even make identifying a body tricky.

For a second, Cullen stared at her, the first of his tears beginning to roll out onto his cheeks. A whimper leaked from his lips. His head dropped, and a quiver ran through his frame. Maggie knew that the brain took time to process news of this immensity, stumbling through various stages of refusal, dismissal, denial, sometimes causing people to behave erratically. She suspected if he'd been given the choice of popping out of existence right here, right now, Cullen would have jumped at the chance.

"How . . . ," he began shakily, "how did it happen?"

"Your wife died from a gunshot wound."

"What?"

"Someone shot her," Loomis said. "Do you own a gun, Mr. Cullen?"

Cullen stared at Loomis, a mixture of fear and disbelief interchanging on his face. "Wait a minute," he said. "You think *I* killed my wife? That's crazy! We loved each other."

"So why was she leaving you?"

Cullen's stricken eyes swung back to Maggie.

"The carry-on in the hall," she said. "Was Dana planning on leaving you, Mr. Cullen? Did you try and stop her? Is that what happened here last night?"

"No!" Now his eyes flicked from her to Loomis and back again. "Look, you've got this all wrong. It wasn't like that. Sure, we were going through a rough patch. Who doesn't? But Dana said she just needed some space, is all. Time to sort out her head. I was cool with that. I didn't *kill* her." He said the word as though it was poison on his tongue.

Loomis loomed, which was something he did without trying. "You didn't answer my question, Mr. Cullen. Do you own a gun?"

"No! Of course I don't! Take a look around if you don't believe me. You won't find one. I've nothing to hide."

"You're consenting to a search of your property?"

"Sure," he said to Loomis. "Have at it. Tear the place apart if you have to. You'll see I'm not lying. You've got to believe me," he said to Maggie as Loomis headed into the adjoining kitchenette. "I didn't kill my wife."

"And I believe you." She didn't. Not yet, anyway. It was a device to elicit cooperation. "But somebody did," she said. "And right now that somebody is still out there. That's why I need your help, Mr. Cullen. Because the more information you provide right now while things are still fresh in your mind, the better picture we have of your wife and who might have wanted her dead. Do you understand?"

He nodded. "I'll try."

Maggie activated the voice recorder on her phone. "How long have you guys been married?"

He let out a tremulous breath. "Four, no, *five* years. Time flies."

"And you've known Dana for . . . ?"

"Six years. We ran into each other in a Walmart parking lot. Literally. She reversed right out into the side of my truck. We exchanged numbers, and we've been together since."

"And you've been here eighteen months, right?"

He nodded. "Dana loves this place. She says it's her little gingerbread house."

"And before here, you guys lived where?"

"Kingman."

Maggie hid her surprise. "In Arizona?"

"Yeah."

She was familiar with the city. Located on a section of the historic Route 66, Kingman was the gateway to Nevada's gambling destinations. Years ago, she and a friend had driven the Main Street of America, from Chicago to Los Angeles, staying in Kingman overnight. The thought that Rita had been living there at the time, maybe within reach of where Maggie had roomed, was incredible.

"Mr. Cullen, what's your wife's maiden name?"

"Burnside."

"Not Grigoryan?"

"No. Why would you say that?"

"It's just another lead we're following. She grew up in Kingman?"

"Yeah."

"Do you have any pictures of her when she was young?"

"Maybe. Somewhere. I don't know. Dana keeps stuff stowed all over the place. You'd have to look."

"I will, thanks."

"She has selfies on her phone, if that's any good."

"Okay. Can I ask why you relocated to Florida?"

"Dana got her dream job down here."

"Doing?"

"Guidance counseling."

"Where at?"

"Crown Pointe."

Maggie's heart missed a beat. "The high school?"

"Yeah." He reached for a cell phone on the arm of the chair. "You know, I really need to call the principal. Tell her Dana won't be coming in."

Maggie put out a hand. "Please. Mr. Cullen. It's Sunday. No one's there. Besides, you don't need to do that. We'll inform the school on your behalf, tomorrow."

With a thud, his hand fell back to his lap.

"Did she like her job, at the high school?"

"Dana loves working with kids. It's all she's ever done. We couldn't have any of our own. She said being a guidance counselor was her way of giving back."

When they were young, Maggie and Rita had talked about their futures, tweaking their aspirations as they'd grown older. While Maggie had contemplated a career in education, Rita had dreamed of becoming an actor. But a few razor-edged words from one of their friends had cut Rita's hopes to shreds, and not long after, an inferno had razed her dreams.

"Mr. Cullen," Maggie said, "does your wife have any enemies?"

Cullen's mouth twisted, as though the thought was unsavory. "No way. Everybody likes Dana. She's the best thing to happen to that school. We're all so proud of her. Me, her parents."

Maggie's heart missed another beat. "Her mom and dad—they're alive?"

◆ ◆ ◆

"Cullen says Dana's parents are still live alive," Maggie told Loomis as she joined him in a small windowless room at the back of the house. The cramped space was being used as a pantry. Floor-to-ceiling shelving crammed with cans and containers, and various bottles and packs of dried foodstuffs.

Loomis was rummaging through the shelves, inspecting inside anything big enough to hide a handgun. "They are?" he said. "Where?"

"Arizona. Not only that. They have two other children as well, both of them sons, both younger than Dana."

"Relevance?"

"Rita had two younger brothers."

"Who all burned to death in the house fire, right?"

"Supposedly."

"Factually."

"Or they didn't."

"Only because you're convinced Dana is Rita."

"She is."

"Which means the ME—and basically everyone else who would've reported the Grigoryans being burned to death—they're all a bunch of liars?"

"You're right. It sounds totally implausible."

"And sarcasm doesn't suit you, Novak." He shook a jar of dried peas. "What've you done with Cullen?"

"Right now, he's being consoled out on the street by a pair of deputies."

"Smart."

"One of us has to be."

Loomis smiled to himself. "Unless you turn over that rock, Novak, you have no way of knowing what creepy crawlies lurk beneath."

Maggie bit her tongue. She didn't want to *get into it* with Loomis right now. Given where they were and why they were here, she didn't think it appropriate. Loomis had his reasons for being pushy with Cullen; far too often in situations like this, the "honest" word of grief-stricken husbands was the last thing that could be trusted. Even blissfully married couples kept secrets from each other. An innocent flirtation with a colleague at the office, a harmless little white lie, a fantasy unrealized. People were imperfect. Being secretive about personal feelings, thoughts, and even actions was human nature. But it was no excuse for rudeness.

"What do you think about Cullen?" Loomis said. "Do you think he's good for this?"

"My gut says no. What does yours say?"

"That it needs more doughnuts." He lifted the lid on a plastic container with what looked like flour inside.

"Guess where Dana worked?" Maggie said.

"NASA?" He stuck a finger in the white powder, stirring it around.

"Crown Pointe."

"Interesting."

"She's their guidance counselor. Which means it's likely she knew Tyler and Lindy."

"The plot thickens. You think this murder is connected with the high school?"

"I think it's something we need to look at. The killer just happening to choose that location to do his dirty deed can't be coincidence. It's possible Dana poked around a little too deeply in some kid's head and dug up something she wasn't supposed to find."

"Tyler's the perfect candidate. I told you he's serial-killer material." He replaced the lid and put the container back on the shelf. "Where were the Cullens eighteen months ago?"

"Arizona. Cullen says they lived in Kingman and that Dana's maiden name is Burnside."

"So . . . Dana Burnside. Not Rita Grigoryan."

"Don't," she said, choosing not to get into the whole name debate again. "The Polaroid picture proves all."

Loomis paused his searching. "To be honest, Novak, Smits nailed it on that one. It's impossible to make out who's in that photo. I know you're convinced it's you and Rita. But it was twenty years ago. How many other girls have taken similar photos in the meantime?" He popped the lid on a jar and sniffed, screwing up his eyes and recoiling from the smell. He put the lid back on. "Even so, I've got to hand it to you. As conspiracy theories go, it's up there with the best."

"I can't believe you still think I'm mistaken. What about the missing pinky?"

"Coincidence?" He rattled bottles. "Look, Novak, we've all got a doppelgänger somewhere. A double. Take me as an example. Everywhere I go, people mistake me for Alexander Skarsgård."

"Alex who?"

"Eric Northman, the vampire in *True Blood*." He saw Maggie's rising bafflement and added, "Never mind. I know you're not big on TV. The point is, Dana and Rita being look-alikes is pretty much all you've got to go on right now. You said it yourself. Dana is from Arizona. Her mom and dad are still alive. The names don't match. If she really is Rita, how do you even begin explaining any of that?"

"Aside from a face-to-face meeting with her parents—"

"Something that the department is never going to fund."

"—I need to interview first responders from the night of the fire."

Loomis smiled to himself again. "You want to interrogate retired detectives over a twenty-year-old incident? Good luck with Smits signing off on that one." He stuffed the jar back on the shelf, clanking bottles. "Now, are you going to help me search this place? It's not every day we get free rein."

At least in that respect, Loomis was right.

Usually, there were two reasons why people consented to their homes being searched by police: innocence, in which they believed they had nothing to hide; and arrogance, in which they believed they had hidden their secret so well that it would remain undetected.

It was important to treat both cases with equal scrutiny, because all too often, both cases turned up more than expected.

Maggie paused as she turned to leave. "By the way," she said, "did you happen to come across a file box or a bunch of documents?"

"Why?"

"Dana's birth certificate. I want to see it with my own eyes."

Loomis shrugged. "I haven't searched the master bedroom yet."

"I'm right about Dana," she said as she left the pantry.

"So prove it beyond reasonable doubt," he called after her.

The master bedroom occupied the rear left quarter of the house, and seemed to be populated by a hundred plush Disney characters.

Rita hated Disney.

Maggie paused in the doorway, an all-too-familiar coolness return-ing to her belly. It struck her, suddenly, that this wasn't just Dana's house; it was *Rita's* house, too. *Rita's private domain.* Home to the grown-up version of the girl she had once shared her own intimate secrets with, and in another bedroom of similar proportions. The last time she'd been inside Rita's bedroom—albeit the one on Oak Street—both the language and the air had been heated, and their relationship had never been the same again.

Was it any surprise that she felt slightly weird just standing here?

Maggie could still picture Rita's other bedroom, with its film noir movie posters and gothic art prints pinned to the walls. The black bed-ding and the bloodred bulb dangling from a wire in the middle of the ceiling.

This bedroom reminded her of the Disney Store.

Feeling like an intruder, Maggie stepped inside.

Even though the decor bordered on sensory overload, the room itself was neat and tidy, if a little claustrophobic. That was the thing about small houses: A finite amount of space could go one of two ways—either cluttered and messy, or organized in such a way as to maximize the best of every square inch. In this case, everything had its place.

Ideally, Maggie wanted to find something to confirm what she already knew: that Dana Cullen was Rita Grigoryan. Not just to satisfy a personal need, but also to prove to Loomis and Smits that she wasn't imagining things. A document explaining Rita's name change, or even a letter made out in her old name would suffice. Of course, it wouldn't point toward who was behind her murder, but it would allow Maggie to pursue a line of inquiry that would otherwise be deemed out of bounds. All too often, breaks in cases came from the least expected sources. Rita had changed her name for a valid reason. It could prove to be significant, a case breaker. The more information Maggie could put at her fingertips now, the better she could sift out the important stuff.

She had learned never to dismiss anything, and especially not something that her gut instinct had an infatuation with. Finding even the smallest gold nugget was always a good indicator that plenty more lay close by.

If the trippy decor was anything to go by, no one would ever believe that Rita had grown up to be Dana.

Maggie began with the nightstand. She put on a pair of gloves, inspecting its three drawers one by one. She found an assortment of personal items in each, including packs and bottles of nonprescription medications and a sparse collection of makeup products. Hair ties, brushes, deodorants, and skin creams. Lying facedown in the bottom drawer: a framed photograph of Dana and Thomas Cullen on what appeared to be their wedding day. The happy couple were hugging each other outside a white wooden chapel, beaming. Blue sky above and rust-colored mountains in the background. They looked like they were madly in love.

Nothing lasts forever.

Maggie left the photo standing upright on the nightstand and moved on, pulling back the louvered doors on the small closet. It was filled with his-and-hers clothing. A sagging rail of dresses and shirts. Above, a single shelf housing cube-shaped storage bins. Handwritten labels: *Arts & Crafts, Christmas, Sewing & Fabric, Paints & Glitters, Keepsakes.*

Maggie reached for the last box and hefted it down, placing it on the bed behind her.

It was crammed with mementos. Souvenirs, picked up at memorable stopovers along life's journey, meaningless to anyone but their owner: a pink visor with flamingos on the plastic bill; poker chips and ticket stubs; beaded bracelets and bird feathers; photos of cityscapes, deserts, mountains; Disney fridge magnets; seashells; hotel soaps; a small alligator head; a vial of sand; a bunch of dried flowers; and dozens of other random items. But nothing to link Dana with Rita.

Her gaze snagged on a file box on the floor between two shoe racks. She slid it out.

Inside, she found a dozen hanging file folders with handwritten labels on the tabs. *Bills, Insurance, Tax.*

She flicked through various documents in the folder marked *Insurance,* finding Cullen's business insurance, private healthcare polices, electrical equipment warranties, regular household cover. She found a letter of cancellation stapled to the front page of a full-term life insurance policy made out in Dana's name. An insurance company based in Arizona. Big red *X*s drawn with a felt pen on each page. The cancellation letter was dated a month ago.

Why did she cancel her life insurance?

An unmarked file at the back of the box contained a year's worth of checking account statements from a branch of Wells Fargo in Kingman, addressed in Dana's name. Maggie fanned them out on the jazzy carpeting. Mostly, the transactions related to small amounts. ATM withdrawals and cashed checks. A few regular direct debits. The largest withdrawal of the year coming in late September, in the amount of $3,000.

Overall, Dana had a healthy balance, hovering in the high four figures. Additions coming in the form of a monthly salary from the Orange County School District.

A receipt was attached to the back of September's statement. Last Friday, Dana had withdrawn $8,000 in cash, reducing her balance to the low hundreds.

Typically, when Maggie came across large withdrawals like this as part of her investigations, it raised an immediate red flag. To her, it indicated one of three things: the account holder was planning to disappear, a third party was pressuring the account holder to settle a debt, or the account holder was being blackmailed.

At a glance, it was impossible to say which, if any, of these scenarios fit Dana's situation.

Maggie took a photo with her phone.

What did Dana need $8,000 in cash for?

The prior healthy balance ruled out a sizable debt, and other than the carry-on in the hall, Maggie had seen no other evidence to suggest Dana was planning on leaving her husband, especially on a permanent basis.

She made a note to question Cullen about it.

She put the file box back in the closet and turned her attention to the eight-drawer dresser under the window.

Its contents were split equally between men's and women's clothing, with Dana's drawers lined in scented paper. Jasmine and rose. Although Maggie had done this a hundred times, searching through someone's drawers always felt weird, and rifling through a person's underwear was definitely the ultimate invasion of privacy. Carefully, she worked her gloved hands through the garments, feeling for anything out of place. Despite Loomis's conviction, she wasn't expecting to lay her hands on the murder weapon stashed away amid Cullen's boxers. But her fingers did locate something flat and oblong at the back of Dana's underwear drawer.

It was a notebook, bound in black faux leather, with Disney character stickers stuck at random all over its cover. Maggie had one just like it at home, minus the stickers: a gift from Rita to mark the start of their senior year.

Maggie laid the notebook on the top of the dresser and opened it to the first cream-colored page.

A Polaroid photo was wedged into the crease of the spine.

It depicted the face of a seventeen-year-old girl, with big sad eyes and scruffy tomboyish red hair.

Maggie's heart skipped again. "Rita."

Like a Pierrot clown, she'd powdered her face white, using black makeup to draw fake tears on her cheeks. Maggie couldn't recall ever seeing Rita like this before, and the ghostly image unsettled her.

Written in thick red ink in the white space below the picture was a single word:

HELGA

And Maggie's heart leaped into her throat.

Although she'd thought about this name and its association with Rita over the years, she hadn't seen or heard any mention of it in two decades. If anything, she'd tried her best to forget it, or at least push it behind her oldest memories where it could do the least harm. But every now and then, especially when her guard was down, it would pop back to the surface, its manifestation squeezing her heart in a cold fist.

Hardly breathing, she levered the photo from the notebook and turned it over. Scribbled on the reverse, and in the same red ink, were the words:

I am dying as I write this,

and dead as you read it.

Maggie gaped, stunned by the sheer impact of the inscription.

Did Dana know she was going to be murdered?

Maggie's phone rang, startling her.

She dug it out, hearing Loomis say, "I'm in the backyard. Look over here," and she lifted her gaze to the window.

Loomis waved at her from the other side of the glass.

Heat burned in her cheeks.

"Drop what you're doing," he said. "Something here you need to come see."

With her pulse still beating way too fast, Maggie buried the notebook back in the drawer and made her way outside into the sunbaked backyard, hoping that her sunglasses would mask the glow in her cheeks.

What had Dana meant by those words?

As with the front of the property, Cullen had landscaped the backyard into an alpine garden, complete with golden gravel, rock mounds, and sprawling magnolia. He'd fenced it in, too, separating the yard from the neighboring properties.

Loomis stood beside an outdoor kettle grill—one of those pod-shaped ovens with three legs. He nudged the toe of his shoe against a red plastic gas can standing next to it. "Empty gas can," he said. "I'm thinking accelerant for burning bodies."

"Okay."

"And then there's these . . . ," he said, lifting the domed lid.

A pair of black work boots stood on the grill plate, their soles caked in brown mud. Even from a few feet away, Maggie could smell the unmistakable tang of swamp water.

"Nice find," she said.

She photographed the boots with her phone. Then, with gloved hands, Loomis lifted up the boots so that she could photograph the mud-encrusted treads.

"Size twelve," he said. "Or I'm a monkey's uncle."

"You do have the ears for it. What's that under the grill?"

Loomis placed the boots on the ground and removed the grill plate.

An oily cloth was bundled in the concave space normally reserved for the charcoal.

Maggie put on gloves and then lifted it out, weighing it in her hand. "Feels heavy." Carefully, she unfolded the cloth to reveal a revolver.

"Looks like a Smith and Wesson six-shooter," Loomis said. "And possibly the right caliber."

Maggie sniffed the muzzle. "It also smells of cordite, which means it's been fired recently. Okay. Let's get the crime scene investigators down here. I think we just struck the mother lode."

Chapter Twelve

DUCKS IN A ROW

From inside the low-lit observation room, Maggie watched Thomas Cullen through the one-way glass as he guzzled water from a plastic bottle. His handcuffed wrists were manacled to a metal loop bolted to the table, which made drinking the water something of a contortionist act. Aside from a bathroom break, Cullen had been sitting in the brightly lit interview room for almost two hours, his impatience more visible with each passing minute.

Once or twice, he'd attempted to make conversation with the deputy standing guard in the corner, to no avail. Several times, he'd called out at the one-way mirror, imploring anyone observing from the other side to release him. But only Maggie was listening, and she had no intention of removing his cuffs.

During the last two hours, Maggie had spent half the time writing up her full homicide report for Smits. More and more these days, her job was as much about the paperwork as it was about the police work. Procedures had to be met at every point. Boxes checked and forms filled out. Too many acquittals and mistrials came as the result of felons being released over a technicality—a vital missing bit of information in a sloppy police report, or an essential piece of evidence falling out of the chain-of-custody—and no prosecutor wanted to go to court hog tied.

Smits was all about the process.

Meanwhile, in light of the discoveries in Cullen's backyard, CSIs from Forensics were at the house, not quite taking the place apart, but as good as. According to Elkin, Dana could have been shot anywhere. Ideally, Maggie wanted the technicians to find evidence of blood spatter, proving that Cullen had used the gun on Dana in her own home before dumping and then burning her body at the lake. Any other incriminating evidence would be a bonus.

But the first thing Maggie had done after returning to the Sheriff's Office was to submit a request to the city transportation authority for intersection camera footage within a ten-mile radius of the death scene. She'd also issued a BOLO to Florida Highway Patrol. If Dana's car had run any reds, or if it was parked on a county road, she'd get to know about it via FHP.

At twelve thirty, Maggie had spoken with the desk sergeant to ascertain if Lindy Munson had turned up to provide her statement as instructed, only to discover that she hadn't. To make matters worse, the number that Lindy had provided came back as unknown. Maggie had tried reaching out to Deputy Ramos—since he had been the one to give Lindy a ride home—but he was off duty until five, and wasn't taking calls. Not to be outdone, Maggie had spoken with his supervisor, who had checked the incident report, confirming that Lindy had been safely deposited at her house at 9:14 p.m.

Maggie had spent the other half of the time in here, in the dark, watching Cullen and wondering if he had indeed killed Dana.

Some might say that Cullen didn't look the part, that he didn't come across as *the murdering kind*, as if such a thing existed. In fact, he looked about as dangerous as a plastic spoon. But Maggie knew that killers came in all shapes, sizes, colors, and creeds. When it came to murder, the benevolent became malevolent in the blink of an eye.

But did Cullen kill his wife?

Unequivocally, the evidence said so.

And Cullen had hinted at the fragility of their relationship, suggesting that tempers may have been frequently frayed.

During Cullen's processing, Maggie had thought long and hard about the discoveries made in his backyard, and the ease with which Loomis and she had unearthed potentially incriminating evidence. Only someone extremely stupid would have left them there like that. But stupidity wasn't the reason why Maggie felt no pity for the man sitting on the other side of the one-way glass. Since being arrested, Cullen hadn't asked once about his wife. No mention of her whatsoever. He was upset, but it was for his own well-being. Not one single soul-searching question, such as: *How did she die? Where did she die? Who did this to my wife? Can I see her?*

It was odd behavior, and it blazed away like a neon sign, because in Maggie's experience innocent spouses did ask those kinds of questions, and repeatedly. It was all part of the brain's struggle of coming to terms with sudden tragedy. It needed answers, reassurance, confirmation. Right now Cullen was behaving like a killer.

"So this is the husband."

Maggie turned as Smits entered the room. He was drinking an energy juice from a can, and he was sweating.

"Doctor's got me on some newfangled meds," he said in response to Maggie's questioning look. "Something to descale my arteries. Bleach, if the missus has her way. Has me sweating like a whore in church." He nodded at the observation window. "Where we at? I hear Cullen declined legal representation."

"He's swearing his innocence."

"That's what they all start out saying."

Outside his home, Maggie had read Cullen his rights and then shipped him back to the Sheriff's Office, where he'd been Mirandized for a second time before being processed, photographed, fingerprinted, and swabbed for DNA. All the while, Cullen had professed his innocence.

"He's insisting he has nothing to hide," Maggie said.

"Does he have an alibi?"

"He hasn't given one. But lack of an alibi isn't consistent with guilt."

Smits almost choked on his drink. "Detective, you found a .38 Special at his house, hidden in a kettle grill. It's the same caliber as the murder weapon. If ever there was a slam dunk, this is it."

"All the same, I'd like to see what Forensics make of the evidence before I come to any definitive conclusion."

Smits wiped his mouth. "Detective, if it looks like a duck, swims like a duck, and quacks like a duck, then it probably is a duck. Your job isn't to determine innocence or guilt. That's for a grand jury to decide. Your job is to collect evidence and present it in a convincing way. Let me hear your working theory."

Maggie kept the agitation out of her voice. "Cullen killed his wife. Either at the death scene or somewhere else we have yet to determine. Crime scene investigators are at his home address as we speak, looking for blood trace and anything else to link him to the murder. Seeing as Dana's car is missing, we think Cullen drove it to the lakeside dump site before setting his wife on fire."

"Passable. With those arms of his, he looks capable of carrying a deadweight."

"We're thinking he then dumped the car elsewhere, to make it look like Dana was nowhere near home when she was abducted and killed."

"By somebody else."

"Yes. We've issued a BOLO on the vehicle. A white Chevy Cruze. If it's anywhere on a county road, FHP will find it before nightfall."

Smits turned his gaze to Cullen. "He had to make his way back home from the lake somehow. It's almost a two-mile walk. You say Loomis canvassed the neighborhood?"

"Last night, with a half dozen deputies. And no one reported seeing anyone on foot anywhere along Ocoee Parkway."

"This guy isn't a ghost. We need to expand the reach and talk with anyone who was in a position to see Cullen walking home last night. I'll get patrol knocking on doors. Have you checked in with the taxi companies?"

"It's on our to-do list. I've also put in a request for traffic camera footage. There's a couple of toll cameras on the Beltway, but I'm not expecting much from them."

Smits sipped his drink. "Things creep at the weekend. Don't hold your breath. What about the handgun?"

"It's with Firearms."

"It's Sunday."

"I called Robbie Zee."

Robbie Zeedeman was OCSO's resident firearms expert. Born in South Africa, he'd acquired most of his weapons knowledge evading gunfire on the streets of Cape Town.

"He came in on his day off?"

"Don't worry, Sarge. He won't be posting overtime. He owed me a favor." Maggie glanced at her watch. "He should be doing the test fire right about now."

"I hear no bullet casing was found at the scene."

"It's not surprising. The lakeshore is heavily wooded. Overgrown. We performed an outward spiral search, but we might need to do a more thorough grid search with metal detectors."

"Unless he threw it in the lake. In which case, you've got to ask yourself, why he didn't toss the gun as well? After all, he tossed the purse."

Maggie had already asked herself the same question. "People do strange things in the heat of the moment," she said. "You can't always explain their actions."

Maggie had once been in hot pursuit of a felon who had dumped his pistol in a baby's stroller as he ran through a park. Luckily, no harm had come to the child. But it exemplified the mindless mentality of people pushed to their limit.

"The swabs for gunshot residue proved negative," Maggie said, her eyes on Cullen.

"Gloves?"

"Probably. Aside from the work boots, we haven't found any clothing that puts him at the scene. We're thinking he ditched the clothes elsewhere. Maybe with the car."

"So why keep the boots?"

"I'm not sure. The crime lab is comparing the casts taken at the crime scene with the treads."

"Sounds like you've got the husband dead to rights, Detective."

"Well, we've a ways to go. Right now he's our prime suspect."

"Isn't that what your partner thought about the Pruitt kid?"

Maggie didn't respond. Smits had a confrontational streak that Maggie refused to rise to. But he didn't push it either; he'd supervised Maggie's work long enough to know that she left no stone unturned.

"So what's bugging you, Detective?" he said. "And don't insult my intelligence by saying there is nothing. I can see it. You've got that itch."

"I'm confused about motive," she admitted. "He admitted they've been going through a rough patch. And I saw evidence suggesting they've been sleeping apart. But even though Cullen comes across as being prickly, he doesn't strike me as the kind of guy who wakes up one morning and decides to kill his wife on a whim. Something drove him to it."

"Marital woes equal crime of passion."

"Maybe. I'm not sure."

"Insurance money? Cullen could have business debts."

"Maybe. We don't know yet. But I don't think he'd risk murdering his wife over a canceled life insurance policy." She glanced at Smits. "I found it in her things. The policy, with a letter confirming cancellation."

"She stopped her insurance."

"A month ago."

"Does the husband know?"

"I'm going to find out."

"Please do. Because I need a strong argument to take to the state attorney."

"About that . . ." Maggie drew a big breath. "I'd like to establish a firm motive before you speak with the prosecutors. Right now, our finding the gun and those boots, it all feels a little too easy to me, too convenient. I don't want them to rush in and formally charge Cullen only to find out later we jumped the gun on this."

Smits went to say something, but the door opened and Loomis breezed in.

"Hey. Sarge. Novak." He waved a manila envelope in the air. "The boot prints are an exact match, and the mud in the treads is the same composition as the exemplar from the beach."

"What about ballistics?" Maggie said.

"Zee is still comparing the slug against his test shots. He promises we'll have the results in ten minutes, tops."

Smits turned to Maggie. "Looks like it's game over for the husband. Now it's your turn, Detective. Go in there and find that motive."

Maggie picked the envelope from Loomis's grasp.

"A confession would be the icing on the cake," Smits added as she put a hand on the door handle.

"I'll do my best."

"Like shooting fish in a barrel," Loomis said with a wink as Maggie opened the door and went inside.

◆ ◆ ◆

When Cullen saw Maggie entering the room, he let out a long sigh. "Finally," he said, drumming his hands on the tabletop, "a familiar face."

Maggie closed the door behind her. "Sorry to keep you waiting, Mr. Cullen. The Sheriff's Office appreciates your patience."

He leaned bare forearms on the table. "You've kept me sitting here twiddling my thumbs. When can I go? There's stuff I need to do."

Maggie sat down in the chair facing him and put the manila envelope on the table in front of her. "Mr. Cullen, you've been arrested on suspicion of murder."

"All right. And I waived my right to an attorney as a show of good faith. I'm innocent. I told you I didn't hurt my wife. So why am I still here?"

"I need to ask you some questions. Get your answers on the record."

"But when can I leave?"

"That's for the state attorney to decide, Mr. Cullen. Can I get you a fresh water?"

Cullen glanced at the empty bottle, shook his head.

"Okay. Then let's get started." She reached behind her, positioning the video camera so that it was aimed at Cullen. "Detective Maggie Novak. Interview with Thomas Joseph Cullen. November one. Mr. Cullen, where were you yesterday evening, the night of October thirty-first, between five and eight p.m.?"

"Between those exact times?"

"Approximately."

"At home. I was there all day."

"Can anyone verify that?"

"No. I was alone between five and eight. Just me and my shadow."

"No trick-or-treaters knocking down the front door?"

"Didn't hear any."

"What about neighbors—did they see you hanging around the house or in the backyard yesterday evening?"

"Hard to say. You'd need to ask them."

"Any disputes with your neighbors?"

"Can't say we've ever met any of them, to be honest. I like my privacy."

"What about Dana?"

"Same goes."

"How long did she work as a guidance counselor?"

"At least the last ten years," he said. "She's great at it, too. I don't know how she does it. Me, I have zero patience with anyone under twenty-one. Kids these days, huh? But she just has this affinity with them, you know? Like she can crawl right inside their head and see what they're thinking."

"Did she get her degree in psychology?"

"Probably." He shrugged.

"You don't know?"

"Dana doesn't speak about her life before we got together."

And it had probably never occurred to him to ask.

"Did she ever mention any of the students at Crown Pointe?"

He rolled his shoulders. "Not that I recall."

"In particular, did you ever hear her mention the names Lindy Munson or Tyler Pruitt?"

He glanced at the ceiling. "Nope."

Someone knocked on the one-way mirror behind Maggie; Smits, she guessed, instructing her to move on.

"Tell me about your Saturday, Mr. Cullen."

He leaned back, spreading his hands as far as the cuffs would allow. "What's there to tell? I don't work Saturdays. Same as always. I catch up on a few things at home. Kick back when I can. Maybe catch a little golf if I'm in luck."

"You said you were home all day yesterday. What about Dana?"

"Sure, she was home all right. Until she wasn't."

"She left when?"

"Not sure. I wasn't keeping tabs. Dana hates me keeping tabs. Four. Maybe a few minutes after."

"Did she say where she was going?"

"I asked her."

"And?"

"She never answered. She just stormed off. Typical Dana. She was in one of her moods yesterday. Time of the month, I reckon. You're a woman; you know where I'm coming from, right? We had a few choice words, and she just up and left."

Maggie refrained from reeducating Cullen regarding female hormonal changes; his opinions seemed carved in stone. "When you say she was in one of her moods . . ."

"Dana sulks. I don't know any other way of putting it. We argue, usually over something trivial like I forgot to start the dishwasher, we fall out, she sulks. Goes on for days. Always the same routine. It can be two or three days before she speaks to me again."

"Do you try speaking with her?"

"That's not the point. She's the psycho. She even saw a shrink to help figure it all out."

"Here, in Orlando?"

"Nope. Back in Kingman."

"When was this?"

"Not long after we got married."

"I'll need the therapist's office details, if you still have them."

"Okay. I'll see if I can dig them out." He jabbed a finger against the tabletop. "I mean it. Anything else you need, just name it."

"We appreciate your assistance, Mr. Cullen. While I remember, has Dana visited with a dentist recently?"

He shook his head. "No way. As far as I know she hasn't seen a dentist since she was a kid. She's got what she calls *dentophobia*, like it's a real word or something. She'd rather lose an eye than have a tooth pulled."

"Okay. Rewind a little here for me. Do you know what the outcome was of Dana seeing the therapist back in Kingman?"

Cullen leaned forward a little, as though he was about to share a secret with her. "Between you and me, I think he saw her coming and bled her dry. He said she suffered from an anxiety disorder and something like PTSD. He used phrases like *persecution complex* and *conjugal paranoia*. Told her it was all in her head. That her troubles stemmed from her childhood. I had to pull the plug eventually."

"Why?"

"Cash flow problems. The guy charged a hundred bucks an hour."

"Mr. Cullen, have you any idea where your wife might have gone yesterday after she left home?"

He sat back, slouching. "Totally and utterly clueless."

"Maybe she was planning on meeting somebody?"

"News to me if she was. Besides, who would she meet?"

"Friends?"

Cullen's mouth twisted. "Don't get me wrong," he said, "Dana's a nice person. She'll do anything for anyone. She says all the right things in all the right places. But she doesn't make friends easily. She hasn't made any the whole time we've been here."

"Why is that, do you think?"

"Trust issues. Hence the shrink. It's just how she's made. She doesn't let anyone enter her inner circle." He drew a loop with both forefingers. "Sealed like Pandora's box."

"What about enemies?"

"Dana is about as inoffensive as Bambi. The shrink she saw, he said she suffered from what he called *sorry syndrome*. I mean, let's get real here. Can you believe there's such a thing? *Sorry syndrome.* Dana apologizes to everyone, even when it's not her fault."

"What about her work colleagues—did Dana socialize with any of them outside of the school environment?"

"Nope. She says, and these are her words, 'Those people are only bearable in small doses.'"

"Did she have trouble with any other teachers?"

"Not exactly." He made a face. "There was this one teacher, last Christmas . . ."

Maggie straightened her spine. "Go on."

"I don't want to speak out of place here."

"We need to know everything, Mr. Cullen."

"It could be something or nothing. I don't want anyone losing their job because I put my foot in it."

Maggie said nothing, using silence as leverage.

"Okay," he said, leaning forward again, as though imparting a secret. "Dana said this teacher made inappropriate suggestions."

"Such as?"

"Sexual innuendo, she said. Came on to her a couple times at the office party. She had to tell him to back the heck off."

"Do you know his name, this teacher?"

Maggie heard a tapping on the glass mirror behind her. Again, Smits wanted her to move on, focus on nailing Cullen to the cross he was already bearing. But Maggie was curious.

"Brandon," Cullen said. "Yeah. I think his name's Brandon, or something along those lines."

"Was Dana overly concerned about this teacher's advances?"

The knuckles rapped on the glass again, this time louder. Maggie raised her hand, indicating she'd heard.

"Dana said she'd handled it and it was no longer an ongoing concern. Not like the dude back in Kingman. Now *he* was one persistent . . ." He glanced at the camera, then back to her. "Am I allowed to say *son of a bitch*?"

"It's your statement, Mr. Cullen."

"Yeah, well, that's what he was. One persistent son of a bitch."

"Was this another teacher?"

Cullen shook his head. "Stalker. He followed her to and from work. Watching her from his car. Even followed her around the mall."

"How long did this go on for?"

"Couple months."

"Did Dana report it to the police?"

"I wanted to, but she said no. Dana hates attention."

"Must have irked you, Mr. Cullen. Someone stalking your wife. Did you approach him about it?"

"I never saw him with my own eyes. She said he drove a black pickup, and he wore a beard. Followed her around town every now and then. That's all I know. I suggested we should get a restraining order, but Dana didn't want any trouble."

"She must have been frightened."

"I guess."

"What happened?"

He stuck out his lower lip. "After a while she never mentioned him again. So I figured he'd grown bored and moved on. Let's be honest. Dana isn't a Disney princess."

No, she's Bambi.

"Are there any witnesses who can corroborate her story, Mr. Cullen?"

"Your guess is as good as mine."

Knuckles sounded on the glass again.

Maggie leaned forward, changing the direction of her questioning. "Mr. Cullen. Earlier, when I asked you about the carry-on in your hall, you said that Dana wanted to spend some time apart."

"Like I said, we've been going through a rough patch."

"What was the reason for that?"

"The usual thing."

"Can you be more specific?"

He snickered. "Pick a card. Plenty of stressors these days. Lately, we've found it hard meeting our obligations."

Maggie thought about Dana's checking account statements and her healthy bank balance before recently. "You have debts, Mr. Cullen?"

"This is America. Who doesn't?"

"Business or personal?"

"Both."

"You own your own landscaping business."

"Last fifteen years and proud of it."

"Things not going great?"

"Middling. Had myself a top-tier reputation back in Kingman." He smiled, seemingly remembering better times. "Desert gardens are my specialty. Cactus. Yucca. All kinds of succulents. Got myself a real soft spot for agave. I like to work with the drought-tolerant plants. But things are different down here. So much moisture to contend with. All the same, I'm making progress. And my reputation's growing."

"We may need to see proof of your financial commitments. Bank statements. Loan details. That kind of thing."

"Whatever you need. You can have access to everything. My accounts are all aboveboard. I have nothing to hide."

Maggie slid a blunt pencil and a sheet of paper across the desk to him. "Write down your bank details for me. And while you're at it, write down the contact details for your in-laws."

"Dana's parents?"

"Unless you've others." She saw Cullen start to scribble them down. "Did you know Dana canceled her life insurance?"

He looked up. "No."

"Any idea why she would do that?"

"Not a clue. She had that policy long before I came along." He continued to jot down details on the paper.

"I also came across Dana's bank statements. She made a large withdrawal recently. Eight thousand dollars." Maggie watched for a reaction.

Cullen swore under his breath, his body language echoing his surprise. "She had that kind of cash?"

"According to her statements."

"I didn't know." He finished writing and slid the paper and pencil back to her.

Maggie glanced at the address in Kingman and the landline number for Mr. and Mrs. Burnside. "Thank you for this." She put the paper in her pocket. "Did you guys argue over the household finances?"

"A little. Just the usual, I guess."

"Is that what prompted her to walk out yesterday, you guys arguing over money?"

He shook his head. "Golf."

Maggie took a beat. "Golf?"

"Yeah. I wanted to golf this weekend. Dana wanted us to spend time together. She said I was being selfish, which seems to be the story of my life these days. It kind of blew up from there."

His wife was dead, and he actually looked miffed with the thought of missing out on walking the links.

"Between you and me," he said, leaning on the table again, "it's not the first time my wife's done this."

"You mean walked out?"

"Every now and then she gets itchy feet. She's like one of those Cape Canaveral rocket launches. One second there's nothing, and she's just sitting there simmering. Then boom! And she's headed for orbit. She packs an overnight bag and goes away a couple days. Says it helps clear her head. Puts things back in perspective."

"How often did Dana walk out?"

"I don't keep tabs. Couple times each month. Every other weekend."

"And was this the norm back in Kingman as well?"

"Nope. Just since we moved out here."

"Has she said where she goes?"

"To be honest, I never asked. Okay, I know I should have. I know I should've been an attentive husband and shown more interest. But hey, I'm just a guy. Last thing I want when she comes back is to get into the whole reason she walked out in the first place. Let sleeping dogs lie. That's my motto."

Maggie resisted the urge to shake her head knowingly at him. "Could she be spending time with her parents?" she asked instead.

"Doubt it. After the first couple times it happened, I checked with her folks. They said they hadn't seen her since the move. If you ask me, I think she holed up in a beach hotel. Drowning her sorrows in a margarita."

"What makes you say that?"

"It's her favorite cocktail."

"No, I mean, what makes you think she went to a beach hotel?"

"I found receipts in her purse."

"For . . . ?"

"Stuff. Mainly from places in Saint Pete's."

"Do you still have those receipts?"

He turned out his lower lip. "Doubt it."

"Okay, so help me out here, Mr. Cullen. Let's go over the basics again, just so that I get the time line right. Yesterday afternoon, you guys had a falling out, and then she left around four. Right?"

"Yup."

"She wanted some breathing space. So she got into her car and drove away. Possibly to a beach hotel in Saint Pete's for the weekend."

"You got it."

"So tell me this. Why did she leave the carry-on behind?"

Suddenly, Cullen looked confused, a deep ridge appearing on his forehead. He blinked several times in quick succession, picked up the water bottle, putting it to his lips before realizing it was empty. He placed it back on the table and rolled his gaze around to Maggie.

"You know," he said, "Dana's right. I go through my life wearing blinders. The truth is, I didn't even notice it was still there until you guys pointed it out."

Either Cullen was a good actor, Maggie thought, or incredibly superficial.

"Is it the same overnight bag Dana packs each time she leaves?"

He nodded.

"Don't you think it strange she left it, right there in the hall like that? It's not as though she could've missed it on her way out or anything."

He shrugged. "Who knows what goes on in the female brain? Baffles the best scientists. All I know is that when one of those sulks of hers descends, she's like a whole different person. All rational thinking jumps out the window. She probably forgot it in her rush to get as far away from me as possible."

"And that's the last time you saw your wife?"

"Slamming the door on her way out."

"What did you do after she left?"

"I slept."

"I thought you said you intended to play golf?"

"I did. But I was tired."

"At four in the afternoon?"

Cullen's frown stayed put. "Maybe I was exhausted from all the sparring with Dana. I curled up on the couch and didn't wake up till this morning."

"You're saying you slept all evening and all night?"

"Right through. Like a baby."

"Is that normal for you, Mr. Cullen?"

"I've always been a good sleeper. Dana says I could sleep through an earthquake. It infuriates the socks off of her. You see, she's a light sleeper. Every little thing wakes her up. I swear, a neighbor only has to fart in his sleep and her eyelids spring open." He smiled, seemingly pleased with his imagery.

"Mr. Cullen, has your wife ever had an affair?" She came right out and said it, principally to gauge his reaction.

And his reaction bordered on laughter.

"Dana having an affair? You're kidding me, right?"

"Spouses cheat all the time. If Dana was having an affair, it could explain her frequent walking out."

Maggie could tell from his trivializing response that the thought had never occurred to him.

"Let me be clear about this," Cullen said quietly as he leaned forward again and prodded a blunt finger against the tabletop. "Dana gets everything she needs from me. *Everything*. She has a nice home. A good job. A husband who's there for her, night and day. She doesn't need to go looking anyplace else for sexual gratification."

"What about you, Mr. Cullen?" she said, turning it around on him. "Have you ever been unfaithful?"

Now his laughter exploded out of him. "That's ridiculous! Me? Sleep around? When would I get the time?"

"Business like yours," she said, "you're in and out of people's homes every day of the week. All those bored and lonely housewives whose husbands are out at the office. You, steaming off sweat in their backyard. Them, fetching you cool homemade lemonade. Are you telling me no one has ever thrown themselves at your feet?"

Cullen's laughter subsided, as though it had been sucked out of him, and he seemed to shrink away from Maggie's question.

Her phone vibrated in her pocket. She glanced at the screen. It was a text message from Smits:

Show him the photos

Maggie picked up the manila envelope and shook out a bunch of 8 x 10 color prints, keeping them on her lap and out of Cullen's line of sight. "Mr. Cullen," she began, "do you own a pair of work boots?"

"Excuse me?"

She placed a photo on the table in front of him. "We found these when we searched your property."

He glanced at the picture. "Sure. They look like mine. Same color laces and all." He looked up at her. "Why?"

"Can you tell me when was the last time you wore them?"

"Friday. A job in Casselberry." He leaned forward, elbows on the table, all traces of his laughter filed away. "What have my boots got to do with any of this?"

"When was the last time you were at Lake Apopka?"

He thought about it. "A couple weeks ago. Maybe longer. My work takes me all over. I'd have to check my records."

"Anywhere on the actual lakeshore itself?"

"Nope."

Maggie placed another photo on the table. It showed the gasoline can standing beside the outdoor grill. "Can you tell me anything about this?"

Cullen glanced at it. "Looks like the gas I use to power my lawn mower."

Maggie's phone vibrated again, this time with a message from Loomis:

Ballistics confirm match ☺

"Mr. Cullen, earlier, when Detective Loomis asked you if you own a gun, you said you don't."

"That's right. Never have. No interest in owning one either. Those things kill."

"Then how do you explain this?" She placed a photo of the revolver on the table, sliding it right up to Cullen's manacled hands. She saw his eyes widen as she said, "This is a Smith and Wesson Model 36. It was recovered from your property this morning. Specifically, from inside your outdoor grill."

She saw furrows break out on his brow. His mouth opened and closed, as though he didn't know quite how to respond.

Maggie placed a finger on the photograph. "Is this your gun, Mr. Cullen?"

Cullen stared at the image, his brow knotted and his mouth working wordlessly.

"Mr. Cullen?" Maggie said a little louder. "Is this your gun?"

He looked up at her as if startled, his expression strained. He pushed the photo back across the table. "I told you. I don't own a gun. Check your records if you don't believe me."

"We are doing so."

But it wasn't the whole truth, because unlike the popular perception usually garnered from TV shows, Maggie knew there was no national firearm database. Although some agencies did keep track of certain weapons and those retailing them, police couldn't simply log in to a common registry and pull up the owner's details from a handgun's serial number.

Even so, Maggie had put a request through to the FBI's National Crime Information Center on the slim chance that the revolver had been stolen before coming into Cullen's possession. It happened frequently in gun-related crimes, and often the check yielded workable results. That said, she wasn't expecting anything back from the NCIC before end of day.

"We found it hidden in your kettle grill," she said, pushing the photo back toward him. "The work boots as well. How do you explain them being there?"

"You're the detective. You tell me." He stabbed a finger at the photo, his lips peeled back. "I swear I've never seen this in my life before."

Maggie laid three of the remaining four photographs in front of him, spreading them out. She pointed at the first. "This is mud we found on your boots. It's a particular type of lake mud, and an exact match to the mud we found at the death scene." She drew his attention to the second picture. "And this is a comparison of the treads on your boots to the prints we also found at the scene. As you can see, they're a perfect match." She pointed to the third picture. "And this is the bullet retrieved from your wife's body, Mr. Cullen. Turns out it came from this gun right here. The gun we found hidden at your home."

Cullen's mouth was agape, his gaze switching from one photo to the next as the color drained from his face.

Maggie sat back, giving him a few seconds to digest the implications before making her closing statement. She glanced over her shoulder at the big mirror on the wall behind her, knowing that Loomis and Smits were watching on the other side, and that what she said next would be crucial in their bid to prove Cullen was the killer.

"Mr. Cullen," she said as she turned back to face him. "I trust by now that you're aware of what this evidence all means, and the seriousness of the situation you now find yourself in. Last evening, your wife was murdered on the shoreline of Lake Apopka. Her killer shot her in the belly, then doused her in gasoline and set her on fire. This morning, we recovered the murder weapon from your property, together with an empty gas can and footwear used at the crime scene. You admit to arguing with your wife yesterday afternoon, and you say no one can confirm your whereabouts during the time in which your wife was brutally murdered." She placed the final photograph on the table, right in the center of the montage. It showed the burned corpse lying on the gurney in Elkin's chilled examination room, the blackened flesh like cold lava in the sterile light. "Right now, all the evidence points to you having killed your wife. It's time to man up, Mr. Cullen, and take responsibility for what you did to Dana. It will make things easier for you if you start by telling me why you killed her."

For a moment, Cullen's gaze remained on the colorful mosaic in front of him while a blood vessel throbbed on his temple. Then she saw him exhale slowly, his posture straighten, composing himself as his gaze rose to meet hers. And in it Maggie could detect no trace of fear. She had hoped the weight of evidence would crush him, squeeze a confession out of him. But Cullen didn't seem fazed one bit by her accusation.

He was silent, his eyes cold and blank. Then he addressed the camera, saying, "These detectives made an illegal search of my property. I didn't give them my permission. I was kept distracted with the terrible news about my wife's murder while they went through my stuff. I didn't give them my consent. I don't own a gun. And I didn't kill my wife. For all I know, these detectives planted that gun." He looked beyond the camera to the one-way mirror. "I want my phone call now. I've said all I'm going to say without a lawyer present."

Maggie gathered up the photos and left the room.

Chapter Thirteen

ALL YOU CAN EAT

The sun blazed down on Maggie as she crossed the parking lot toward the chain restaurant on West Colonial, her police badge swinging like a pendulum on its chain. In the bright afternoon light, the cheap Halloween decorations still strung around the restaurant's entrance looked more jokey than scary.

It was a little after three in the afternoon, and despite the glorious sunshine, dark rain clouds bruised the western sky.

A storm was on its way.

Maggie pushed open the glass door, a welcome blast of icy air blowing the heat from her skin.

"I need to speak with Ronda Munson," she said to the hostess responsible for assigning tables. She showed her badge. "I believe she works here."

The hostess spoke into her headset—to the manager, Maggie assumed—and then told Maggie that Ronda would be right out.

Maggie nibbled at the insides of her cheek while she waited.

With Cullen now in custody, Smits had instructed her and Loomis to spend the rest of their shift tying up loose ends and finishing off their reports, so that he could present an airtight case to the state attorney come Monday morning. Maggie had left Loomis poring through E-PASS toll camera footage sent over from the Central Florida Expressway Authority, while she drove to the restaurant alone. As far as Smits was concerned, they'd caught Dana Cullen's killer, and now it was a matter of demonstrating to the prosecutors that they had all their ducks in a row.

But Maggie had reservations.

She conceded that the evidence in favor of Cullen having killed his wife was solid. No one could dispute the fact that they had found the murder weapon on his property. Maggie had seen murderers convicted on far less circumstantial evidence. Even so, she knew that when it came to homicides and motives, not everything was black and white. Their finding the revolver squirreled away in Cullen's backyard seemed a bit too easy for her liking. It stank of him being set up to take the fall for the murder. Ideally, she'd like to see more evidence to corroborate Cullen being the actual killer. But no case was perfect.

When she'd voiced her concerns to Smits, he'd told her that arrogance made people stupid, and that Cullen probably never thought for one minute they'd check the outdoor grill. She'd argued that a third party could be trying to frame Cullen. But he'd told her to take the win, and be grateful for the upturn in her conversion rate while it lasted. He'd gone on to dismiss Cullen's closing statement as the words of a desperate man.

Still, Maggie was in conflict.

Granted, Cullen didn't seem like the sharpest knife in the block, and he did exhibit conceited tendencies, but she wasn't convinced he was naive to the point of allowing them to search his home, knowing full well that the murder weapon could be found with such ease.

As always, her gut told her to probe the gray areas.

Maggie wanted to explore other avenues before hammering the final nail in Cullen's coffin. He'd mentioned a stalker back in Kingman, as well as a teacher here in Orlando who was obsessed with Dana. Both hinted at motive. Maggie needed to dig deeper, not only for her own peace of mind, but to make sure an innocent man didn't go to jail.

Sometimes, the trail to the truth ran through a labyrinth of lies.

Case in point, before heading out to the diner, she'd called the number for Dana's parents that Cullen had given to her in his interview. The number had gone to an answering machine. Maggie had let the machine activate a dozen times, each time listening closely to the recording of a man's voice, saying, *Hey there. You've reached Vince and Barb. Leave a message and we'll get right back*, convinced that the voice in the recording was identical to her memory of Big Bob Grigoryan's from her childhood.

How was it possible for the whole family to survive that night, and yet no one knew that they did?

Maggie had chewed cud over that question on her drive down to the restaurant, knowing that there was a whole other history behind Dana that even her husband was unaware of.

Did the fact that Rita had cheated death twenty years ago have some bearing on her death this weekend?

Maggie stopped her prowling as a skinny woman with bleached-blonde hair and heavy makeup approached her from the bar area.

Too heavy for a Sunday afternoon, Maggie thought.

Ronda Munson—Lindy's mother.

She looked to be in her midthirties, with acute angles where most women had curves. Sharp features that seemed to be drawn on, and eyes that might have been lost altogether if not for the thick black eyeliner. A purple hickey glowed darkly on the slant of her neck.

"Thanks for coming out here," Maggie said. "I'm sorry to bother you at your place of work. I appreciate you're busy and all."

"It's okay. I was about to take my break anyway. The manager said you're police?"

Maggie flashed her badge. "Sheriff's Office."

The woman nodded without looking at it. "What's this about?"

"Can we talk outside?"

"Sure."

They made their way outside behind the restaurant, to a stand of trees in the corner of the parking lot, where the shade sucked a little of the oppression out of the heat.

"Storm's brewing," the woman said as she tapped a cigarette from a pack. "Do you mind?"

Maggie shook her head.

The woman lit the cigarette, taking a long drag before breathing out smoke like it was pure euphoria. "I could get hit by a car tomorrow," she said, as though feeling the need to justify her smoking. "What can I do for the Sheriff's Office?"

"Mrs. Munson—"

"Ronda, honey. Please." She pointed with a red-painted fingernail at a name tag pinned to her shirt. "Mrs. Munson is my mother-in-law. It's strictly Ronda."

Maggie smiled. "Okay, strictly Ronda. Can you tell me what happened? I was expecting both you and your daughter at noon."

"Excuse me?"

"At the Sheriff's Office. Lindy was supposed to provide a statement about last night's events."

Puzzlement pinched the woman's face. "First I heard about it. Is Lindy in trouble? I can't afford any bail money."

"She witnessed an incident yesterday evening. She was instructed to come in at noon today. She didn't mention it?"

Ronda sucked on the cigarette. "I haven't seen her since yesterday morning."

"A deputy dropped your daughter off at home around nine last night."

"Sorry, hon. I was here, working the late shift." She blew out smoke. "Somebody's got to make ends meet."

"What about your husband?"

"What about him?"

"Was he home last night?"

"Not unless somebody dug him up from Woodlawn Cemetery. He's been dead going on ten years."

"I'm sorry."

"I'm not."

"Any other older children?"

The woman smirked. "Lindy's my one mistake." She tapped ash onto the pavement. "She told me she was staying out last night, and I knew better than to try and stop her. Lindy's a free spirit. Just like her father. I've tried doing my best by her. Keep her grounded. But she's a rebel, you know?"

Maggie did. *Rebel* was the same word her brother had used to describe her when they were kids, especially when she had pushed boundaries and ignored curfew times.

"Lindy was with a boy," Maggie said.

"Doesn't surprise me. She knows how to work that treadmill. Which one was it this time?"

"Tyler Pruitt."

"Tyler Pruitt." She seemed to think about it. "No. Never heard of him. Then again, she doesn't exactly introduce them to Mommy."

"They were hanging out in the woods near Crown Pointe."

"Devil's Landing?"

Maggie was taken aback. "You know it?"

"Who doesn't? Seems to be my daughter's place of choice these days. In that respect, she's just like her mother."

"You were a student at the school?"

"With above-average grades and doing great. Up until Lindy came along, that is, and ruined everything." She slid an arm across her waist, hugging herself.

"I was there, too, a couple of years before you."

Ronda shrugged, as if it meant nothing to her.

Maggie switched tack. "Did Lindy ever mention the school's guidance counselor? Her name's Dana. Dana Cullen."

"No."

"Do you know where Lindy is right now?"

"No idea, hon." She sucked a final breath through the cigarette, then dropped it on the ground, grinding it into the concrete with the toe of her shoe. "Maybe with this Pruitt boy?"

Chapter Fourteen

FROM THE DEEP

Maggie remembered a quote from a book she once read: *Daylight has a way of diluting the demonic.*

The author was right. Under the smiling sun, the woods separating the high school from the lake had lost all of their nighttime eeriness. Gone were the spooky shadows and the cackle of cicadas. In their place, a gentle autumn breeze meandered through the trees, and black crows cawed as they wheeled against the late-afternoon sky.

As far as Maggie could see, there was no trace of the overnight police activity. No black-and-yellow police tape to map out the crime scene boundary, and no hint of barbecued flesh tainting the air.

It was as if the murder had never happened.

She didn't park right away.

Instead, she followed Ocoee Parkway as it looped from the highway to the school and back again, driving no faster than a crawl, imagining Thomas Cullen traversing this same route early yesterday evening, either with his wife's body dripping blood on the upholstery, or with her still alive and unknowingly traveling to her doom.

Maggie knew that if they could locate Dana's vehicle, it could disclose which scenario was correct.

A raccoon crossed the street in front of her, glancing her way with jet-black eyes before scurrying into the underbrush.

Maggie had spent the last few hours canvassing business owners and residents along the two-mile stretch of roadway between the Cullen house and the crime scene. In all, she'd spoken with a handful of people, showing each the image on her phone of Cullen, taken during his processing at the Sheriff's Office. No one recalled seeing anyone on foot and heading north into Paradise Heights yesterday evening. Maggie didn't subscribe to the idea of Cullen calling a taxi back home after murdering his wife, which left, in her opinion, only one viable option: Cullen had driven Dana's car to and from the lake.

But where was it now?

Maggie parked the sedan in the same spot where Tyler's red Charger had been a matter of hours earlier, and climbed out onto the curb.

The sandy trail sloped downhill from her feet, disappearing into the trees. Lake water visible through the meshed branches, glittering in the afternoon sunshine. It all looked different than she remembered, more compact.

Twenty years ago, the slope from the school down to the tree line had been gradual, the trail much longer as it snaked across the undeveloped land. The construction of the new roadway had flattened out the incline, raising it in line with the school, and now the trail was a quarter its original length, the slope falling steeply away from the road.

Maggie made her way downhill, finding the going easier in daylight.

All things considered, the walk through the woods was pleasant. Dappled sunshine slanting in through the swaying canopy. Lizards scurrying and birds tweeting. Palmetto fans and fuzzy firs. A scent of pine trying to mask the musk of standing water. But for all its natural beauty, Maggie knew this place harbored an equal amount of unnatural ugliness. Bad things had happened here. And not just recently.

She came to the end of the trail, pausing before entering the clearing proper.

In her youth, someone had erected a wooden sign here, staking it in the ground, as though making claim to the small patch of land that lay beyond. On rough wood, they had written the words Devil's Landing in bloodred paint, adding runs and drips for dramatic effect. The sign had long since rotted away, or been uprooted and flung into the trees, but the name remained stuck in the social consciousness, like a barb.

The clearing looked bigger in daylight, its dome-shaped canopy less imposing. Several logs were positioned around its edges, acting as benches for kids with reasons not to be in school, their bark worn smooth and shiny by years of use. The same logs that had been here when Maggie was a teen. Crime scene investigators had left them in place, but they had raked the sand clean, removing all the trash accumulated in the trees and in the tangled vines.

The clearing looked pristine.

But Maggie could see a faint shadow in the sand where Dana's body had lain, a darkening caused by the soot of burned human skin.

Why did your killer choose to leave you here?

Maggie dropped to her haunches, placing a palm against the sand. It felt cool to the touch and less gritty than it looked. When she lifted her hand, it came away covered in a fine coating. She wiped it off on her pants before making her way over to the narrow beach.

For their working theory to grow legs, Maggie needed to understand not just why Cullen had decided to kill his wife, but also his reason for choosing to burn her here at Devil's Landing. Rita had hung out here with Maggie, doing all the same boundary-pushing things that Dana had probably counseled seniors on. She'd known about this place. But how did Cullen know about it? Did Dana tell him?

Cullen was from Arizona. Still relatively new to the area. Granted, he'd lived in the vicinity of Lake Apopka for the last eighteen months, but what reason would he have for ever coming down here? The nearest houses were a few hundred yards back along the parkway. Even if Cullen had tended to a backyard overlooking the lake, he wouldn't have been able to see the small beach, let alone know that a convenient hideaway lay behind it. The sandy trail leading into the woods wasn't obvious from the roadway either, and unless you walked the trail in its entirety, you wouldn't know that it ended here, at the shore.

How did Cullen know this place existed?

Maggie went over to the narrow beach, her heels sinking in the soft surface.

The casting of the boot prints had left rectangular lines in the mud. Blobs of what looked like dried pancake batter speckled the brown beach—dental stone, mixed on-site and poured into the molds.

She edged up to the waterline, then leaned out as far as she could, looking to her right, toward the gated community that Loomis had canvassed Saturday night.

No houses were visible.

Not even a single rooftop poking above the trees.

If she listened, she could pick out the distant sounds of civilization carrying over the water: children playing in sprinklers, and moms calling for calmness while dads cleaned cars, stereos booming.

Of course, it was possible that Dana had mentioned Devil's Landing to her husband during an innocent conversation, never knowing that he'd made note of its location for future use.

Maggie scanned the open water.

In daylight, the lake no longer looked black as tar. It was the color of tea, stained brown from rotting vegetation. Diamonds glinting on its rippling surface. An egret wading through the shallows. A lone heron slicing across the blue. On the far horizon, she could see a thin smudge of buildings, but no discernible detail.

Standing here, surrounded by foliage and water, with the sun beating down and no other human beings in sight, she could quite easily be on a desert island.

Miles from nowhere.

The perfect dump site.

Her gaze landed on the small mud mound.

It seemed closer in the day. An elliptical hump of silt covered in swaying reeds. Dark lake water swirling around it.

The mound had changed location in the last twenty years, she realized. She remembered it lying more to the left, and more at an angle to the shore. Time, wind, and current had all conspired to migrate its position, bringing it level with the beach.

A memory came back to her.

The last winter they spent together, she and Rita had made the mound their own. Each day, after school, coming down here, holding their shoes aloft as they waded out to the mound. Flattening out an area of the reeds at its center, so that they could sit and talk, and sometimes spy on their fellow seniors making out in the clearing. Occasionally skinny dipping when no one was around. Two girls dreaming of things to come. Making plans and making waves. Watching the sun as it set, turning the water into a lake of fire. Laughing and cuddling. At one point, Rita leaning in to her, kissing her on the mouth, her lips hot and moist, her hand cupping Maggie's breast. And Maggie returning the kiss with a passion that surprised her, unable to breathe, her lungs aflame, her head spinning. Then breaking free, pushing Rita away, picking up her shoes and splashing back across the shallows, her heart beating wildly in her bosom.

Maggie realized she was holding her breath, and she sucked in a lungful of air.

Their friendship had changed that day. Something broken. Unspoken. Something irreversible. Like a comment that couldn't be unsaid. A distance setting in. A feeling of something missing that had stayed with Maggie all her adult life. Like internal scar tissue left over from an operation. Every now and then, niggling under the skin.

Maggie's heart was pounding.

A mullet leaped out of the lake a few yards away, making her jump as it belly flopped back into the water.

Chapter Fifteen

GOOD COP, BAD MOTHER

Steve parked his Tahoe alongside the silver minivan in the driveway of the Loomis residence and, as he and Maggie got out, said, "Let's hope dinner isn't ruined."

If it was, Maggie had only herself to blame. It was almost eight p.m., and they were running late, mainly due to her getting home later than intended.

Steve leaned on the bell, and Loomis answered the door.

"We come bearing gifts," Maggie said, holding two wine bottles aloft.

Loomis took one of the bottles. "French Grenache," he said with an admiring nod. "Nice pick, guys. You're forgiven." He waved them inside.

The Loomis house smelled of cooking and scented candles. Discreet lighting and a gentle pulse of folk music breathing in the background. Children's toys scattered randomly along the hallway and up the staircase.

"Where're the twins?" Steve asked as Loomis closed the door behind them.

"Hopefully, chasing fluffy sheep through dreamland," he said. He handed the wine back to Maggie. "Abby's slaving over a hot stove in the kitchen. I've got a new video game to show Steve. Do you mind if I steal your boyfriend a minute?"

"So long as you give him back when you're done."

Maggie found Abby peering through the glass of the oven door, her ash-blonde hair hanging in a side ponytail. She glanced over her shoulder as Maggie entered the kitchen. "Oh, hey, Maggie," she said with a big smile. "You made it."

"Sorry we're late." She waved the Grenache. "If it's any consolation, I brought pain relief."

"You're a lifesaver."

"Wine glasses?"

"Corner cupboard."

Maggie retrieved a pair of glasses and poured the wine. "You know, you didn't need to go to all this trouble on our account," she said. "We could've called for takeout on the way over."

Abby pulled on a pair of fish-shaped oven mitts. "And renege on a Sunday tradition? Have you met my husband?" She nodded toward a baby monitor standing at the corner of the counter, its blue LEDs flashing. "Do you mind checking the rug rats for me? I really need to take this out, as in *now*."

"Sure."

Glass in hand, Maggie made her way upstairs, stepping around plush toys as she went. In the semidarkness of the children's bedroom, she could make out the shapes of animal decals on the walls and a huge rainbow print connecting a pair of white cribs together.

Maggie inspected the blond-haired babies sprawled on their backs.

Harper, the baby girl, was fast asleep, her little mouth forming a perfect oval and her little hands rolled into chubby fists. Logan, the baby boy, a tiny version of Loomis, was wriggling on the mattress, whining softly, eyes screwed shut while his little legs pedaled the air.

Maggie sipped her wine.

"Did you ever want one of your own?"

She turned to see Steve silhouetted in the doorway, leaning against the jamb.

He came to her, sliding an arm around her waist from behind.

"I thought you were drooling over Loomis's latest video game?" she said.

"The console crashed. It's rebooting." He nuzzled his mouth into the curve of her neck and nibbled her skin.

"Careful," she said. "You'll spill my wine."

"You didn't answer my question."

Maggie turned around in his embrace. "Me and babies, you mean? Just stop for one second and look at this picture." She raised an eyebrow. "What's the odd thing out here?"

"For starters, you're not your mother."

"I'll take that as a backhanded compliment." She screwed a finger under his ribs. "Besides. Don't make any plans. I don't have a maternal bone in my body, and you know it."

"I'm just saying. Your biological clock is ticking, Maggie. If you were considering having children . . ."

"You'll be the first to hear about it," she said, pecking him on the lips.

Logan began to cry. Steve reached around her. Gently, he rolled Logan onto his side, and the baby stopped crying.

"Someone's got the knack," she said.

"Got to practice when you can. You never know when it might be useful."

They made their way back downstairs, Maggie wondering just how serious Steve was about the whole parenting thing.

They hadn't discussed it in depth; they were barely six months into their relationship and had yet to broach a lot of subjects. Whenever it came up, Maggie tended to reroute the conversation, expertly avoiding most situations that could lead into the topic of her and babies. It wasn't that she was anti-children. She loved her nieces and nephews. It was that she'd never factored kids of her own into her life plan.

The dinner was good and the company great. They ate too much pot roast and drank too much wine, talking through a variety of topics. Inevitably, the conversation rolled around to the reason why Maggie and Loomis had been distracted from their loved ones for a chunk of the weekend. The Halloween Homicide Case. And Loomis proceeded to give a detailed overview of their case. By default, Maggie was always reluctant to talk shop outside of the office. She believed that most civilians found police work uninspiring, and rarely was casework conducive to cordial conversation. But Steve was inquisitive, and Loomis seemed bent on discussing it, leaving Maggie little room for maneuver.

She listened, happy to let Loomis do most of the talking. Every now and then interrupting with bits he missed, or supplementing his recap with details relevant to the story.

Eventually, the conversation took a welcome detour into new territory, and the overall atmosphere lightened.

It warmed her heart to see her favorite people getting on like this. No awkward silences. No one pretending to be anything they weren't. Just friends being friendly.

But her dead friend was never far from her thoughts.

Embrace the good times when you can—as her father used to say.

As they were clearing the dishes off the table, making room for dessert, Maggie's phone vibrated in her pocket.

It was a text message from dispatch. She read it with a frown.

"What's up?" Loomis asked, picking up on her change in mood.

"Patrol found Dana's car," she said. "We have to go. *Now.*"

Chapter Sixteen

PRESSURE COOKER

Where's the fire?" Loomis said as he rushed down the hallway after Maggie.

"Dana's car could hold vital clues," she said as he caught up.

"Which will still be there in the morning."

"Except we're not working tomorrow. Remember?" She reached the front door, pausing to face him. "We need to check it for evidence. Don't give things time to spoil."

She went to open the door. Loomis put a hand out, preventing her. "It's immaterial either way," he said. "Smits has all he needs."

"Only if Cullen is guilty."

"Wait. Now you're thinking he's not?"

"I think it's possible somebody is trying to frame him. And I don't think any of this is as cut-and-dried as it seems. I know murderers often behave irrationally, and they do some pretty strange things, but I've never come across one who did such a bad job of hiding the murder weapon, and then allowing us to find it. It was like Cullen was dished up to us on a plate."

"And I totally agree. But how many times have we scratched our heads over a killer's flimsy motive? People kill people for the weakest excuses. Someone looks at somebody the wrong way. Somebody takes exception to another person's status. You name it. Sometimes people are just wired wrong upstairs and they do crazy stuff. You can't decode crazy."

"And I can't ignore my gut instinct." She ducked under his arm and squeezed through the gap in the doorway.

Loomis followed her outside, darting around in front of her and blocking her path.

"Novak, please," he said. "Hold up. We're having dinner here. We're being chatty and sociable and having a nice time. It's fun. We don't get to do this kind of thing often enough. What you're doing here, right now, this can wait."

"Abby and Steve agreed we should go."

"Only because they were being polite and they know what you're like."

Maggie balked. "What I'm *like*?" She made a face, waiting for him to expand. She saw the struggle in his eyes, knowing that he wouldn't back up his claim.

He blinked at her through his alcoholic haze, clearly unable to find any words that wouldn't inflame. "Just come back inside," he said at last.

"No."

"I made ice cream."

She frowned. "*You* made ice cream?"

"Hey, don't sound so skeptical. I got skills."

"What flavor?"

"Double chocolate pecan. Admittedly, a calorific calamity. But something to behold. Come on, Novak. You know you're tempted."

"I know I need to see Dana's car, and it can't wait till Tuesday. You coming with?"

"Yes. But . . . I'm just a teensy bit on the tipsy side of sober right now."

Maggie smirked. "Get over yourself, Loomis. You've had two glasses of wine. You must be the only cop from New York who can't hold his liquor."

"What can I say? I'm sensitive."

She waggled her fingers. "Come on. Give me your keys."

"You've been drinking, too."

"Cast-iron constitution from my dad's side. I'm fine. Come on. Hand them over."

He dug the keys out of his pocket. "Okay," he said. "You drive the minivan. But on one condition. No speeding. This isn't your Mustang."

"Relax," she said, popping the locks. "I wouldn't dream of it."

◆ ◆ ◆

Maggie drove Loomis's minivan west toward Apopka with her foot all the way down on the gas, only easing up for slower traffic and the occasional red light.

Loomis sat in the passenger seat, holding on tight, offering driving tips and moaning about insurance premiums.

According to dispatch, Dana's white Chevrolet Cruze had been abandoned on a secluded service road near Lake Apopka, in an area of district-owned conservation land hugging the eastern shoreline. The location was a five-minute drive from Paradise Heights, lying within walking distance of the Cullen family home.

Between complaining about Maggie's driving, Loomis attempted to get her to open up about her feelings regarding Rita. But she told him she didn't want to discuss it, not just yet.

"I'll just keep hounding you until you cave," he said.

"You should know by now that I never give in."

"Like a dog with a bone. I know. Be your undoing, Novak."

"Maybe."

They left the highway at the signpost for Lake Apopka Wildlife Drive and followed Lust Road as it sloped downhill a quarter mile before slipping under the Maitland Boulevard overpass. Woodland stretching away on either side. Apart from a distant sparkle of red and blue up ahead, no other lights were visible anywhere.

"Ideal place to dump a vehicle," Loomis commented dourly as he gazed out at the darkness on either side. "And only a stone's throw from civilization. You ever been out this way before, Novak?"

"Not for a long while."

In fact, it seemed like a lifetime ago. So much had changed in the meantime, but not everything.

"This road runs straight as a die for another mile or so," she said. "Right to the shoreline. When I was young, we rode horses through here in the summertime."

"Privileged upbringing."

She glanced at him. "They don't have horses in New York?"

"Only at the racetrack and the police stables. You don't get to ride them."

After New York, Florida must seem like an alien world to Loomis, she thought, *and with more strange wildlife than you could shake a stick at.*

The road widened after a few hundred yards, forming a disc-shaped turnaround spot for vehicles at the entranceway to Wildlife Drive. A sheriff's cruiser sat at an angle in the center, its roof lights flashing and its headlights partly illuminating a large metal gate closing off the road ahead, and a big white visitor information board fixed to the aluminum bars.

Maggie tucked the minivan behind the cruiser, and a familiar face greeted them as they climbed out.

"Well, if it isn't Deputy Ramos," Loomis said as he approached them. "What are the chances?"

"My patch. My shift. Pretty good, I guess." He nodded greetings at Loomis, but his gaze was on Maggie.

"Show us what you've got," she said.

"All right. This way."

Ramos walked them around to the front of his cruiser, to where its powerful headlights lit up a burned-out vehicle standing in a rusty puddle on the rim of the turnaround. Oil and burned paint flakes floating on the murky water. Maggie took out her phone and snapped a picture.

"No one mentioned the vehicle had been torched," Loomis said with a note of disappointment. "Who found it?"

The deputy pointed off to one side. "There's a fruit farm a little ways back. You don't notice it in the dark. The owner picked up on the smoke around eight o'clock and came out here to investigate. When she saw it was a vehicle on fire, she called nine-one-one."

Maggie glanced at her watch. "That was over two hours ago." She took another flash-lit photo, then one of the closed gate and the noticeboard.

"Firefighters from Apopka FD arrived within minutes," Ramos explained. "But the connection with your homicide wasn't made right away. I was attending to a neighbor dispute when the report came in. Dispatch logged it as a possible stolen vehicle. I got here about an hour ago. Of course, I was aware of the BOLO you guys put out earlier. So I checked the tags. Sure enough, that's when I realized it was your victim's car."

"Nice work, Deputy."

A smile brightened up his face. "Well, I appreciate it, ma'am. Means a lot coming from you."

"I'll get the stuff," Loomis told Maggie, rolling his eyes as he walked away.

"My partner is feeling a little off-center right now," Maggie explained as she saw the deputy's puzzlement. "Just ignore him. I do." She nodded at the closed gate. "The noticeboard over there. It says the drive is open Friday through Sunday."

Ramos directed his flashlight at the visitor information, revealing black text on a white background. "That's right. And closes an hour before sunset."

"Which means it was open to visitor traffic till around five thirty today, right?"

"Right." His gaze came back to hers. "The killer dumped the car *after* sunset. Otherwise, visitors would've seen it earlier and called it in."

"Exactly what I'm thinking. Plus, as you can see, there's a serious lack of street lighting around here. It's pitch black after the sun goes down." Maggie retreated a few paces so that she could see back along the length of the service road. "Even better, this spot is secluded from the highway. No direct line of sight. It's completely hidden."

"The killer knew about this location beforehand. He could be from the neighborhood."

Loomis returned with flashlights and two pairs of plastic overshoes and gloves. He handed Maggie her share. "You got sights on being a detective?" he asked Ramos as they put them on.

Ramos's smile was self-explanatory, showing teeth. "Yes, sir. Someday. Soon, hopefully."

"You put in for the exam yet?"

"Matter of fact, a couple of weeks back. I know I'm young and relatively new to the job. But I've plenty of experience, mainly with the Military Police. I'm willing to do whatever it takes to reach the top. I'm really proud of my conversion rate. Number one in Sector Three."

"Nice."

"Ideally, I want Homicide."

Loomis nodded. "Deathtectives all the way, right?"

"You bet. Any kind of recommendation would go a long way to making it a reality. If that's all right with you guys. Working Homicide is my dream job."

Maggie caught Loomis's raised eyebrow, but Ramos missed it.

"Well," Loomis said as he snapped on his gloves, "good luck with that. These days, there's a higher chance of winning the Powerball than a place in Homicide Squad. But don't let those sky-high odds deter you."

"No, sir. I won't. Thank you."

Maggie flicked on her flashlight. "Okay, Deputy Ramos. Thanks for your input. We'll handle it from here."

He nodded and returned to his cruiser. Maggie waited until he had shut himself inside his vehicle before turning to Loomis and quietly saying, "What's with all the passive aggression?"

Loomis shrugged. "I have no idea what you mean."

She showed him a frown.

He sighed. "Don't bust my balls here, Novak. What can I say? The dude's a bit on the intense side, to put it mildly."

"He's young and he's eager. Give him a break. We've all been there. You can't shoot a guy down in flames for being keen."

"Still . . ." Loomis glanced over his shoulder and faked a smile at the deputy. "That cheesy grin of his gives me the creeps."

"What's new? Since the twins came along, just about everything freaks you out. A Pop-Tart pops out of the toaster and you jump out of your skin."

Now he smiled genuinely. "Those babies will be the ruination of me for sure."

Maggie pointed to the public noticeboard fixed to the gate. "We have a big problem here. The time line's all wrong. Wildlife Drive was opened to visitors today until around five thirty. That means Dana's car must have been left here and set on fire *after* the gate closed."

"Okay."

"So Cullen can't be the one who dumped it. He's been in our custody all afternoon."

"He has an accomplice."

"Or he's being set up and the real killer dumped it here."

Loomis looked toward the burned-out wreck, the beam of his flashlight throwing twisted shadows onto the trees behind it. "If the real killer is out to frame Cullen, dumping Dana's car *after* we detained him is a pretty dumb move on their part. It reeks of an amateur."

"You're forgetting. People don't think like police. For us, it's all we know. We work on time lines, working out who did what and when. Regular folk don't think that way. Most people are poor planners. Killers are no exception."

"Either way," he said, "it's a dead giveaway. Someone else is involved in Dana's murder." Loomis took out his phone. "Best let Smits know before he talks to the prosecutor."

Maggie put a hand out, stopping him from dialing. "Hold that thought," she said. "We both know Smits won't budge without incontrovertible proof. If we go in there half-cocked and it turns out we haven't done our homework, he'll have us working desk duty the rest of the month. Let's see what evidence, if any, we can find here first."

Dana's car had been abandoned on the compacted white sand that fringed the turnaround. Sand that was now waterlogged and clayey and pitted with overlapping boot prints. Sooty puddles and ash in the trees. Off to one side of the wreck, a single yellow metal barrier barred access to an overgrown side road.

"Bad combo," Loomis said. "Fire *and* water damage. Not exactly prime conditions to preserve potential evidence, that's for sure."

Maggie stepped over a puddle. "Never say die."

He snickered. "A saying that always strikes me as weird considering we're Homicide."

The blaze had reduced the Chevy to a shell of mangled metal and glass fragments, intense heat evaporating the paintwork and turning the base metal into a pitted brown-black husk. Melted plastic and incinerated upholstery. Had it not been for the manufacturer's logo and brand name on the bodywork, it would have been impossible to determine the exact make and model by visual inspection alone.

Maggie aimed her flashlight inside, peering through the empty frame of the driver's window. This close, the noxious stench of liquefied plastic was almost overpowering. Clawing at the nose. Not surprisingly, there wasn't much left of the interior—just exposed metalwork, springs, and crumbs of glass. She inspected the floor space, looking for signs of foul play. Although fire destroyed hemoglobin, it had to work hard to completely disintegrate pooled blood. When it came to trace evidence, the old saying that blood was thicker than water was never more applicable. When exposed to concentrated heat, pooled blood tended to coagulate, turn syrupy, and then harden into a glaze. Only an inferno with a sufficiently high temperature and a long lifespan could completely cremate blood and remove every last trace of it. If Dana had been shot before being put in the car, or shot inside and bled out on the upholstery, Maggie was hoping that the fire had been doused in time to save at least some recoverable blood evidence.

But she didn't expect finding it to be easy.

Contrary to popular belief, wounds stopped spouting blood the second the heart stopped pumping. Residual traces seeped for a while, but once the body was inert, time and gravity pooled the body's fluids to the lowest points, causing the distinct bluish-purple discoloration known as *lividity*.

The only way they might find blood trace here was if Dana had been alive inside the car after being shot, her bullet wound pumping blood onto the seat.

But she could see no visible signs.

"Let's check the trunk," Loomis said.

The back of Dana's car was illuminated in the cruiser's headlights. Paint flakes swirling in the beams. Maggie tried the release catch, but the lid refused to pop.

Loomis hit it with the side of his fist, trying the catch again, but the lid remained sealed. Either locked or welded shut with the heat, or both.

"I'll be right back," Loomis said, heading back to the minivan.

Maggie took pictures with her phone while she waited—close-ups of the buckled license plate and the keys still dangling in the ignition.

"This ought to do the trick," Loomis said, wielding an oversize crowbar.

"You keep *that* in your family car?"

"You'd be surprised what I keep in my car." He hefted the iron. "Step back from the vehicle." He wedged the chisel end into the lid seam beside the locking mechanism, and applied some brute force. At first the lid wouldn't budge, but as he leaned his weight into it, the metal groaned, creaked, and suddenly it jumped open an inch. Smiling to himself, he handed the crowbar to Maggie, hooked his fingers into the crack, and heaved the lid all the way up on its protesting hinges.

The first thing that hit her was the smell, followed a fraction of a second later by the realization that Lindy Munson was curled up in the trunk.

Chapter Seventeen

IN HARM'S WAY

Maggie woke with a start, her pulse pounding and sparks flying in her vision. Momentarily disoriented, she lay deathly still in the dark, sucking in air and trying to fathom what had shaken her from her sleep. A fine coating of sweat lacquered her skin, and a dull ache throbbed behind her eyes.

Where was she?

It took a few seconds for her ricocheting senses to recognize her surroundings as the hard-edged topography of Steve's bedroom, with its door in the wrong place and its big picture window overlooking the Golden Bear golf links.

It came back to her: she'd been dreaming of Rita.

Not the caring, considerate, ever-smiling image of the girl from her childhood, with her luminous freckles and her tomboy haircut, but the charred corpse from Maggie's worst nightmare, the ghastly remains of Rita Grigoryan, creeping toward her across the chilled tiles of the ME's examination room, her boiled-egg eyes unblinking as she reached with witchy fingers for Maggie's throat.

Gasping, Maggie pushed herself up on one elbow.

Steve lay beside her in the bed, his chest rising and falling with the sluggish beat of the overhead fan.

She watched him for a moment, willing her speeding heart to slow.

Rita's premature death had haunted Maggie for years, branding her memories. Time had helped heal things over, but Dana's murder had wrenched open those old wounds, forcing the painful past into the present and rewinding Maggie's feelings all the way back to the moment she'd first learned that her former best friend had died in horrific circumstances.

Was it any surprise she couldn't sleep?

She sat up, swinging her legs out of bed as lightning flashed outside. Cool-blue light illuminated the bedroom, flickering wildly for a few seconds before plunging her into darkness again. Six seconds passed before a deep rumble sounded in the far distance.

Feeling headachy, Maggie pushed to her feet and padded into the bathroom. She found Tylenol in the mirrored medicine cabinet and guzzled two down with tepid water from the tap.

Lindy Munson was dead.

The recollection came back to her with a jolt, overriding her thoughts of Rita. She quaked, clinging to the vanity until it passed.

Lindy Munson.

Broiled in the trunk of Dana's car.

Maggie felt nauseous.

She and Loomis had waited a difficult hour for the cavalry to arrive, both of them unable to put into words the horror of what they'd found.

At some point during early evening, the killer had ditched Dana's car on the service road and then set it on fire with Lindy in the trunk, stripped down to her underwear and hog tied with plastic zip ties. Until Elkin had taken a look, it was impossible to say if she had been dead in the trunk before the blaze, or if she'd still been alive when fire had engulfed the car. Either way, the enclosed space had acted like an oven, roasting her flesh and steaming off moisture, blistering her skin until it had peeled and split and turned bright crimson.

The thought of Lindy cooking to death had put Maggie's head in a spin, and by the time she had handed over control of the death scene and driven Loomis back home, it was after one in the morning, and her brain hadn't stopped hurting since.

"You okay?"

Maggie looked back toward the darkened bedroom. "I didn't mean to wake you." She went back into the room. "I have to go."

"Go? Go where, Maggie? It's still dark."

Maggie scooped up her clothes from the back of a chair. "There's something I need to do."

"Can't it wait?"

"It won't let me sleep." She pulled on her underwear, shirt, and jeans.

"It's the middle of the night," he said, as though she hadn't realized and his pointing it out might change her mind.

"I won't be long," she said, going around to his side of the bed. "I'll be home in time for breakfast." She leaned down and kissed him on the mouth. "Go back to sleep."

She found her boots and pulled them on.

"At least let me drive," he said, sitting up.

"It's okay."

"I don't mind."

"I do. Your blood alcohol level is probably still off the chart. Seriously, Steve, I'll be fine." She opened the bedroom door.

"Be careful," he said, lying back down. "There's a thunderstorm on its way."

◆ ◆ ◆

Diamond raindrops freckled the windshield as Maggie drove out of Keene's Pointe, the wipers kicking on and screaking across the glass.

First Dana, and now Lindy.

At least one, maybe two killers.

She wanted answers, *needed* them, in the same way an addict needed her next fix. It left her *wired*.

This was how it was with her.

Whenever things felt unsettled, a good night's sleep was impossible. Maggie wasn't sure if it was the whisper of those murdered that kept her awake, or her gut as it tried to alert her to things awry.

Unlike some of her fellow detectives in Major Case who quite happily left their work at the office, Maggie had never been able to fully detach. Casework distracted her, even when she knew she should be concentrating on her life outside the workplace.

Steve had tried several times to counsel her out of the habit, to reprogram her brain waves. His claim was that less was often more, and her being able to step away for a while would lead to a fresh-eyes approach. But she couldn't change how she worked, the same way he couldn't suddenly fall out of love with surfing. Some things were written in the DNA.

Her science-minded father had always maintained that "a photon is both a particle and a wave. Remove either one and you take away both. Like it or lump it, it is what it is, and there's not a damn thing we can do about it."

She turned into Chase Road, her foot hard on the gas. The Mustang roared, eating up the asphalt like a panther stretching its legs.

Truly, the last thing she had expected to find in Dana's car was Lindy's body. How was she even going to begin to tell Ronda Munson that her daughter was dead, and in such a nightmarish fashion? Maybe she wouldn't have to. The Sheriff's Office had community relations people, trained to communicate with the families of victims. More than likely, the task would be taken away from her and given to someone better qualified. Someone less emotionally entangled in the case.

Still . . .

Maggie couldn't shrug off her sense of responsibility to the girl, or to her mother.

Heavier rain began to patter the windshield. Maggie flicked the wipers fully on, the rubber blades sluicing off rainwater.

Lightning flashed, outlining towering thunderheads. Deafening rain drumming against the Mustang's soft top.

Maggie kept her foot down.

Lindy's murder pointed to several possibilities and several puzzling scenarios, all contributing to Maggie's restlessness. She went through them, one by one, as she drove through the rain, the streets all but abandoned.

Possibility one: Cullen murdered Dana and then Lindy.

In this setup, Cullen had killed Dana early Saturday evening before later abducting Lindy from her home in Pine Hills while her mother was at work. Cullen had killed Lindy, hiding her body in the trunk of his wife's car. Someone else—as yet, an unknown third party and Cullen's accomplice—had driven Dana's car to the Wildlife Drive dump site on Sunday evening and torched it with Lindy's dead body inside. One killer. One aiding and abetting accomplice.

Possibility two: Cullen murdered Dana but not Lindy.

Similar to the first scenario in that Cullen killed Dana, only in this one, the mysterious third person had abducted and killed Lindy. Then, with Cullen removed from the equation, the second killer had dumped Dana's car with Lindy's body in the trunk. Two killers working as one.

Thunder broke across the sky, rattling the Mustang's roof. Visibility reducing and rain bouncing off the roadway.

Both these scenarios raised further questions. But right now, Maggie was all out of answers. Of course, she could speculate, spin scenes in which Cullen and his accomplice did their dirty deeds. In her profession, speculation was a valuable tool. It acted like a mental sieve, filtering out the detritus, focusing on the important facts.

What did she know with absolute certainty?

She knew that, together with Tyler, Lindy had found Dana's body, and that she had played the damsel in distress to Maggie and the camera. She knew that when she had confronted Tyler in his bedroom, he'd confessed that the date at the lake was "her idea," implying that Lindy had set the whole thing up.

Did Lindy take him there knowing what they'd find?

The thought was an unnerving one. Right away, it spoke of Lindy having insider knowledge regarding Dana's murder.

Is that what got her killed?

Did she know too much and became a liability?

It also suggested a premeditated involvement that put her alongside Cullen on the guilty pedestal.

But why would Lindy want Dana dead?

"If Dana was Lindy's guidance counselor," Maggie said out loud, "that's their primary connection. Best to start there."

Everybody had secrets, Maggie knew. Secrets that nobody wanted the world to know about. Secrets that might bring shame, or ridicule, or even retribution.

Did Dana hit a raw nerve in one of Lindy's counseling sessions, uncovering a secret that put her life in jeopardy?

In not so many words, Ronda Munson had suggested that, when it came to sexual relationships, her daughter was licentious. In other words, she slept around. One of those popular girls who used her body to control the boys. Maggie remembered several of the girls she'd known when she was at school behaving similarly. In fact, Kristen, one of her closest friends in senior year, had slept with every member of the school football team, and several all at the same time. She'd said it empowered her as a woman. But Maggie knew it was all an act, set up to hide her insecurities.

"Did Dana question your promiscuity, Lindy? Is that what happened?"

It was possible that Dana had tried to reset the teen's moral compass, and Lindy had taken exception to her interfering. She'd teamed up with Cullen to dispose of his wife. And then Cullen had brought in a third party to silence Lindy.

"Weak as station-house coffee," Maggie said with a scoff. She tilted the rearview mirror so that she could see her own eyes. "Will you please stick to what you know? There's no way Lindy would murder Dana over loose morals."

Unless . . .

"You were sleeping with a teacher. Is that it, Lindy? Did Dana find out and threaten to expose you?"

It wasn't beyond the scope of imagination. Lindy was a good-looking girl. Coming of age and bursting with youth. Dressed to kill and flirtatious, too; Maggie had witnessed it firsthand. With Lindy's moral compass freewheeling, it was possible it had misdirected her to the bed of an older male. A predator waiting to take advantage of vulnerable girls. Dana had discovered Lindy's indiscretion, prompting the teenager to take lethal measures to protect herself.

Did Lindy kill Dana so that she could hide an affair?

The thought was chilling, because it pointed to a cold-hearted killer who would go to any lengths to protect her wrongdoings. Add that to the fact that Tyler had told Maggie he had been instructed to bring what was, in effect, a kill kit to the lake, and suddenly Maggie could imagine Lindy playing a major role in Dana's death.

Which led to . . .

Possibility three: Cullen didn't kill anyone.

Instead, Lindy had killed Dana, and then, to throw the police off her scent, she'd framed Cullen for his own wife's murder. She'd then orchestrated the discovery of Dana's body, using Tyler as her alibi, believing it would immediately rule her out of any other involvement.

Maggie made a mental note to find out if Lindy had had access to a handgun.

The traffic lights at the intersection with West Colonial were blazing away on red. Pink-blue lightning flooded the sky as she rolled the Mustang up to the line. The rain was torrential now, battering the bodywork and throwing the wipers into a frenzy.

Lindy killed Dana.

Maggie mulled it over as she waited for the signals to change.

It was a fascinating proposition, and if it were true, then Lindy was dangerous. But it didn't explain everything. And it didn't fill the gaping holes in the theory. For starters, why did Lindy insist Tyler bring the kill kit to the woods? And who killed Lindy?

The lights changed to green, and Maggie accelerated through the intersection.

She was going to get wet.

◆ ◆ ◆

Sitting in her car, she waited for a gap in the rain that she knew would never come.

Across the street, a thick shawl of rain shrouded Dana Cullen's picture-book cottage. Obscured behind raindrops the size of golf balls, bouncing a yard high in the street, the noise earsplitting.

Briefly, lightning crackled, turning night to day and painting details on featureless shapes. Forget the theme parks; Florida's thunderstorms were some of the wildest rides in the state, with light shows to beat any Fourth of July fireworks.

Not for the first time, Maggie asked herself what she was doing here.

It was the middle of the night, a tropical storm tearing up the heavens. The only people out and about at this hour were those with no choice.

She had a choice.

She'd chosen *this*.

What was she thinking? She should have been at home with Steve, in bed and cuddling up. Of all places, she shouldn't be here. This was madness.

But Maggie couldn't help herself.

A twenty-year-old debt was being called in.

She put on a pair of latex gloves from the crime scene kit stowed in the glove compartment, and grabbed her flashlight. Then, with her jacket held over her head, she ran through the downpour to the back of the house.

She was soaked within seconds.

It was pitch black in the backyard, deepened by the overhanging trees. Spanish moss dripping. Warm rain drumming against the patio and kicking up the gravel. She felt her way to the back door. It was open. She let herself inside, dripping water on the floor tiles.

She shook off her coat and left it draped over a stool at the breakfast bar.

Then she stopped, reminding herself that she could turn around at any moment and never come back.

No choice.

Although the residence wasn't designated as a crime scene per se, it had been deemed a point of interest in light of Cullen's arrest, and a weekend judge had signed off on Forensics taking the place apart—if so doing led to a successful murder prosecution. As lead investigator, Maggie had every right to be here, even at this unconventional hour, but it didn't stop her from feeling like an intruder.

Her flashlight projected sharp shadows across the small kitchenette and into the chintz-laden living room.

Forensics had spent most of the afternoon here, sifting through the neatly stored contents with a fine-tooth comb. Every nook and cranny inspected, including the small attic and the cramped crawl space. Techies in white coveralls turning over every rock in Cullen's beloved alpine garden, emptying out his tool shed and removing his outdoor grill for further analysis. Every possible hiding place checked, meticulously, and luminol used to locate any possible blood trace.

Forensics had come away empty handed.

No clothes in the laundry stained with gunshot residue. No box of 9 mm bullets hidden behind the bleach bottles under the kitchen sink. No blood in the drains. Nothing to add to the incriminating items collected from the property earlier in the day.

The lack of corroborating evidence hadn't daunted Smits one bit. Following Maggie's interview with Cullen, Smits had decided they had enough circumstantial evidence to present to the state attorney. In his opinion, with or without a definite kill site, the burden of proof had been met, and the case against Cullen looked airtight. Formal charges could be brought.

But Maggie had clung to her doubts, unable to resist cleaving to her gut instinct.

A droplet of rainwater ran down her face, and she brushed it away.

Although Cullen was probably guilty of being a pitiful excuse for a husband, in light of Lindy's murder, Maggie wasn't sure that he was solely responsible for his wife's death, or that he had even played a part in her killing at all. Right now, she couldn't put her finger on it, but something felt amiss.

Trailing wet boot prints behind her, Maggie followed the beam of her flashlight deeper into the house.

The carry-on was still in the hall near the front door. She carried it through to the master bedroom, laying it down on the bed and unzipping it.

Forensics had already processed the luggage, but Maggie wanted to see it for herself. It was likely that the carry-on was the last thing that Dana had handled before leaving home and never coming back. Maggie's gut had been telling her to check it from the moment she'd first laid eyes on it from Cullen's doorstep.

She emptied the contents onto the bed.

Two changes of clothes, Lycra gym gear—including sneakers with thick white sports socks jammed deep inside—accessories, a makeup bag, toiletries, and a sealed plastic pouch containing various medications.

Dana had packed for a weekend away. Cullen was probably right: a beachside hotel with fitness facilities. A private getaway from her golf-mad hubby.

If Dana had remembered to take the carry-on with her, Maggie wondered, would they have found it tossed in the lake or crammed in the trunk of Dana's car with Lindy?

Maggie inspected the makeup and pill bags, then prodded around the interior, looking for anything hidden away behind the red silky lining.

Why did Dana forget to take the carry-on with her?

Finally, Maggie pulled the socks out of the sneakers, raising her eyebrows at the thick rolls of crisp hundred-dollar bills stuffed into the shoes.

"Sneaky," she said, tipping them out onto the bed.

The rolls were wrapped tight with paper currency bands. Four rolls with $2,000 written on each in black marker. Maggie was in no doubt that this was the same $8,000 that Dana had withdrawn from the Wells Fargo on Friday.

"Where were you going with this much in cash?" she wondered out loud. "What was it for?"

Maggie took photos with her phone. Then she put the bank rolls to one side and packed everything else back in the carry-on.

She turned her attention to the primary reason for her coming back here at stupid o'clock: Dana's notebook.

It was still in the dresser where Maggie had left it.

She sat down on the corner of the bed, opening the notebook, straightaway the flashlight picking out the word *Helga* written on the Polaroid photo tucked inside the front cover.

Maggie's stomach tightened.

She hurried past it, wanting to know what the rest of the book contained.

Mostly, poetry and personal observations, by the looks of it. Poems tackling segregation and subjugation, a feminist roster. Views on anti-establishmentarianism and nihilism, all very dark and dismal. Personal accounts of activities at school and after.

Dates in the top right corners, going back twenty years, to the start of their senior year.

These were Rita's thoughts.

Obsessively, Maggie kept turning pages, occasionally pausing to read a verse or two, marveling at the complexity of the writing and the way that Rita was able to express herself with such clarity. Although Maggie could take or leave poetry, she appreciated the word wizardry involved.

Something was pushing open the pages in the middle of the notebook.

Maggie flicked through to it, her fingers finding a small white envelope that was being used as a bookmark. It looked old, its edges yellowed and worn, the flap tucked in at the back, and a recipient's details written in red pencil on the front.

Lightning flashed, lighting up the bedroom, and thunder roared, vibrating in her chest as a chill rose in Maggie's belly.

The name and address on the envelope were hers.

◆ ◆ ◆

The address corresponded to her home on Wineberry, and at first Maggie was unable to explain it.

A decade ago, when she'd made the decision to buy the family home from her divorcing parents, it had been met with negativity from both of Maggie's siblings. Up until then, Maggie had rented an apartment in the city, but she'd never considered it permanent, or homey. Not like the four-bed, three-bath house on Wineberry, with its rich Novak history and its roots reaching all the way down to the fossil record.

Nora had told her it was a bad idea, Maggie buying the house, and that the family needed a clean break after years of parental squabbling. If that meant selling the house to strangers, then so be it. And Bryan had simply told her that she was being selfish as usual, and that Maggie's opting to buy the house where they'd all been raised was her way of cheating both him and Nora out of their rightful inheritance. Of course, their fears had been unfounded and misguided; Maggie had insisted on paying top dollar for the property, with every penny of the profits being split equally between their warring parents. How their mom and dad then chose to distribute their share of the estate to the three children somewhere down the line was their choice, not Maggie's. But even ten years later, her ownership was still a bone of contention with Bryan especially, and he never let her forget it, arguing that due to the depressed housing market, she'd snapped it up for a song. The fact that the house had almost doubled in value since then only added fuel to his fire.

But she wasn't for giving it up anytime soon.

What was her address doing on the envelope?

Did Dana intend to send it to her, only to be killed before she could? If so, why did it look so old? It even smelled musty. The only explanation Maggie could think of was that this was an unsent letter, dating from before the Grigoryan house fire, when Dana had been Rita.

Which meant . . .

Maggie pulled out the envelope's flap. There was a folded piece of paper inside. She tipped it out.

Lightning flickered again, thunder rolling as she opened it.

In red ink, three uppercase words were written across the paper, underlined several times:

LEAVE ME ALONE

Maggie recoiled as each word seemed to reach up off the page and punch her on the nose, so hard that tears broke out in the corners of her eyes.

Leave me alone.

She'd only ever heard Rita say those words once, in person, to her face, on a late summer's evening a few weeks before the fatal fire, and they'd never left Maggie since.

Leave me alone.

The last words Rita had ever spoken to her.

And their power both then and now was utterly crushing.

Something banged somewhere in the house.

Maggie looked around to the open bedroom door, holding her breath and listening. She could hear the storm raging outside, rain drumming against the windows and the roof.

Then she heard a man's voice cussing out loud. And adrenaline burst through her system. She stuffed the note back in the envelope, and the envelope back in the notebook. And a fraction of a second later, her police training kicked in. She doused the flashlight and leaped to her feet, hovering in the doorway to listen, to assess the situation, and to weigh her options.

She could hear movement coming from the direction of the kitchenette, what sounded like a cupboard door banging shut, a man's voice muttering words she couldn't quite make out. She figured someone must have noticed the heavy police activity in the daytime, assuming that tonight the house would be empty and easy pickings.

Maggie reached for her Glock, only to realize that she'd left it locked in the trunk of her car, in the gun safe. To make matters worse, her cell phone was in her jacket pocket at the breakfast bar.

Right where the intruder was.

She asked herself, did she want to tackle a burglar in the dark and in an unfamiliar setting?

But she couldn't just stand here while somebody ransacked the house.

Maggie smoothed her damp hair back from her face.

The intruder didn't know she was here, least of all that she was unarmed. Announcing her presence might prove deterrent enough, give her time to call for back up. Often, the declaration that a police officer was on the premises was sufficient to subdue a trespasser, or to send him fleeing.

The glow of a flashlight sent long shadows scurrying across the end of the hallway ahead of her.

Silently, Maggie moved toward it.

More bangs and cussing coming from the kitchenette.

It sounded like cupboards were being opened and their contents rummaged through.

She paused where the hallway joined the living room, peeping around the edge of the doorframe as lightning flashed outside.

A man was silhouetted against the bright kitchen window.

She saw him freeze in the sudden light, as though he had seen her peeping.

"Police!" Maggie shouted. "Get down on your knees! Hands above your head!"

Thunder boomed, shaking the wooden walls.

It seemed to act like a starting pistol.

The intruder took flight, clattering through the kitchenette toward the back door.

Maggie made her choice and ran after him.

Spears of steel rain fell vertically from the black sky, striking the patio and bouncing as high as her head, louder than a hundred crashing cymbals.

Maggie paused to grab her bearings, rain pouring, drenching her. Everywhere she looked, reduced visibility. She had no idea which way the intruder had fled.

Thunder and lightning erupted simultaneously.

Maggie spotted him clambering over the side fence. She hollered at him to desist, but he disappeared into the neighboring yard without so much as a glance in her direction.

With her clothes clinging to her skin, she splashed her way across the yard. She leaped at the fence. The white-painted wood wasn't white-painted wood at all. It was vinyl. And it was slippery. Her first attempt at vaulting it was met with her slithering down into a heap on the gravel, knees bruising. She tried again, hooking her fingers over the apex and hauling herself up, feet scrabbling for purchase, the fence panel wobbling precariously as she rolled over the top and landed heavily in a muddy puddle on the other side.

Lightning lit the broiling clouds.

The intruder was a good thirty yards away already, headed toward the back of the neighbor's property, his heels kicking up rainwater.

Unlike in Cullen's yard, there was no fence here to denote the boundary, just mowed lawn stretching away into the adjoining yards. Maggie took up the chase again, splashing across the grass as rain needled her face.

She saw the intruder reach the street and begin to cross it on a long diagonal, running like the devil was snapping at his heels. Through the driving rain, she could just make out that he had on a dark hoodie with the hood up, dark-colored pants, and sneakers with red soles.

Maggie hit the harder asphalt, increasing her pace on the firmer surface.

Twenty yards and closing.

Although it was completely doable, Maggie had never considered herself a marathoner. She had the stamina for it, and she could tune out everything to focus on the long game, but the thought of running for hours had never appealed to her. There were far more productive things she could do with the time, she thought, other than grinding down her knee cartilage.

Running down fleeing wrongdoers, on the other hand, came with a certain adrenaline-fed rush. An immediacy. And already she could feel the heat pluming inside her, fueling her sprint.

The rest was a matter of attrition.

Stick at it long enough, and she was confident she could wear him down, grab him while he fought for breath, powerless and unable to resist arrest.

Maggie tucked her elbows in and dipped her head, following his long diagonal route across the street.

Ten yards and closing.

She saw the intruder veer suddenly into a front yard and disappear into the deep shadow at the side of the house. She cut across the lawn a second or two later, running at full speed and almost losing it on the slick grass.

A deafening thunder volley broke above her. And as brilliant lightning flickered, she saw him darting around the back of the house.

Five yards and closing.

Any second now and she'd be close enough to tackle him from behind. She was trained to apprehend suspects, knowing what pressure to apply where, which soft spots incapacitated, which nerve junction to plant her knee into.

The thought spurred her on.

What she hadn't bargained for was what happened next.

As Maggie rounded the corner of the house, something like a baseball bat struck her squarely on the chest. The impact stopped her in her tracks, scooting her feet out from under her and sending her crashing to the ground. She hit the grass hard, spread eagled on her back, the air knocked from her lungs, momentarily stunned.

The clouds lit up again, thunder detonating across the sky. And in the shuddering light she saw the intruder looming over her, his hooded silhouette as black as space.

She blinked as rainwater drilled at her face. "Police," she managed to gasp. But it didn't make a difference.

He kicked her in her side.

Pain burned through her ribs.

Instinctively, she drew up her knees, curling into a ball, trying to protect her head as another kick landed. Waves of agonizing fire sweeping through her.

Then her training took over.

As the foot swung again, she caught the heel in her fingers. In the same instant, she twisted, deflecting the foot aside and using its own momentum to push it away and upward. His balance shifted, forcing his weight onto his other heel. Maggie exploited her advantage, rolling to her knees and forcing the leg even higher. She heard him cry out with surprise, his arms barreling as he toppled backward like a felled tree, his foot still in her grasp.

Maggie ignored the pain flaring in her side, scooting to her feet and using both hands to twist the foot sharply to one side. He yelped again, this time with pain. She stomped her own foot on his stomach, silencing him. Then she twisted the whole leg around, forcing him to go with it and roll over onto his belly. Once he was facedown, she released the foot and planted a knee in the small of his back. Again, he howled.

"Police!" she shouted above the din of the rain. She grabbed his wrist and yanked his arm up his back. "You're under arrest! Do not resist!"

But he did.

Her assailant was strong, stronger than she anticipated.

He used his free arm like a piston. An impressive one-handed push-up that lifted them both up off the ground. Spine snapping straight and bucking her off.

Maggie landed awkwardly on the grass, one leg tucked under itself. And then it was his turn to take advantage. He scrambled on top of her before she could move, his weight pressing her down into the sodden earth.

She cried out as pain tore up her trapped leg.

She tried to defend herself, to dig her fingertips into his eyeballs, or into any soft tissue she could find, but he swatted her hands aside, raising his fist and bringing it down to her face like a hammerhead. Clenched knuckles scuffing her jaw and rattling the teeth in her mouth. Paralyzing pain bursting through her skull. Sparks flying in her vision. Maggie had taken quite a few knocks to the head in her career, but each time it happened it was like the first, the severity of it shocking. She saw him hoist the fist again, readying to deliver the knockout blow.

Is this it? she wondered as rain pelted her face. Is this how her life was destined to end—at the hands of some stranger, here in someone's backyard, flat on her back in the mud, in the middle of a thunderstorm, unable to put up even the weakest defense?

Lightning flashed, flickering for long brilliant seconds.

And in its cold light she glimpsed a sliver of her assailant's face for the first time, a hint of a face that she thought she recognized.

"Tyler?" she gasped. "Tyler, is that you?"

The attacker hesitated. Rain cascading over his shoulders. His fist still poised to deliver its killer strike.

Maggie blinked. "Don't."

Chapter Eighteen

CLOUDY, WITH SPELLS OF POOR JUDGMENT

Maggie looked up from her phone as the ambulance's rear doors swung open and a gray-haired man in a windbreaker climbed inside, bringing a swirl of rain and an air of authority in with him.

"Go easy on those pain meds," he said as he traded places with the attending paramedic. "I need my detective pin sharp and able to answer questions."

Maggie switched off her phone and rammed the ice pack back under her jaw. "Captain," she said with a slight nod.

"Detective."

Captain Wes Corrigan was Maggie's section commander at Major Case. Now in his late fifties, Corrigan was all about his *people*, as he liked to refer to those under his command. And like most hands-on leaders, he didn't suffer fools gladly.

"Sir . . . ," Maggie began, but Corrigan cut her off with a hand slice.

"No apologies necessary, Detective," he said. "When I hear an officer is down and it's one of my people, I don't hesitate to run into the maw of hell if need be, even at this ungodly hour."

Bold words. But coming from Corrigan, it was a standard-issue statement, and Maggie suspected it came from a point of procedure rather than a place of empathy. Although he was trying to appear concerned for her welfare, she could sense he was irked at being dragged out of his bed at four in the morning.

She couldn't blame him.

His gray eyes glanced down at her chin. "Other than the obvious welt, what's the damage?"

She touched a hand to her waist. "Bruised ribs and a slight concussion." The paramedic had given her something for the pain, then let her breathe oxygen for a few minutes, but she still felt achy, light headed, her muscles cramping every time she inhaled. "Good news is, I'll live."

She knew it could have been much worse. They both did.

"I hear a good neighbor called it in," Corrigan said.

"Kindly souls still exist."

Storm watching, an elderly woman had been at her bedroom window when the fight had broken out in her yard below. She'd banged a fist against the window and shaken her phone at Maggie's attacker, bringing the assault to a premature and welcome end.

"She spooked him, just at the right moment," Maggie said.

"She probably saved your life. You should send her some flowers."

Maggie tried to smile, but it came out a wince.

"I hear you ID'd the attacker as the Pruitt kid," Corrigan said.

"Yes, sir."

Not only had the captain been apprised of her present situation, he'd also familiarized himself with her case, it seemed. No surprise. Even though it had been late when they'd found Lindy's body in the trunk of Dana's car, Loomis had called Smits at home, bringing him up to speed, and everyone in Homicide Squad knew that Smits was an information conduit for Corrigan. No one could sneeze without it going up the chain.

The captain's eyes narrowed. "Atrocious weather conditions. Everything happening in a blur. You're sure you got a clean look at your attacker? Eyewitness says he wore a hood. On a scale of one to ten, how confident are you it was him?"

"Eight. Maybe nine."

She saw conflict stir in Corrigan's eyes.

"The truth is, sir, I glimpsed a partial at best. But I'm sure it was Tyler."

And the more she'd thought about it in the aftermath of the attack, the more convinced she was that Tyler was the culprit. Same height and build. Same bigger upper body. And she was sure she'd seen sneakers with red soles lying on the floor of Tyler's bedroom yesterday morning. On top of all that, her gut was shouting out his name. But gut instinct was inadmissible.

Corrigan brushed raindrops off his collar. "And you made it clear you were police?"

"Twice. It didn't stop him."

He shook his head, sprinkling raindrops. "No respect these days."

A deputy in a rain-spattered poncho appeared in the ambulance doorway. In clipped words he explained to Corrigan that his men's sweep of the vicinity had proven fruitless; the attacker was long gone. Corrigan thanked him, and as the deputy departed, he swung his gaze back to Maggie.

"It's my understanding you had this Pruitt kid in custody yesterday."

Maggie nodded, going dizzy. "For assaulting Lindy Munson."

"Who you found dead a few hours ago."

"Yes, sir. I believe it demonstrates Tyler has no qualms when it comes to hitting women. If we bring him in . . ."

"*When* we bring him in," he corrected. "Your BOLO is out. If this kid did attack one of my people, rest assured he's going down for it."

Regardless of her assailant's true identity, Maggie knew that the second he struck her, he'd elevated his status from intruder to attacker. To add fuel to the fire, assaulting a police officer came with the unenviable position of making him the focus of every member of law enforcement in the state.

"What was he doing there?" Corrigan asked.

"Looking for something."

"Did he find it?"

Maggie shrugged, then wished she hadn't. "I disturbed him, so it's unlikely."

"Flip side, Detective. What were *you* doing in the Cullen house in the middle of the night?"

"Following up on an earlier discovery."

It wasn't the whole truth, but she was hoping it was enough to excuse her unorthodox behavior. Better to get out in front of it on her own terms than allow Corrigan to wonder about her wider motive.

She saw him raise an eyebrow, and she explained about her finding the notebook in Dana's dresser, her intention to inspect it when they were there earlier in the day, only for that plan to be postponed in the wake of Loomis uncovering the work boots in the outdoor grill.

"I couldn't sleep," she said. "Not after finding Lindy like that. I thought I'd put the time to good use."

"By coming down here and snooping around on private property."

"Our search warrant has a twenty-four-hour window, sir. My actions were within protocols."

"But outside the scope of normalcy. Besides, don't preach to the converted, Detective. My concern is your clumsy timing and your disregard for safety. What were you thinking?"

"I think I was reacting," she admitted.

It wasn't like her. Rarely did she let emotion influence her decisions. In fact, Maggie had learned how to keep her emotions separate from her work. It was a necessary evil. Self-preservation. Some cases were heartbreaking. To let emotions interfere would be a disservice to the victims and their families. Plus, a detective couldn't do her job if she was an emotional wreck all the time. It hadn't been easy learning to completely dissociate when situations warranted a cool composure, but she'd mastered it.

Only, now things were personal. The Halloween Homicide had opened up a crack in her steely exterior, and she wasn't sure if her reactiveness was down to her emotions leaking out, or the outside world leaking in.

"Despite everything," Corrigan said, "you showed initiative and dedication. And I value that in my people. Let this be a lesson, Detective. Even something as innocent as a notebook could be your undoing."

Corrigan didn't know the half of it.

Maggie swallowed against the constant lump in her throat. "About that," she said. "I'd like to take a proper look at the notebook, before Sergeant Smits talks to the state attorney."

"Why?"

"I'm thinking it could contain substantiating evidence."

"To cement the husband's guilt? From what I hear, your sergeant has all he needs. This is an open-and-shut case."

"With all due respect, sir, I'm not sure it is."

Corrigan glanced at his watch. "Okay. Make it quick."

Briefly, Maggie explained her new theories in light of the second homicide, and how it was possible that Cullen might be innocent altogether.

"The notebook contains the victim's private thoughts," she said. "It goes to her state of mind. I'm thinking she could name names and even point us in the right direction. Plus, we know for a fact that Cullen didn't torch his wife's car. He was in our custody at the time. Someone else is involved here. That, in itself, gives his defense ammunition to blow our case wide open."

"You think Sergeant Smits should hang fire?"

"I think I don't want the state attorney tossing my case because our evidence can be explained away by a reasonably decent defense."

He nodded contemplatively. She knew what he was thinking: Cullen was in custody, the physical evidence pointed to him having killed his wife, Smits had arranged an audience with the state attorney tomorrow morning, and the department badly needed a win.

"All right," he said at last. "How much time do you need to examine this notebook?"

"A few hours, tops."

"You have until noon. That gives you the morning to come up with corroborating evidence confirming the husband's guilt, or his innocence, either way. I'll instruct Sergeant Smits to hold back on speaking with the state attorney until then."

"Thanks, Captain." She was grateful for his latitude, but she wasn't sure how she'd fit everything in. Monday had now become her day off, and she'd already promised to spend it at the beach with Steve.

But then, that's not what this was all about.

Corrigan got up to leave, pausing at the doorway. "The second victim," he said. "The girl. She was just seventeen, right?"

"Yes, sir."

"Have the parents been informed?"

"There's just the mother, sir. And no. Not yet. The body is still waiting processing."

He hung his head, his expression grave. "This is a screwed-up universe. A parent should never have to experience the death of a child. It's goes against nature. Leave this with me. I'll pay the mother a visit."

"Captain, I . . ."

Corrigan raised a halting hand. "I won't hear any more of it, Detective. You have plenty to keep you busy. This is my burden to bear. Now, go home and get some sleep. You're going to need it."

Chapter Nineteen

THE PRINCIPAL

Y ou don't have to do this," Steve said to Maggie as they turned off the highway at the sign for Crown Pointe High School. "You were injured in the line of duty. Could've been killed. Nobody is expecting you to go above and beyond here."

"Only me," Maggie said.

It was after nine a.m., and they were in Steve's Tahoe, making a detour to the school before heading off to the beach. After last night's storm, Orlando had woken to blinding sunshine and another hot day. And Maggie had woken with her side as stiff as a board and a constant ache in her jaw. A slight twinge in her left leg as a result of it having been trapped under her while her attacker had pinned her down. More Tylenol hadn't fixed the issues, and Maggie was hoping that things would ease off as the day wore on.

"I see you couldn't resist bringing a beach read along," Steve said as they drove along Ocoee Parkway.

Maggie glanced at Dana's notebook protruding from her purse on the floor at her feet. Owing to exhaustion and her subsequent crashing at Steve's place, she'd only managed to read about half of it. So far, no mention of marital unrest or Dana fearing for her safety in any way. Nothing to cement Cullen's guilt.

"What are you hoping to find?" he asked. "Evidence of murderous intent?"

He still sounded a little pissed with her, she thought. But she chose to let it go, knowing that if the shoe were on the other foot, she'd never let him hear the last of it.

"I'm not holding my breath," she said. She didn't add that her inspection of Dana's notebook was more for her own peace of mind than to prove Cullen's culpability, and that the remainder of the book was calling out to her like liquor to an alcoholic.

The truth was, it was *her own guilt* that she needed to address here, or hopefully assuage. And Steve would never understand her teenage behavior, even if she laid bare everything on his therapy couch. He would try to tap into her core, to uncover the reason behind her one mistake. He'd attempt to decode it, to analyze it, to neutralize it, but he'd never *accept* it. Once her fatal error in judgment was out in the open, it would always be there, standing between them, like an elephant in the room, taking up precious attention.

Either with or without therapy, there was no explaining away the things she'd done.

She took a swig from a water bottle, wondering if any of the hundreds of students and teachers at Crown Pointe this morning had any inkling of the vicious murder that had taken place at the lake less than forty-eight hours earlier.

"Don't spend all day doing work," Steve said as they turned into the school parking lot. He found an empty space reserved for visitors. "You need your rest. Doctor's orders." He glanced sidelong at her, offering a supportive smile. "Patient first, detective second."

Maggie didn't have the heart to tell him that it was the other way around, and nothing he could say would ever change that.

No matter how many times they went over it, he'd never fully understand that her work couldn't be confined to office hours, or that as a woman she had to excel just to be considered equal. Criminals didn't operate on a nine-to-five basis. Cases evolved naturally, with no consideration to time constraints or vacation days. As such, an investigator had to be flexible in her schedule and her approach, willing to put in the legwork if she wanted to reach the finish line first. In other words, if Maggie wanted to be one step ahead of the bad guys and on a level footing with her male counterparts, she had to be willing to go the extra mile in order to catch her man *and* the eyes of her bosses.

She saw Steve's supportive smile slip a little.

She knew he was putting on a brave face on her account, but she sensed he was still upset with her for limping home with her ribs blackening, a whisker away from being pulverized by her attacker. In the predawn light, she'd resisted the compulsion to be standoffish as Steve had fussed over her awhile, both understanding and disapproving at the same time. On one hand, concerned for her welfare, and yet critical of her behavior on the other. To his credit, he'd kept his frustration mostly at bay, but she knew her assault had made him feel powerless. Men had a built-in need to protect their women, and her injury had put a big dent in his machismo.

Spartacus nudged her ear with his wet nose.

The dog was in the back seat, panting despite the air-conditioning. Not for the first time since they'd set out, he put his big paws on the back of Maggie's seat and tried to lick the side of her face.

"See," Steve said. "Even Spart can sense you're overdoing things."

Playfully, Maggie rubbed her knuckles against the dog's muzzle, his hot tongue curling around her wrist. "He's just excited about getting to the beach eventually. Aren't you, boy?"

Steve brightened. "Makes two of us."

Maggie gave Steve a wholesome smile even though she felt torn in half. Surfing was Steve's *thing*, and always had been, long before Maggie had come onto the scene. She'd agreed to a day of rest and recuperation while he sat on his board, seeking out what he called *the perfect wedge*. The last time she'd agreed to go on a beach day with him, she'd had to pull out at the last minute. It was the only reason she wasn't insisting they stay home while she chased Dana's killer.

"I'll be as quick as I can," she said, opening the passenger door and climbing out.

She signed in at the school admin office, then waited two minutes for Principal Wendy Ellis to come fetch her. Maggie had called ahead. She didn't go into detail over the phone.

Ellis was a tall brunette. Green-tinted eyeglasses propped on a hook nose. Noticeably long fingers. The first thing she said as they shook hands was, "If one of our students is in trouble with the law, we possess the know-how and the integrity to sort it out."

Even from those first few words, Maggie could tell that Ellis was one of those people who saw silver linings when everybody else saw rain clouds.

"I need to speak with you about Dana Cullen," Maggie said, getting right to the point of her visit.

"Dana? Why, has something happened? I notice she hasn't come in yet."

"Can we talk in private?"

"Certainly."

Maggie followed Ellis into the principal's office, with its big corner windows looking out into a communal courtyard of benches and trees. Even though it had been more than twenty years since Maggie had last stepped foot inside the principal's office—albeit in the old school—the fear she'd felt back then suddenly came rushing back, squeezing her gut.

"We're so lucky to have Dana," Ellis said as they sat. "She's excellent at her job. The best counselor we've had in ages. All the students think very highly of her. If she's in some kind of trouble and the school is in a position to help her out in any way—"

"Dana is dead," Maggie said.

Ellis's jaw dropped.

"I'll need to see her office," Maggie said before the principal could ask any questions Maggie didn't want to answer. "If that's okay."

Ellis nodded. She looked like the wind had been knocked out of her. "Who else knows?"

"It's an ongoing murder investigation, which means I'm not at liberty to discuss the details."

"She was murdered?" The color vanished from her face. "Who would do such a thing?"

"I need to ask that you be discreet about this. And that includes limiting who you tell."

"But the students . . ."

"You can inform them in due course." Maggie thought about the moment she'd heard of Rita's death, announced at school, and the ensuing emotional chaos. She placed her business card on Ellis's desk. "In the meantime, until we give you the all clear, please hold back on making any kind of an announcement."

Ellis nodded. She lifted up her glasses, wiping tears from her eyes with her overly long fingers.

"Do you need a moment?" Maggie asked.

The principal shook her head. "No. It's just a lot to take in. Dana was a good person. Well liked." She sniffed, composing herself. "I know it's too soon to say, but I promise you we will all learn something from this. The whole school. Something positive. You have my word. Dana's death will not be in vain."

"There's something else," Maggie said. "And again, it calls for absolute sensitivity."

"Discretion is the better part of valor." Ellis made the statement without missing a beat, as though preprogrammed to respond that way.

Maggie nodded, all too familiar with the school's motto and its expectations. "Two of your students found Dana's body. Lindy Munson and Tyler Pruitt."

Ellis reacted as though someone had slapped her across the face. "Lindy and Tyler?"

"Is something wrong with that?"

"It's just that they are the last two students I'd put *together*." She pronounced the final word as though it left a foul taste on her tongue.

"What can you tell me about them?"

"They're both midlevel achievers, with average stats. Their attendance is good. Lindy is one of our more popular students. She's head of our varsity cheerleading squad. She has a large entourage of friends and followers, whereas Tyler seems to prefer his own company." Ellis pointed to a framed photo on the wall, one of many highlighting both school and student achievements, mainly in athletics and on stage. In the picture, the orange-suited cheerleading squad were huddled together, with the blonde-haired Lindy in the middle, hoisting a trophy above her head, her grin stretching from ear to ear.

Maggie felt her stomach curl up. She couldn't tell Ellis that Lindy, too, had been murdered this weekend. Not while Lindy's mom had yet to learn of her daughter's cruel fate.

"Did Lindy and Tyler ever visit with Dana in an official capacity?" Maggie asked.

"We encourage all our students to receive guidance counseling."

"Maybe they visited more often than the norm?"

"I'd have to check."

"I'd appreciate that."

"I don't recall Dana ever mentioning either Lindy or Tyler specifically to me."

"Is it standard practice for the guidance counselor to speak with you about private sessions?"

"No. But if she had any serious concerns . . ."

"Did Dana record her sessions, do you know?"

"Not electronically. That would violate students' rights. We make sure all records kept are in handwritten form only."

"I need to see the files on Lindy and Tyler."

Maggie saw Ellis withdraw, probably at the thought of the implications coming from allowing a third party and someone unrelated to the school system to view what were considered protected documents.

"Alternatively," Maggie said, "we can pursue a court order, which will only delay our investigation. Either way, you have my assurance that any and all information will be treated in the strictest confidence."

It was textbook phrasing, but it usually did the trick.

Ellis smiled. "I'm sure we can sort something out."

"Thank you."

They got to their feet.

"One more thing," Maggie said as she followed the principal to the door. "Dana's husband mentioned a member of the faculty showing an unhealthy interest in her. Do you know anything about that?"

"No, not at all. Did he say who?"

"A teacher by the name of Brandon."

Ellis paused with her hand on the door handle. "Brandon?"

"I don't have his last name."

"You must mean *Bianca* Brandon. And she's certainly not male."

Maggie didn't let her surprise show, kicking herself that she hadn't considered a female source for the interest in Dana. "I'd like to speak with her," she said.

"I'm afraid that's not possible. She left us a month ago. Said she was moving out west. And she didn't leave any forwarding details."

◆ ◆ ◆

Maggie sealed herself inside the guidance counselor's office, her back pressed to the glass of the door, her breathing deep and her ribs aching as she surveyed Dana's place of work.

It felt odd being here, like it had when she was in Dana's bedroom, as though she was trespassing on sacred ground.

Rita's unexplained reincarnation into Dana and then her subsequent murder had yet to fully penetrate, she knew. The news was still relatively brand new, and it had yet to filter through all of Maggie's emotional layers. Once it reached her core, that's when the real test would come.

Even so, over the last thirty-six hours, Maggie had come to realize that there was a lot of baggage surrounding Rita that she hadn't dealt with over the last two decades. A weight that would take some effort to lift. Of course, she'd been younger back then, naive. Unable to contemplate with wisdom.

Steve would say it wasn't her fault.

Biologically, the average human brain only truly matured in its midtwenties. Until then, it simply didn't possess the mental connections to think like an adult. And that was why the average teenager didn't deal. They dismissed instead. Because self-preservation had to be selfish; otherwise, the human race would cease to exist.

Now that Maggie was able to look back at her actions with mature eyes, it was clear she hadn't taken ownership of the events preceding Rita's death, never mind the death itself.

Maggie had buried her past under the present and planted a future on it.

Steve would be quick to reassure her that she needed time to process the weekend's revelation. Time to adjust, for her emotions to catch up.

But that wasn't the primary cause of Maggie's unease right now.

Every time she thought about what she'd done to Rita, back then, in the handful of months before her friend had supposedly burned to death, Maggie's mind seemed to jar, stutter, her thoughts fleeing for the hills before she could corral and tame them.

It wasn't like her.

Not one bit.

Usually, she was as focused as a laser.

But her emotions were diffusing the beam.

Maggie realized she was holding her breath and let it go.

"This isn't about you," she told herself.

But it was hard not to *feel.*

With no windows and only a single strip bulb to illuminate the room, the guidance counselor's office was small. Yet, as with Dana's home, everything had a place. Alphabetized books on shelves. Neatly stacked folders in trays. Framed certificates on the walls, including a photo of Dana shaking hands with Principal Ellis.

Maggie went over for a closer look.

In the picture, Dana was dressed in a gray skirt suit, her lank hair scraped up in a scruffy bun, a smidgeon of makeup warming up her sallow complexion. At a glance, she looked happy, her smile mirroring the principal's grin, but those eyes . . .

Unmistakable sadness.

"What did we do to you?" Maggie breathed.

A filing cabinet occupied a corner, chockablock with student files. Maggie pulled open the drawer labeled *H–M* and flicked through to the *M* section. No file labeled Lindy Munson between Jonny Munro and Katrina Murphy. She checked through all of the *M*s just in case it had been misfiled, then scooted back a little, seeing if Dana had filed it under *L* instead. Still, nothing. She moved to the next drawer down, only to discover that the file for Tyler Pruitt was also inconveniently missing.

Either Dana had never filed anything for Lindy and Tyler—which was a stretch—or she'd deliberately removed their files. The question was: *Why?*

Maggie turned her attention to the small wooden desk, and in particular to the laptop on its polished surface. Dana had stuck Disney stickers all over the gray plastic casing. The screen lit up as she lifted the lid, asking for a password. Hopingly, Maggie tried a few random guesses, but no luck there. After mulling it over for a minute, she called Ellis on the internal phone.

"Those files I asked to see," she said, "the ones for Lindy and Tyler—they're missing,"

"Missing? Did you check?"

"I did. They're not here. Do you have any idea why this is the case?"

"I don't. We keep files on every student. They're used to store teacher observations as well as counselor records. Even if those files are empty, they should still be there."

"I'm looking at Dana's laptop. Do you know the password?"

"Let me see . . ."

Maggie heard several clicks of a computer mouse, followed by the tapping of keyboard keys. Then Ellis came back on the line. "Helga."

Maggie's belly burned.

She hurried Ellis off the phone and then entered the password. The lock screen gave way to a blank desktop. No gazillion icons cluttering the screen. No unusual wallpaper to give psychologists a bone to gnaw on.

Maggie navigated to the Documents folder, scanning through what seemed like an endless list of internal memos and school curriculum material. Nothing leaping out at her. Everything work related and official.

She inspected the other Library folders, finding them either empty or containing default files.

She opened the email app, finding nothing but junk mail.

Even the trash can was empty.

It was as though, supernaturally, Dana had sensed her demise was on its way and cleaned everything out.

Did you know you were going to die? Maggie wondered as she closed the lid.

◆ ◆ ◆

Steve and Maggie were headed south on the toll road when Loomis rang Maggie's phone on FaceTime. Loomis had recently discovered the app, and video calling had quickly become his choice of communication when they were both off duty.

"Hey there, punch bag," he said as his image came to life on the screen. He was in his sunny kitchen, a mug of coffee in hand. "How's it going? Bruised ribs hurt like . . . fudge."

"Fudge?"

"Small humans in the immediate vicinity." He angled his phone so that she could see the twins sitting in their high chairs, spooning slop at everything except their mouths.

Loomis came back into the frame. "I just got off the phone with Smits. He wanted to know why I didn't have a handle on what my partner was doing at three o'clock this morning."

"What did you say?"

"I told him to go fudge himself."

"For real?"

"Absolutely not. What do you think I got, Novak—a death wish?" He took a sip of coffee. "I told him you're emotionally invested right now, and that because this case has a personal element, you're supremely focused. So much so that it's keeping you up at night."

"It is." She'd managed to grab less than a handful of hours' sleep the whole weekend, and it was beginning to show. "Did Smits tell you everything about what happened at Cullen's place?" she asked.

Both Loomis's tone and his expression became less lighthearted. "You got lucky," he said. "Next time you plan on a midnight excursion, call me first, okay? It'll save us both from the earache." He sipped coffee. "So what's with this cash you found stashed in Dana's running shoes? Escape or extortion?"

"The carry-on suggests escape," she said. "But we found no travel documents in her purse, or accommodation reservations."

"Staying with a friend covers that."

"If you believe Cullen, she didn't have any. The more I think about it, Loomis, the more I'm thinking she needed to settle a debt quickly, or satisfy a guilty conscience."

"I like the way you think, Novak."

"So do I," Steve said.

"Please concentrate on driving," Maggie said to him, and followed it with a smile. "What is clear," she said to Loomis, "is that Dana didn't need the cash in order to leave her husband. The money came from her own private account. It was hers already to do with as she pleased. She didn't need to withdraw it to fund an escape."

"Okay, then somebody was blackmailing her."

"Possibly."

"It could explain where she was going with all that paper stuffed in her kicks. To meet her blackmailer."

Maggie nodded at Loomis's image on the screen. She'd already given the exact thing some thought, but hadn't been able to come up with a reason why somebody might be blackmailing Dana.

First impressions indicated she'd led a pretty humdrum life, consisting mainly of work and the occasional weekend runaway. Their search of the Cullen household hadn't turned up any third-party demands for money, either from a blackmailer or from loan companies. No clipped communications put together out of newspaper headlines.

"If she was hoping to pay someone for their silence," Maggie said, "it all went awry the moment she forgot the carry-on."

"And that's why the blackmailer killed her." Loomis nodded. "It's a nice theory, Novak. It means Cullen is innocent. But right now, other than the money you found, we've no reason to consider blackmail. By the way, I hear you clocked the Pruitt kid."

Maggie touched the bruise on her chin. "Pretty sure it was him."

"What do you think he was doing there?"

"Definitely looking for something. Right before I spooked him he was rummaging through kitchen cupboards."

She saw Loomis snicker. "You know what teenagers are like, Novak. Their hungry switch is always on. Besides, it's equally possible he was planting something."

"Like what?"

"Like more incriminating evidence for starters. Fresh as the morning dew."

"Which implies Tyler is the one framing Cullen, and therefore the killer."

"Like I've been saying all along."

"No, you haven't. I know you, too, Loomis. You hedge your bets by saying everyone's guilty until proven innocent. That way, you're never wrong."

His snicker came back. "Get the fudge outta here, Novak."

"Anyway, after visiting the school, I'm thinking it could've been Tyler's psych file he was looking for."

"Whoa. Hold up. You were at the school? I thought you guys were headed to the beach?"

Steve leaned over. "We are. At least, I hope we are."

"We are," Maggie said. "It was just one small diversion; that's all. Now, stop ganging up on me. I hate bullies."

She proceeded to tell Loomis about her talk with Principal Ellis and her subsequent one-woman tour of Dana Cullen's office.

"Turns out both files are missing," she said. "I'm thinking Tyler's may contain something he doesn't want anyone to see."

"Explains his breaking and entering."

"But not how he knew the file wasn't in her office."

Loomis sipped coffee. "Any theories? I know how much you like them."

"Only two, so far."

"The day is yet young."

"Either Tyler already checked the office and presumed she'd taken it home with her. Or he was there for a different reason."

"Which brings us all the way back to him playing a part in Dana's murder. And I hate to say it, Novak, but I told you so. I also have a third theory for you. The kid was there looking for the money you found."

"Tyler blackmailed Dana."

"Only to kill her when she showed up penniless."

"Blackmail her over what exactly?"

"The affair she was having. Like you said to Cullen in his interview. All those weekends away from home. Very suspicious. Maybe Tyler bumped into Dana at one of those beach hotels. Figured the guy she was with wasn't her husband. Threatened to tell Cullen if she didn't meet his financial demands. Let's face it, Novak, the kid's a nut job. And dangerous. Anything's possible with someone like that. Plus, that ride of his isn't paying for itself."

Maggie tried to fit the probability into the equation. It felt a little clunky, needing more elements to balance things out.

Loomis came closer to the camera. "Smits said the kid's in the wind."

Following Maggie's attack, a patrol unit had been dispatched to Tyler's address. Tyler wasn't home. And his grandfather claimed not to know his grandson's whereabouts. Countywide, an *attempt to locate* order had been issued on Tyler and a BOLO put on his bloodred Charger. Several times already this morning, Maggie had checked in with dispatch to see if Tyler had been picked up. So far, he was successfully evading detection.

"Never fear," Loomis said, seemingly picking up on her thoughts. "Driving that kind of car, he won't be on the lam for long. Sooner or later we'll spot him."

She saw him glance behind him at the twins.

"I'll do what I can from this end," he said. "Abby is taking the yearlings here on a baby club playdate. I have the entire afternoon all to my lonesome."

"And you haven't been invited?"

He laughed. "Later, Novak. I'll call if I get any news. Meanwhile, enjoy your beach day, you bums. And wear sunscreen. It's going to be a hot one."

Chapter Twenty

COOKING THE BOOKS

Out of all the famous surfing spots dotted along Florida's eastern coastline, Sebastian Inlet was probably the least well known. And that was its draw.

Maggie and Steve left the Tahoe at the beachside parking lot and picked out a sheltered spot at the head of the beach, where the grassy dunes surrendered to flatter sand.

"Looks like that storm tail is kicking up some great swells," Steve commented as he changed into his wet suit.

Maggie took his word for it. To her, the ocean looked far too choppy to surf. Gray, frothy breakers rearing up before smashing against the beach. Several surfers already shooting the curls, and crashing haphazardly into the waves. Beyond, the remnants of last night's steely thunderheads parading the horizon.

It was a beautiful spot, but Maggie's thoughts were back in the city. "You'll be okay?" he asked as he hefted his board.

"I have phone calls to make," she said, "and plenty of reading material to keep me occupied. Now go. Find that perfect wedge."

Maggie waited until Steve had reached the water before she settled down in one of the beach chairs they'd brought with them. Despite the sea breeze, it was punishingly hot, and even in the shade of the beach umbrella, Spartacus was panting, his tongue dangling like a red rag out the side of his mouth.

Maggie kicked off her deck shoes and buried her toes in the soft white sand. She had always liked the feel of the beach under her feet, the surface heat contrasting with the coolness just a few inches under. It brought back happy memories of childhood vacations to Cancun: her father strutting around in his swim shorts like Sean Connery in *Thunderball* while their exasperated mother fanned her face and rolled her eyes; Nora being scared of the water and freaking out if she so much as got splashed; Bryan being eaten alive by sea lice and wearing his bug bites like a rite of passage.

None of the children aware that their mother had been having affairs even then.

Maggie opened Dana's notebook on her lap and turned to the midpoint, marked by the envelope addressed to her.

At best, she had an hour to read what remained before time would force her to contact Smits, either with new information to support Cullen's guilt, or without.

With the bill of her OCSO ball cap pulled down, and the rumble of the rollers in the background, she started to read Dana's notebook from where she had left off earlier.

Spartacus let out a long sigh and flopped onto his side.

In their youth, Rita had shared many a convoluted verse with Maggie as they sat in the trees by the lake at the end of Rita's street. Swinging their legs and dreaming of things to come. Sunlight glimmering off the lake, and the rough bark chafing their thighs.

Even then, Maggie had considered Rita's poems a little too dark for her taste, filled with nightmarish themes and supernatural undertones. Although Rita had never described herself as such, she was an all-out goth, dressing in black and wearing the kind of grim reaper makeup that most grown-ups declared demonic. Rita hadn't cared. Subscribing to the subculture had separated her from the crowd at school and divided adult opinion—neither of which had deterred her from following her own flame.

While others had caroled in the choir, she had sung the lead.

Rita had been the first of their friends to smoke a cigarette, to get a tattoo, to initiate the first move in any sexual encounter.

Some people called it outspoken, or unruly, or sluttish.

Maggie called it courage, or character.

It was one of the things about Rita that Maggie had been attracted to, and one of the things that had pushed her away.

How did Rita the butterfly retrogress into Dana the chrysalis?

Maggie hadn't given it much thought at the time—her age and inexperience limiting her from seeing outside the box—but in retrospect, she had to hand it to Rita: Despite the ridicule, the name-calling, the social segregation, the attempts to clip her wings, she had remained true to herself. And it took balls to stand tall in a hail of hate.

The second half of the notebook was filled with more poetry and personal observations, spanning Dana's thirties. Page after page of her internalizing. Most of it as dark as Maggie remembered, but in a different way.

Whereas Rita's early poems had been forged from her firebrand spirit, questioning morality, society, oppression, and suffering, this later batch seemed much more philosophical in nature, examining life's bigger themes of purpose, reproduction, and passing over. Maggie wanted it to be uplifting, to reveal that the rebellious Rita had still lived at the heart of Dana, but the poems were woefully depressing, and they left Maggie feeling downcast and melancholy.

No mention of her husband, or of her work at the school.

Another Polaroid photograph separated the last written page from a few dozen blanks at the back of the book. As with the Polaroid jammed into the beginning, this one was another close-up of Dana's face, only much more current. This time, Dana the school counselor, with her skin painted white to match the classic Pierrot clown, her lank hair held back with bobby pins. In red ink on the white space beneath the picture was a single question mark:

?

Was Dana suffering an identity crisis?

Maggie laid both Polaroids side by side, amazed at the stark differences. The seventeen-year-old girl and the thirty-eight-year-old woman, a lifetime of sadness between them. The dainty and the dumpy. From flawless to fractured in the space of twenty years.

A choking lump in Maggie's throat. She looked away from the photos, blowing out air.

On the water, surfers sat on their boards, some stroking away from the shore while others paddled furiously. She spotted Steve out near Monster Hole, and she raised a hand, not knowing if he could see her.

Spartacus snored at her feet.

She drained half a bottle of cool water, her thoughts rewinding to the time of the Oak Street fire.

Rita had excelled at all things arty. Not just creative writing, but theatre, too, her acting skills winning her the leading roles in several school stage productions. She'd planned on going to Hollywood after graduation, of becoming an actor, and no one and nothing was going to stop her.

But something had. Something unseen, unpredictable, and beyond her control. A fire. Creeping through the house in the dead of night and demoting her dreams to dust.

At the time, the official account was that the Grigoryan family had all perished in their sleep.

But Maggie now knew it was a lie.

The fire had clearly happened; through stinging tears, Maggie had seen the blackened, skeletal timbers, the remnants of a happy home reduced to rubble, the sooty sludge slipping down the street and into the storm drain. She'd stood on the corner the next morning, her knees trembling, her heart quaking, knowing that she could never put right the wrong she'd done.

Why make everyone believe they died?

Whenever Maggie was presented with such a puzzle, she always flipped it around, coming at it from a new angle. In this case, the question wasn't so much *Why lie?* but *Who stood to gain from the lie?*

Rita hadn't died that fateful night, and neither had the rest of her family. Maggie was absolutely convinced of this now. The fire had been a smoke screen, hiding their relocation to another state.

What would make a family fake their own deaths?

Maggie knew that Rita's father had been a prominent accountant in the city, known for his outlandish TV ads and his garish billboards. It was possible he'd come unstuck somehow with a client, perhaps after misappropriating funds. She remembered Big Bob dripping in gold jewelry, the latest sports car on the drive, and the whole family enjoying regular European vacations.

Was he skimming off the cream? Did this impropriety come to light, forcing him to flee with his family to Arizona?

In the aftermath of the house fire, Maggie couldn't recall ever hearing about Big Bob Grigoryan syphoning off millions of dollars from a client. Certainly nothing in the papers or on the local TV news stations. Embezzlement did explain the change in surname from Grigoryan to Burnside, but it didn't explain the burned bodies recovered from the house fire on Oak Street.

If the Grigoryans didn't burn to death in that fire, who did?

Sipping more water, Maggie placed a call to the ME's office.

Much of her work these days was undertaken on the phone or online. Unavoidable. Luckily, Maury Elkin was on his midmorning break and able to take her call.

"If you're phoning about the girl . . . ," he began.

"I'm not," she said, keen to avoid discussing Elkin's dissection of Lindy over the phone.

Images of Corrigan sharing the bad news with Lindy's mom had kept invading her thoughts all morning. She'd pictured his sitting her down, consoling her in his gruff manner while telling her, bluntly, that her daughter was no more. Lindy's mom, teary and chain-smoking, wordless as her world imploded and black mascara drizzled down her cheeks.

Maggie's stomach had turned each time the image had invaded her thoughts. And each time, she'd scolded herself for letting Corrigan do her job for her.

"I'm calling about a bunch of twenty-year-old autopsy reports," she told Elkin.

"You called the right person."

Maggie explained about her attempt the day before to access the Grigoryan family's autopsy reports online, and failing.

"That was a long time ago," he said.

"And before your time, I know."

"Makes no difference. If they're not in the database, they'll be in deep freeze. All our paper files went into cold storage during the switchover from the old facility. Did you submit a report request?"

"I got kind of sidetracked, to be honest."

"Don't worry," he said. "I'll check right now."

"Thanks, Maury."

"No problem. Always happy to serve the greater good."

She heard the sound of keystrokes, a mouse clicking, then Elkin saying, "This is strange. We don't seem to have any records relating to the Grigoryan family."

"Maybe it was before computers."

"Was there such a time?"

"I believe so, in the dark and dismal past. I remember hearing scary stories about it as a child."

She heard him laugh. It raised her spirits a little.

"That's all well and good," he said, tapping more keys, "except for the fact that everything in cold storage is cataloged in the database. We're talking records going back before you and I were twinkles in our fathers' eyes. All serial numbered and cross-referenced."

Maggie sat up in the beach chair. "You're saying the files are missing?"

"No, Maggie. I'm saying they don't exist."

"But . . ."

"Even if they were inexplicably missing, the catalog entries would still be in the system. And there's nothing."

"The reports were never filed." Maggie's thoughts began to spin.

"Not so fast," Elkin said. "My guess is, the reports were never *done*. And I'll tell you for why. Preston Dobbs was the chief examiner back then. Dobbs was the epitome of fastidious. You should read his notes sometime. They make quantum physics papers seem like easy bedtime reads. If those bodies came through District Nine, trust me, Maggie, there would be extremely detailed reports to prove it. Since we don't . . ."

"They were sent someplace else."

"Which then begs the question of *why?*"

"The obvious answer," Maggie said, "is to hide foul play. But that's not the half of it, Maury. There were a dozen firefighters at the scene that night, as well as paramedics and police. Neighbors. Eyewitnesses who saw those body bags being wheeled out on gurneys. According to reports, five partly cremated corpses were removed from the ashes that night. And now you're telling me that none of them made it to the coroner's office."

"Sounds like something out of a good horror chiller, doesn't it? However, there is one other possibility."

"Fake corpses." Maggie was already there, her heart rate quickening. There were no reports because there were no real bodies. "You can't do an autopsy on a mannequin," she said. "It's the DoJ."

Spartacus lifted his head, one eyebrow raised at her.

"Sounds like you've reached the middle of your maze, Maggie," Elkin said. "I'll leave you to find your own way out, if you don't mind."

"Not at all. I know you're busy, and I appreciate the brainstorming session. Thanks, Maury."

"Anytime."

Next, and with the adrenaline beginning to surge, Maggie called Nick Stavanger, her neighbor, on his desk phone at the *Orlando Chronicle*.

Nick sounded busy, and grumpy. Then again, grumpy seemed to be his default setting of late. She could hear the chatter of people and the clatter of keyboards in the background.

"You left me standing at the altar," he said as he answered. "Forced me to drink more scotch than is good for me or anyone else for that matter."

"Nick," she said, cutting right to the chase. "I need to pick your brain."

"What's this? No polite persuasion first? No easing me in and warming me up with a seductive fib about how much you value our friendship?"

"You know we're besties. Now and forever. It goes without saying."

"All right. Better. But you owe me an evening with a movie, and soon."

"How do you figure that one out?"

"Because it's long overdue. We're beginning to lose touch. Drift. I'm lonely."

"So get a pet."

"With my allergies? And besides, I'll only forget to feed the little critters. And then they'll go the same way as the indoor plants I forget to water. Compost all the way down."

Maggie found herself smiling.

The last time she'd agreed to a movie night in with Nick at his place, he'd made her sit through the whole of *Titanic* as well as the supplemental documentary. Worse still, he'd provided a running commentary all the way through, with spoilers.

"Okay," she said. "We'll do a movie. But on the condition I get to choose which one this time."

"Deal. So long as it contains an element of dancing and a handsome leading man, I can live with that. Okay, let's hustle. What do you need my help with?"

"Do you still speak with Casey?"

"You know I don't still speak with Casey. That ship has long since sailed and floundered on the rocks."

"I was hoping things might have changed."

"Does the sun shine at night? Casey and I haven't spoken in . . ." Maggie heard his words trail away, sensing that he was beginning to grasp the true nature of her question. "Okay, Detective. What do you need Casey for?"

"I was wondering, does he still work at the US Marshals Service?"

"As far as I know."

"I need you to call him for me," she said, braced to cringe if Nick's response came back acerbic.

"What part of *we don't talk anymore* don't you get?" he said, his tone only slightly strained. "I'm not sure he'll even take my call."

"Try, for me?"

She heard him sigh heavily. "If this was anyone else other than you . . ."

"I know, I know. It's expecting a lot. I get it. Honestly, I do. I wouldn't ask if it wasn't important. I'm sorry, Nick, for putting you in a position. It's just that . . ."

"What else are friends for, right? Okay. What is it you need from him?"

"Confirmation."

"About . . . ?"

Keeping it simple, and insisting that she was speaking off the record, Maggie told Nick about Dana Cullen's murder and the victim's previous life as Rita Grigoryan, as well as Maggie's brand-new emerging theory that the house fire on Oak Street twenty years ago was staged.

"Why?" he interrupted before she was done.

"As part of a bigger cover-up."

"You know I despise conspiracy theories."

"I know you like a good mystery."

"Fair point. Continue."

She told him about the lack of autopsy reports, and hearing Rita's dad, Big Bob, on the answering machine, and how it confirmed to her his true identity. She refrained from going into too much case detail; she didn't want Nick mapping out column inches in his head just yet. She knew he'd ask for an exclusive later. And he'd get it, of course, no questions asked. He always did. But he'd have to wait.

"Aside from magic and miracles," Nick said when she was finished, "what are we thinking here?"

"WITSEC."

"Witness protection? Interesting."

"It's just occurred to me, after speaking with the ME. The Grigoryan family are in the Witness Security Program. It neatly explains why their deaths were faked in the house fire, the family's relocation, and the name change."

"And you need Casey to confirm it, one way or the other."

"If possible, yes. Without landing himself in hot water, that is."

"What's wrong with submitting an official information request? I'm sure the DoJ will play ball with OCSO on matters of this nature."

"Because it could take weeks, that's why. Plus, this way, two birds are killed with one stone. I get the information I need faster . . ."

"And I'm forced to speak with my ex. You're terrible at matchmaking, Detective."

"You'll thank me later."

She heard him pause.

"Nick?"

"No, you're right," he said. "Thinking about it, WITSEC makes perfect sense."

"Why do I feel there's a *but* coming?"

"There isn't. I was just flashing back to being twenty-five again and writing stories from the mail room. The Grigoryan fire was hot news back then—forgive the pun. Big Bob was a huge character in this town. People were stunned by the tragedy. I remember my editor mentioning Big Bob and the Moreno family in the same breath more than once."

"The crime syndicate?"

"One and the same. What do you know about the Moreno clan?"

"To be honest, not a lot. They were before my time. I do know they ran organized crime from Miami to Jacksonville. A drug empire built on slashing prices and the throats of anyone who got in their way."

"The very definition of a cutthroat reputation. Correct. It was never made public, but a few people at the paper suspected Big Bob was their accountant."

Maggie scooted to the edge of her seat. "I never knew."

"It was just an in-house rumor, and hardly anyone took it seriously. But now that you've brought it up, in this context, I'm inclined to believe it."

Maggie's thoughts shifted up a gear. "Big Bob turned state's evidence. It's the only way his family would be offered witness protection."

"Which makes sense when you know that the Moreno kingpins were sent to Supermax less than six months after the house fire."

"They were? How did nobody make the connection?"

"I guess because the house fire was old news by then. Look, Maggie, this is excellent stuff. When can I print it?"

"You can't!"

"And that particular word combo isn't in my vocabulary."

"I mean it, Nick. Do not print this. Wait for my all clear."

"But this is twelve inches of pure pleasure above the fold."

"Nick, I said *hang fire*." Her phone vibrated in her hand. "Looks like my sergeant is trying to get through. I have to go." She disconnected the call, then drew a big breath before answering. "Hey, Sarge. What's up?"

"I'm at the courthouse," he said in her ear. He sounded in a bad mood, flustered. "Before you butt in like you usually do," he said, "just listen. This is important. Pay attention. I just got off the phone with the Feds. They got a hit on the gun report you submitted."

Maggie pressed the phone tight to her ear. "That's great."

"Not so fast, Detective. The serial number comes back to a gun that was reported stolen over twenty years ago. A gun registered to Ronald Novak of Wineberry Court."

Maggie's heart blazed, and she almost dropped the phone.

"Do you have an explanation," Smits continued, "for why your father's revolver was used in a homicide that you just happen to be investigating?"

Chapter Twenty-One

GIVE AND TAKE

Maggie was still staring disbelievingly at her phone when she sensed Steve coming toward her.

"That look on your face," he said as he stabbed his board into the sand. "Should I be worried?"

"Smits just pulled me off the case."

He picked up a towel, rubbing it over his hair. "What? Why would he do that?"

"Conflict of interest." She stuffed her phone in her pocket. "I need to go."

Steve put out a hand. "Hey, Maggie, wait a sec. Go where? Back to Orlando? But we just got here."

"It's my dad . . ."

"Your dad?" He dropped the towel and came to her. "Is he okay?" His hands were cool against her bare arms.

"No. Yes. I mean, he's probably fine. At least, he is right now. I'm not sure how long it's going to last, though. Not when he hears what I have to say. Have you seen my purse?"

He pointed to the back of her beach chair. She went to grab it, but he held on to her, preventing her from going very far. "Maggie, listen to me. You're not making much sense. Has something happened to your dad?"

She looked up at him, mind whirling. "Remember I told you about the murder weapon we found in the kettle grill—the gun that killed Dana Cullen?"

"Yes."

"It's his."

"Your dad's? But that's . . ."

"Crazy impossible, I know." She shook her head, as though the action would anchor her runaway thoughts.

"Wait a minute. He didn't . . ."

"No!" It was laughable, the idea that her father had anything to do with Dana's murder. But Maggie wasn't laughing. "I really need to go," she said, slipping free from his grasp.

"Did you try calling him?"

"You know what he's like. He never answers his phone."

"Do you want me to come with?"

"No," she said more forcefully than she meant. "I've messed up your day enough as it is."

"I don't mind."

"I do."

She knew it was too much to ask of him to abandon his day of surfing. Not when he was already here. She'd vowed to treat Steve's feelings with equal respect. It would be unfair to expect him to keep sacrificing while she kept taking. Sooner or later, that kind of setup broke apart.

"Then take the car." He said it without hesitation.

She paused gathering up her things. "What about you?"

"Don't worry about me. I'll catch a ride home with one of the guys."

"You're sure?"

"Positive." He retrieved the car keys from the cooler and handed them to her. "It's a full moon tonight. And the guys are talking about a midnight surf. Go, see to your dad. Keep me posted. I'll pick up the car in the morning. Just do me a favor?"

"Anything."

"Take Spart with you?"

Chapter Twenty-Two

BACKSEAT DRIVER

Maggie spent most of the drive back to Orlando trying and failing to reach her father by phone. Knots in her stomach and questions stacking up in her thoughts. For the life of her she couldn't figure out how her father's revolver had ended up being used to kill Dana.

But it had.

Robbie Zeedeman's ballistics test had matched the bullet that Elkin had retrieved from Dana's corpse to the gun found in Cullen's backyard. And the FBI had matched its serial number to her father's revolver, stolen from the family home when Maggie was just seventeen.

Maggie kept asking herself, *What are the chances?*

One in a million? More?

How many guns were there in the state of Florida alone? And how many of those had been used to commit murder? What was the likelihood of her father's revolver being used to kill the grown-up version of her childhood friend?

"Miniscule," she told Spartacus, who was snoozing on the back seat.

He raised an ear and an eyebrow simultaneously, then settled back down when he realized no treats were in the offing.

More than twenty years between the gun's disappearance and the Halloween Homicide. Two decades in which the gun had stayed under the radar, as good as lost, forgotten.

Where has it been all this time?

Not in Cullen's outdoor grill, that's for sure.

At speed, Maggie took the on-ramp to I-95, setting the Tahoe's cruise control at eighty.

What did she remember about the theft of the gun?

Maggie had a hazy recollection of the gun going missing, but nothing significant about the actual details of the theft itself—probably because she hadn't been privy to it at the time.

Like many teenagers, Maggie had been wrapped up in herself, engaged in a life of self-service, happy to move within her own sphere of influence, taking the mechanisms of her family home for granted. It wasn't her fault. At seventeen, she lacked the brain connections to properly think like an adult. She came and went as she pleased, mostly oblivious to anything that didn't concern her directly. Even something way out of the ordinary, like the theft of her father's gun, hadn't broken through the minutiae of regular life. As a result, she had no memory of the house being broken into, or of the police coming to visit afterward. She did remember her parents arguing about the gun being stolen, it seemed for weeks after, chiefly because her mother had been particularly critical of her father's blasé gun security, and it had put her in a prolonged bad mood that had affected Maggie.

For years, Maggie's father had kept the revolver in an antique lockbox on a shelf in his closet. A small wooden case with swirling patterns in the walnut veneer and shiny brass corner braces. Throughout their childhood, the box had been off-limits to the children.

Touch at your own peril and suffer the consequences.

Maggie remembered her father fetching the box every now and then, setting it carefully on the coffee table in the living room, where he would spend what seemed like all afternoon polishing the steel and lubricating the cylinder, all the while giving them a lecture about the physics of propellants and the ballistics of projectiles.

She remembered Bryan sitting cross-legged on the carpet, his tongue licking fervently at his lips, his eyes as big as goose eggs as he watched their father at work, fingers itching to get ahold of the gun. By default, boys were fascinated with firearms, and Bryan's excitement was palpable whenever he was allowed to spin the empty cylinder and snap it back in place. In those days, Bryan had worn a toy pistol around the house, stuffed in a Billy the Kid holster, always ready to defend the homestead from marauding Indians. To Bryan, their father's revolver might as well have been Jesse James's original Smith & Wesson. Something to be idolized. Used.

But Maggie had been drawn to the box itself, marveling at its craftsmanship and its red felt interior. Originally a Victorian humidor, their dad had told them. A gentleman's cigar box, handed down from the time of his great-grandfather. Even now, if she closed her eyes and concentrated, Maggie could still smell the rich, aromatic tobacco.

A horn sounded, and Maggie realized that she'd let the Tahoe drift slightly into the adjacent lane. She corrected, checking her mirrors.

A mile later, she left I-95 at Cocoa. Once she was going west on 528, she phoned Loomis.

"You've got to be kidding me," he said after she updated him about the revolver. "That's pure madness."

"I know. It's crazy, right? My dad's gun, the murder weapon. I can't wrap my head around it. I'd all but forgotten he even owned a gun."

"I mean your exclusion from the case," Loomis said. "What's Smits thinking?"

"That right now I'm contagious, and therefore his only option is to remove me from the investigation."

Loomis was a quick study; she didn't need to add that if she stayed on the case a moment longer, her association with the murder weapon would definitely allow for reasonable doubt, if it didn't do so already.

The prosecutor would state that *Detective Novak was removed from the case the second it was discovered that her father's revolver was used to kill the victim.* The defense would argue that she'd handled the gun, both before and after its theft, which made it tainted goods, and by the lead investigator's hands. Inadmissible.

"It gets worse," she said. "Smits canceled his appointment with the state attorney."

"He . . . what?"

"Think about it. He had no choice."

With the gun effectively excluded, the evidence against Cullen was no longer as clear and convincing. With just the muddy work boots, the burden of proof could no longer be met.

She heard Loomis curse.

"You are aware," he said, "that once Cullen's lawyer gets wind of this, his client will probably walk."

"Maybe it's a blessing," she said, negotiating traffic. "Like I said. The more we find out, the less I'm inclined to think Cullen is guilty of anything other than being a bad husband."

"So where do we go from here, assuming we're still working this case?"

"We are. But I can't be seen to be anywhere near the investigation right now."

She'd thought about it for all of ten seconds as she'd driven the Tahoe out of the beach parking lot. Publicly, she'd accede to Smits's bidding, standing down from the case. Given her relationship to the murder weapon and its rightful owner, it was the sensible thing to do. Privately, however, there was no way she was stepping aside and turning her back on Dana's murder. Defeat wasn't in her. One way or the other, she had to see this through to its conclusion, especially now that things had become even more personal.

More than ever, she needed to know who killed Dana, and why.

She told Loomis about her conversation with Nick.

"Witness protection sounds plausible," he said when she was done. "But I'm still missing relevance here. How does this fit in with our case?"

"Revenge."

"All right."

"It's like this. The more we uncover, the less I believe Cullen pulled the trigger. And Lindy turning up dead like that just proves someone else is involved. The Moreno family are dangerous. That's why I believe the Grigoryans were placed in WITSEC."

"And you're waiting on Nick's contact to confirm it?"

"Yep. It's the perfect cover-up. Everyone thinks they died in the fire."

"Only, twenty years later, Rita comes back to town. Albeit with a new identity."

"Except, I recognized her at a glance. Instantly. Rita has been back in Orlando eighteen months. It's likely someone else recognized her as well in that time."

"Someone in the crime family. Now I see where you're coming from. You think they had her killed."

"I know it's not a one-size-fits-all solution. But I think it's something we need to consider. Dana was their way to get to Big Bob."

"Then why kill her? Why not put pressure on her to reveal her father's location?"

"Maybe they did and *then* killed her. Maybe the killer is on his way to Arizona right now. We need to warn the DoJ."

"Whoa," he said. "Take a beat, Novak. You're moving faster than the speed of sound. Don't let this run away with you. Right now, this is all supposition. We have no way of explaining how some random hit man came to use your dad's revolver."

"Unless Rita had it all this time."

"You mean, *she* stole it?"

"It's a possibility. I don't know. I'm thinking out loud here, Loomis. Maybe she tried to defend herself with it, and the killer used it against her."

She heard him mull it over, knowing he wasn't buying it.

"How about we let Nick get the confirmation from the US Marshals Service first," he said, "before we move things up to the next level? Okay?"

"Okay." She let out a tense breath. "I'm also going to need you to take the wheel, for now. Publicly, at least."

"No problem. What about you?"

"If Rita didn't steal the revolver, I'm going to find out who did."

Chapter Twenty-Three

A SPECIAL NEED

A chill stippled Maggie's flesh as she left the Beachline at Exit 31. She drove northeast for a few miles before taking the Seminole Expressway to Oviedo. She switched the air-conditioning down a few notches, but the chill clung to her skin like damp clothing.

What connection was she missing?

Ten years ago, after an unpleasant divorce had alienated the grown-up children and split their loyalties, her father had used his half of the capital generated from Maggie's purchase of the family home to buy himself a fixer-upper on the shoreline of Red Bug Lake. Back then, he'd lectured in physics at the University of Central Florida, and had done so since before Maggie was born. At the time of the divorce, the lakeside property had been one of the closest available to the campus at the price he could afford, allowing him to buy the place outright. And Maggie had been visiting him here every two weeks since.

She turned right after the park, Spartacus sitting up as the Tahoe slowed.

The scenery hadn't changed much over the years. If anything, the street looked even more tired, weeds in the sidewalks and fences flaking. Properties still devalued after the market fall, and pockets pinched.

Spartacus jumped to his feet, tail whipping the back seat as Maggie pulled up outside her father's house. Then she hesitated, her gaze scanning the sagging eaves and the bug screens jammed up with dead flies, all at once recalling the moment her parents had sat the family down to announce their separation a decade ago. Her mother blaming her father for loving his precious physics more than he did his wife. Atoms instead of anatomy. Her father blaming her mother for seeking solace outside of their marriage.

It had been hard not to become embroiled in the blame game. Hard not to take sides, or to join in with assigning fault. Hard not to let emotions dictate action. Maggie had resisted, determined to remain neutral even though it wrenched her heart to hold her tongue when Bryan and Nora couldn't hold theirs.

Spoiled Nora—always outspoken, always needing to be heard, to be consoled, to be *understood*.

Sensible Bryan—continually pushed and directed and rewarded for very little in return.

And Maggie—*Magpie*, as her father liked to call her—mostly overlooked and left to her own devices. The reason being: Unlike her siblings, Maggie didn't need pampering or supporting. She could look out for herself, and always had.

"Life's too short not to be happy," she said to Spartacus, echoing the words her father had said as he'd handed her the keys to the family home all those years ago. "Never settle for second best."

The dog poked his head between the front seats and licked her on the chin. She winced as his tongue touched the graze where Tyler's ring had scuffed off skin.

Her phone vibrated. It was a text message from Loomis:

Cullen is footloose and fancy free

In other words, pending further investigation, Cullen had been released without charge.

She got out of the car, letting the dog join her on the sidewalk. She told him to stick to her like glue, and he obeyed, following her up the driveway to her father's front door.

Unsurprisingly, her father didn't answer to her repeated knocking. Lately, he'd become a bit of a recluse, staying home and preferring to keep a low profile, even with his neighbors. She cupped a hand against the living room window and peered inside. The TV was on, showing an afternoon movie matinee. Jack Nicholson in a straitjacket. No signs of her dad.

Maggie returned to the front door, trying the handle. The door opened. She let herself inside.

"Hello?" she shouted in the hallway. "Dad? It's me. Maggie. Are you home? I have the dog with me."

She waited for a second, listening, hearing the sound of running water coming from the bathroom. She moved toward it, the dog keeping close.

She paused at the bathroom doorway.

"Dad? You in here?"

When she got no answer, she peeped inside. The showerhead was on, blasting cool water into the tub. She went inside, turning off the water.

There was a disposable razor on the sink top, and blood spots in the sink, stark against the white porcelain.

She called out to him again as she returned to the hall, going through to the kitchen. Dishes stacked up in the sink and bread crumbs on the countertop. Potted herbs on the windowsill, withered and brown and beyond salvation.

Still, no sign of her father.

The back door was partly open. She went outside. The large grassy yard looked empty. Spartacus caught a whiff of something and bounded off toward a glint of lake water visible through the trees at the end of the property.

Maggie put on her sunglasses and followed.

She had always considered the large yard as the real reason her father had settled on the house by the lake. Astronomy had always been his main hobby, and the private yard was the perfect spot for setting up his telescope and stargazing.

She saw Spartacus scamper onto the wooden jetty that jutted out into the lake. Claws clattering as he ran across the planks. She spotted her father, sitting in a lawn chair at the end of the dock. He opened his arms as Spartacus rushed up.

"Well, hello there," he said, letting the dog lavish him with licks. "I missed you, too."

Maggie and Steve had only brought the dog to see her father a handful of times over the last six months, but the first time had been enough for the two of them to form an unbreakable bond.

"Hey, Dad," Maggie said as she stepped onto the jetty. "I've been calling you the last hour."

He ruffled the dog's hackles, eliciting more wet-tongue kisses. "No wonder my ears were burning."

It was hot and muggy down near the water, no air movement in the shade of the trees. Insects attracted to the stagnating mud and damsel flies buzzing. The slender white bodies of dead cigarettes floating in the reeds, unlit and never smoked.

"I got you the phone in case of an emergency," she said.

"And that's precisely when I'll use it." He urged the dog to settle down. "You know I hate talking on the phone, Magpie. It's invasive. Communication is an art form, and technology is killing it. Who writes letters anymore?"

Maggie leaned against the wooden rail and smiled.

For someone who had spent the larger part of his adult life standing in front of a class lecturing, her father had all the hallmarks of a hermit.

He'd gotten worse since he'd turned seventy last year and retired. He'd submerged himself in a solitary existence, to the point that he only ever left the house to pick up groceries or to run errands. He never socialized anymore, and he had no interest in any activities outside of his domain. Maggie couldn't remember the last time he'd come over to the house on Wineberry, or visited with her brother and sister, for that matter. She knew it wasn't good for him, and it worried her.

She pointed to the dried blood on his chin. "You cut yourself shaving."

"I did?" He touched his fingertips to it. "Blade's getting old. Much like its owner." He motioned to Maggie's chin. "Seems I'm not the only one. You in the market for a new blade, too?"

She touched the scuff on her jawline, the chafed skin sensitive, itchy. "I ran into something harder than me."

"Let's hope he learned his lesson." He took a cigarette pack from his shirt pocket and tapped one out, sniffed it, but didn't light it. He'd given up smoking a dozen times since retiring. "So, Magpie," he said, "talk to me. What's the matter? It's a weekday afternoon. You shouldn't be here. Did somebody die?"

Maggie folded her arms.

Beating around the bush with small talk had never been her father's way. It was a directness that used to fascinate Maggie and infuriate her mother. To his scientific mind, things were quantifiable, measurable, either observable or unobservable, and everything in between was useless filler.

"Do you remember the revolver you used to have?"

"The .38 Special?" He shook his head in the way that people do when they pull up a fond memory. "My oh my. Where'd you dig that up from? I haven't thought about my old revolver in years. Antique, you know. Like me."

"It was used in the act of a crime." She came right out and said it, steering clear of the word *homicide*, mainly because she knew he would hold himself partly responsible for the killing. After all, it was his gun. Stolen after her mother had raised hell about its poor security. *Somebody's going to get badly hurt someday.* That kind of guilt never went away.

"I don't remember much about it being stolen," Maggie said. "I was hoping you could help fill in the blanks."

Her father leaned forward in the chair, planting both elbows on his knees. He looked thinner than when she last visited. Skin and bones. "Well, I remember it was the first weekend in March. Your tenth birthday, if I recall."

"You mean Nora's birthday."

"I do?"

"Dad, I was seventeen when the gun was stolen. And my birthday is in November. Nora is seven years younger than me. It was her party."

For a second or two, he stared at her from under a heavy brow. Then he pointed at her with the two fingers holding the unlit cigarette. "Right. Yes, you're absolutely right. Thanks for correcting me. It was *Nora's* birthday. She was the one turning ten."

"When did you first notice it was missing?"

"Later that same day. After all those noisy kids had gone home. The lockbox was turned around the wrong way on the shelf. I always had the lock facing out, see? This time it was facing *in.*"

"And that's when you found it gone."

He nodded. "I didn't tell your mother right away. Oh boy. I spent a frantic hour going over every inch of the house, hoping to find it tucked behind a cushion or in a drawer someplace. Your brother always had a *thing* for the Special."

"You thought Bryan took it?" She was surprised, but then realized it made sense.

Bryan had been twenty-one at the time, old enough to buy ammunition and sneak the revolver out of the house for target practice. In later life, the shooting range had become one of her brother's favorite haunts. Maggie wasn't sure how many guns her brother had in his personal armament, but she did know that he and a group of his buddies often took part in alligator hunts down in the Glades.

"Bryan was my first suspect," her father said, sniffing the cigarette again. "But he wasn't home all day. And I know the Special was there in the morning, because it was the first Saturday of the month."

Like a ritual, like clockwork, religiously, her father had serviced the revolver at the start of each calendar month, even if it had remained unused and locked up since its last clean. It was good practice, he'd said, passed down by his father, along with the gun itself. *In a shootout, a dirty gun will get you killed quicker than you can spit*, he used to say. Maggie could still recall the distinct smell of the oil cloth and the hypnotic ticking of the greased chamber as it spun around and around and around.

"I think he was avoiding Nora's party," her father said, bringing her thoughts back to the present. "Couldn't blame him, mind you. All those giddy girls running amok. Frightening for any man."

Vaguely, Maggie remembered sitting under the tree in the back of the yard with a bunch of her own friends, drinking soda and grouching while Nora and her high-octane partyers ran around like maniacs, screaming and being generally annoying. Her mother and several other attentive moms, overseeing the cake ceremony and the trite party games. Her father keeping a low profile with the other dads, amusing themselves in his workshop. Maggie, under strict instruction to *enjoy* the party, and sticking it out for as long as she could before boredom had set in and she and her friends, armed with fistfuls of candy, had slunk off.

"Of course," he continued, "I didn't find it anywhere in the house, or anyplace else for that matter. Finally, I plucked up the courage to tell your mother, and after she raised the roof, she called the police." He broke the cigarette in half. "She wasn't happy."

Maggie could imagine it being the case. Her mother wasn't known for her sense of humor, or for a tolerance for those who had one. When Maggie was young, one of her father's favorite snipes had been *With one look, your mother could kill Schrödinger's cat.* Apparently, it was a physicist's joke, and Maggie had only gotten it later, with age. Her mother never had, seeing it as an insult only.

Her father flicked half the cigarette out onto the water. "Only struck me months later who the real culprit was."

Maggie pushed away from the rail. "Who?"

"That feral friend of yours."

"Rita?" Fire burned in her lungs. "I was thinking the same thing, too."

But her father made a face. "What? No. Not Rita. Rita was a good kid. We used to talk for hours."

"You did?" It was news to Maggie.

"Sure. She possessed a healthy appetite for learning."

"And where was I when you were having these chats?"

"I don't know, Magpie. Probably in the shower, or running errands for your mother. There was no harm in Rita. God bless her. I mean the other one. I don't recall her name. She was tall, blonde, and flirtatious."

"Kristen?" The fire in Maggie's lungs spread outward, searing her bruised ribs.

"That's her. Real piece of work, that one." He flicked the other half of the cigarette out into the lake, and settled back in his chair.

Maggie was stunned.

There had been a time when they came as a package: Maggie, Rita, and Kristen. A trio of best friends, going everywhere together. As inseparable as triplets. Loud, brash, and daring. They spoke the same language, and they gate-crashed the same parties. Together in class and after school, hanging out at Devil's Landing and drinking beer with the boys. An invitation to one acting as an invite for all three.

The union had lasted most of one semester.

But then everything had changed, suddenly, and Maggie's world had never been the same after.

Kristen Falchuck.

"As trustworthy as a fox in a henhouse," he added.

Maggie was shocked, not least because Kristen had never seemed the type to steal anything. In fact, as far as Maggie remembered, Kristen had never wanted for anything. She was an only child, with a deceased mother and a doting daddy. She needed only to snap her fingers, and it was hers.

"Dad, are you sure?"

"Ninety-seven percent, give or take."

"But there must have been a dozen or more parents coming and going that day. What convinced you it was Kristen?"

"Because I bumped into her in the house while everybody else was outside in the yard. She said she was looking for the bathroom, but she was headed out of the master bedroom, all red-faced and jittery."

"Did you tell the police?"

"I gave them the names of every soul at that party. Never heard a thing. It was only when the topic came up again months later that I remembered bumping into her that day."

"I'm not sure she even knew you had a gun, never mind where you kept it, or where the key was."

She saw the corners of his mouth lift up. "The lock was for aesthetic purposes only. You could pick it with a spoon handle. Mark my words, Magpie. She's the one that stole the gun. Any idea what became of her?"

Chapter Twenty-Four

EMPLOYEE OF THE YEAR

Thirty minutes later, Maggie was standing in the polished marble lobby of a hotel at Grande Lakes, waiting to speak with Kristen Falchuck. She'd left the dog with her father, both of them lazing on the dock.

In the short space of time that she had been here people watching, she'd clocked the clientele as made up mostly of moneyed folk. Coiffed vacationers in designer golfing gear, plucked straight from the pages of this month's *Vogue*. She was in no doubt that one night's stay probably cost more than she made in a week.

She told herself it was never going to happen.

She helped herself to a complimentary water, thankful for the breeze blowing in from the entranceway.

After navigating congested city traffic, Maggie had arrived at the classy resort on John Young Parkway feeling hot and bothered. Unless she had no other choice, she tried to avoid the well-trodden tourist tracks that crisscrossed the city. A staggering seventy million people visited the area each year, drawn to the world-famous theme parks and the state's favorable climate. But tourism was a double-edged sword. On one hand it brought jobs, wealth, and commerce, but on the other, it affected transportation and the quality of life of every resident in the region.

A woman in a trim blue pantsuit approached across the plush carpeting. Maggie bounced to her feet. The woman looked around Maggie's age, her chestnut hair swept up in a neat bun, and her lipstick, Maggie thought, slightly too orange in hue for the olive tone of her skin.

"Marlene Gonzalez," she said, stretching out a skinny hand.

Maggie shook it. "Detective Novak, Sheriff's Office. I spoke with one of the receptionists. I'm waiting to speak with the general manager."

The woman smiled. "That's me. How can I help you, Detective?"

Maggie drew back a little. "*You're* the general manager? There must be some kind of mix-up. Is there more than one?"

"I wish. I could certainly benefit from cloning."

"This is the Marriott, right?"

She pointed with the flat of her hand. "If you need the Ritz-Carlton, it's next door."

"No. The woman I'm looking for said she was the GM here at the Marriott."

"When was this?"

"A couple of years ago."

"Well, I've been here five years myself now. And before me, Jerry Shears was the GM. Do you have a name?"

"Kristen Falchuck. But her last name could be different. She's about six foot. Short blonde hair."

"Yes. Kristen. I know her. She served in one of our restaurants."

"She's a waitress here?"

"Up until this weekend. Kristen quit Saturday. We're sad to lose her. She was a hardworking member of our team."

"Did she give a reason why she quit?"

"Actually, she didn't. At least, not to my knowledge. She left a text message saying she wouldn't be returning to work this week, and that was it. I tried calling her several times, but she didn't pick up. Is she in trouble, Detective?"

"I'm afraid I can't say. How long was Kristen employed here?"

"If I were to hazard a rough guess, I'd say eight, maybe nine years. I'd have to check our records for an exact start date."

"As a server?"

"Yes." She smiled at a family as they passed by. "Walk with me back to my office, Detective? We're a little exposed here."

Maggie nodded, knowing that a police officer asking a bunch of questions in the lobby wasn't exactly in keeping with the hotel's pristine image. They crossed the spacious foyer, passing a bar area. Through tall windows, Maggie could see palms swaying in the breeze.

They arrived at a door marked GENERAL MANAGER, and Gonzalez ushered her inside. The office had everything an office needed, yet was sorely lacking in character. No photos of Gonzalez with celebrity guests, and no personal touches to make it feel inviting.

"Any causes for concern in the time she was here?" Maggie asked.

Gonzalez closed the door. "If you mean was there any time Kristen failed us in her duties, then the answer is an emphatic no. Kristen was always willing to go the extra mile to make our clients feel special."

"No prior mention of her being unhappy in her work and that she was considering quitting?"

"Not that I'm aware." She sat down behind her desk, accessing a computer terminal.

"Don't you find it odd," Maggie said, preferring to stand, "that she didn't give a reason?"

"We don't require one. The hospitality industry has a high personnel turnover. Seasonal workers. College students. Temporary employment, especially in server roles. People use it as a stepping-stone. Only a hard-core few like Kristen stay in one place as long as she did."

"Why is that?"

"Sometimes, it's lack of qualifications or confidence. Better the devil they know. What I find odd is that Kristen quit, period."

"How so?"

"Because she topped our customer review charts. She was in line for a substantial bonus. And I know money was tight for her. So, yes, I'm surprised she quit so suddenly, especially knowing that if she'd stayed with us another month or two, a thousand-dollar windfall would've been hers."

"And she definitely knew it was in the pipeline?"

"We make a big deal out of customer satisfaction surveys. Kristen was our shining star. Had she stayed, this would've been the fifth time she'd won the bonus."

"She's good at her job."

"Better than good. She excels. Kristen has a way with people. She's perfected the meet and greet. It's hard not to fall in love with her, figuratively speaking." She glanced at the computer screen. "Here we go. Kristen was with us almost ten years. No sick time and an impeccable punctuality record. She really is something to behold. I only wish every one of our employees was a Kristen Falchuck."

Chapter Twenty-Five

SOUVENIR

The mobile home on Sunset Drive in Kissimmee was an oblong wooden box about the size of two shipping containers welded together. Painted olive green, with decking on one side and a brown picket fence separating it from the neighboring homes.

Maggie got out of the Tahoe, lingering on the roadside while she assessed the scene.

The mobile home park reminded her of a cemetery that had all its coffins above ground.

At first, Gonzalez had hesitated at the thought of giving up Kristen's home address. Then Maggie had let it be known that she was investigating a homicide, and that the Sheriff's Office appreciated the hotel's expeditious assistance in the matter, and any communication with the Marriott HQ would only speak positively of Gonzalez.

Ten minutes later, here she was: Sun Friendly Community Village—a designated area west of Main Street in Kissimmee that consisted of several parallel rows of mobile homes, some as good as derelict, some with little gardens, and some rentals awaiting occupancy. All shades of color, shapes, and sizes.

In her youth, Kristen had had big aspirations to *make it* as an artist. Kristen was *into* sculpture in a big way, crafting abstract creations out of inorganic trash. Kristen had dreamed of owning her own art gallery on the West Coast, of hosting cocktail parties for the rich and the influential, of mixing with the jet set, her sculptures taking pride and place in municipal buildings across the nation.

But Kristen had never realized her dream.

Maggie didn't know Kristen's true story, only that she had ended up here in this little wooden house with its assortment of wind chimes dangling from the eaves. And the sight of it made Maggie feel sad for her.

Did *she* play a part in Kristen's failure?

Within days of the house fire on Oak Street, Maggie had called an immediate end to their friendship, never wanting to see Kristen again, or have anything to do with her. In Maggie's eyes, Kristen had been equally to blame for Rita's death. And Maggie couldn't bear being in her company anymore. Not after what they'd done. On every level, their actions were unforgivable, and Maggie couldn't cope with Kristen's black-and-white "She deserved it" attitude on top of her own cowardice.

Something had to give, and that something had been their friendship.

For more than fifteen years they went their separate ways—Maggie opting for law enforcement while Kristen sold her handmade wares at local flea markets—only chancing on each other again in a fitting room at the Florida Mall a couple of years ago. Catching up over coffee. Kristen telling Maggie that although she still created artwork, albeit on a small scale, she now worked in the hospitality industry. Kristen had always had a persuasiveness about her. One of those people who could convince others that her way was the best way. Seated in the food court at the mall, Kristen had introduced herself to Maggie as the general manager of the Marriott at Grande Lakes. Declaring that life was better than ever, and that she couldn't hope to be happier.

Kristen had lied.

Probably, due to embarrassment, or awkwardness with the truth, or just because it made her sound more important than she felt.

She'd pretended to be someone she wasn't.

Maggie had given Kristen her card, encouraging her to keep in touch, but she'd never heard from her again. That said, Maggie had never tried contacting Kristen either.

Locking the Tahoe behind her, Maggie stepped up onto the decking. She banged a fist against the frame of the screen door. All around her, wind chimes jingled in the breeze. She knocked again, this time harder, longer.

"She ain't home," a man's voice called from behind her.

Maggie turned on her heel.

An old-timer was leaning out of the window of the neighboring residence, watering succulents in a window box. He looked to be in his eighties, withered, a tight mat of gray hair clinging to the dark skin of his head.

"You're wasting your time," he said. "She's gone."

"Do you know where?"

"Why you interested, lady?"

Maggie held up her badge. "I'm with the Sheriff's Office, sir."

He glanced at her star, then continued to water his flowers. "Gone, as in cleared out and ain't never coming back."

"What makes you say that?"

"'Cause I'm her landlord and I say so. Girl was four months past due on her rent. We had words. I told her she was forcing me to take legal action. She wasn't happy. Saturday afternoon was the last I saw of her. Ain't been back since."

"And she was your tenant for how long?"

"Long enough." He began to draw himself back inside the house.

"Wait," Maggie said. "Please, sir. One last thing."

He hesitated with his head half-in, half-out.

"What kind of car does she drive?"

"A black one."

"Do you know the make?"

"I don't. Have a good day," he said and disappeared behind the window.

Maggie turned back to the door, tempted, for a moment, to try the handle.

Kristen had quit her job suddenly during the weekend. Plus, she'd not been back home since before the murder. If Maggie's father was right about Kristen being the one who had stolen the revolver . . .

A sudden gust of wind jangled the wind chimes. A melodic jumble of notes coming from all but the one hanging closest to the door. Curious, Maggie looked closer. The wind chime was composed of a metal loop with wooden tubes suspended on nylon threads. Rudimentary animal glyphs engraved in the wood.

It didn't jangle with the rest of them because its sail was missing— that curvy slice of wood or metal designed to catch the breeze—with just a snapped thread hanging forlornly in its place.

A familiar coolness bloomed in Maggie's belly.

Stepping into the shade, she signed into Major Case's cloud storage on her phone and flicked through the photos in the Halloween Homicide folder until she came to the image of the artifact she'd found in Dana's purse on Saturday night.

Sure enough, when she held the image up to the wind chime beside the door, it was a perfect match.

The coolness in her belly sent a chill creeping up her spine.

Immediately, two possibilities sprang to mind: either Dana had stood right here and for some reason taken the sail, or Kristen had met up with Dana elsewhere and given it to her.

Regardless of the correct answer, the fact that Maggie had found the sail in Dana's purse proved one thing.

Both Dana's and Kristen's lives had somehow come back together. And Maggie had been oblivious.

◆ ◆ ◆

To Maggie's surprise, her first reaction was rooted in jealousy. A deep, inexplicable rush of envy that struck her like a fist in the throat. It came as a shock, knocking her off-balance, primarily because it was the last emotion she'd ever expect to feel when it came to Dana or Kristen. Even when the three of them had hung out together—and three was generally considered *a crowd*—there had been no cause for any jealousy between them, even when they'd voiced differences in opinion. But here it was. Hot and fierce. Burning a hole in her papery heart and setting her thoughts on fire.

What had she stumbled on here?

Kristen missing and Dana dead.

It didn't take a leap of imagination to picture their inflammatory meeting and what happened next.

Maggie's second reaction was incendiary. Her knees buckled, and she had to put a hand against the doorframe to steady herself.

Dana and Kristen had met, and probably recently.

Why else was the sail in Dana's purse?

A chance encounter. Some random fluke that brought their paths together again, briefly crossing them. Kristen inviting Dana back here, and perhaps giving Dana the sail as a mark of their newfound friendship. Or Dana vocalizing her pain to Kristen, this time as an adult, with all the prowess and power gained from her guidance counselor training. Stealing the sail as a memento of her victory over Kristen.

It sounded feasible, except . . .

Maggie couldn't imagine Dana even speaking with Kristen again, let alone accompanying her back here to this one-bedroom box in Kissimmee. Not after what they'd done to her all those years ago, shattering their friendship. Even twenty passing years was not sufficient time to glue all those broken pieces back together again, hoping that things would stay intact under pressure.

All of a sudden, Maggie felt microscopic, as though the universe had noticed her for the first time and was taking an interest. Billions of eyes seeing right through her adult skin to the child inside.

Confess, it demanded.

Maggie brought up her contacts list. She needed to speak with someone who would understand what she'd done and not hold it against her. Someone who would listen to what she had to say without standing in judgment.

She called Loomis.

"Hey," he said from the screen. "I was about to call you."

"I think I know who killed Dana and why," she said before he could expand on his comment.

"For real? Um, okay. I'm listening."

"Not over the phone," she said. "It's complicated. I need to tell you in person. Where are you at?"

"Walmart on Turkey Lake. Is everything all right, Novak?"

"No. Anything but. I need a stiff drink." She stepped down off the decking. "Meet me at the Whiskey. I'll be there as soon as I can."

Chapter Twenty-Six

BURGERS AND BOILERMAKERS

The bar and grill in Dr. Phillips, a suburb at the western end of Sand Lake Road, was one of Loomis's favorite places to eat, boasting "the best gourmet burgers in town," according to him and their in-house marketing. Maggie pushed through the door, entering into a dimly lit cavern that offered coolness on two levels: chilled air and a hip black decor. The place was narrow and deep, smelling of barbecue and liquor. A full bar along one side, and an assortment of patrons at the tables. Mirrors on the walls and just enough neon to keep it from being tacky.

Maggie spotted Loomis seated close to a small stage area in back. Plated burgers, two pints of beer, and a pair of shot glasses on the table in front of him. She took a deep breath and crossed the barroom, a heavy-metal rock song banging at her eardrums as she went.

She'd spent the twenty-minute drive trying to convince herself that, despite her repeated refusal to believe them, the facts here were undeniable.

Dana was dead and Kristen was missing.

"You'll be late for your own funeral," Loomis shouted over the music as she approached.

She dropped into the bench seat, her back to the wall.

"Took the liberty of getting us burgers and boilermakers," he said. "All hail Monday afternoons." He pushed one of the plates toward her. "The Southerner," he said.

Maggie lifted the bun lid. "No onion?"

"As prescribed." He took a hearty bite out of his own burger, purring and rolling his eyes as he savored the patty. "So what's with the long face?"

"I spoke with my dad."

"And?"

Maggie told him about her conversation.

"Did Kristen know he kept the gun in the closet?"

"I never told her. In fact, I can't remember ever telling anyone about it. Even Rita."

"What about Bryan? Could he have mentioned it?"

Maggie shrugged. She had no memory of Bryan ever talking to Kristen. It didn't mean it never happened, though. He was four years their senior; he moved in different circles. But she did remember the way he used to look at Kristen whenever she was at their house, and the way she'd flirt with him.

"I think Kristen killed Dana," Maggie said.

"How'd you figure that?"

"Because . . ." She let out a breath, her heart suddenly drumming in her chest. "Oh boy."

Loomis paused with his burger halfway to his mouth. "What's up, Novak?"

"This." She sat herself upright. "It's why I wanted to speak with you face-to-face. To avoid any confusion."

"Should I be worried?"

"Just be understanding. If possible. That's all I ask. And nonjudgmental. That will help immensely. If you can. We were kids. Just seventeen, and stupid. Very stupid. I know it's no excuse. And I'm not looking for any sympathy here. I was wrong, okay? Dead wrong. I know that. What I did, it's unforgivable."

He dumped his burger back on the plate. "Okay, Novak. You have my undivided attention. What did you do?"

Maggie stared at him, unable to find the words.

After a few silent seconds, Loomis picked up the two shot glasses and dropped them into the beers. Then he pushed one of the pint glasses toward her. "Drink," he said. "All of it, all the way down, in one, and without stopping for breath. Then, you confess."

In unison, they picked up their drinks and guzzled the mix of cold beer and malty whiskey. The chill of it temporarily dousing the flames in Maggie's chest, the alcohol not merely crossing her blood brain barrier, but bursting all the way through it.

They slapped their empty glasses down as one.

Loomis belched.

Maggie said, "I ruined Rita's life."

◆　◆　◆

Beforehand, Maggie had expected her confession to be a release. Finally getting it off her chest after all these years of it weighing her down would open up a feeling of freeness and a sense of relief. Instead, it came as a collapse, coming down around her like the demolition of an old institution that had harbored wicked secrets. Once the dust settled, more effort would be needed to clear the rubble away.

Maggie wasn't sure if an anticlimax like this was the typical outcome in such colossal confessions, or if it was the result of the alcohol suppressing her mood. Either way, Loomis seemed slightly disappointed.

"You mean you bullied her?" he said, looking at her through partially closed eyes. "Isn't that kind of run-of-the-mill schoolyard stuff?"

"Trust me. This wasn't playful teasing. It was bad. What I did, it put Rita through hell."

"I thought you and Rita were inseparable."

"We were. But things changed after Kristen came along. She was a latecomer. She moved here from Savannah in our senior year. At the start of the second semester."

"And you did the honorable thing of letting her hang out with you guys."

"It was easy. Kristen was nice. The three of us hit it off right away."

"So what went wrong?"

"I'm not sure how it all started. But bit by bit, Kristen and I started doing more stuff together, slowly but surely leaving Rita out."

"You ostracized your bestie."

Maggie pondered it while Loomis chewed his food, her gaze on the foamy dregs sliding down her glass. Although her memories of that time were fairly intact, she'd buried them deep in the dark recesses of her mind, and the discomfort attached to them was still light sensitive. "I guess I didn't realize that by letting Kristen in, I was pushing Rita out."

"The folly of youth is thinking we know everything before we've experienced anything."

Maggie looked up at him.

"I got no idea where that came from," he said, smirking. "Seriously though, Novak. Don't be too hard on yourself. Everyone has some questionable history behind them. We've all done stuff we're not proud of, especially when we were young. Kristen was a bad influence on you, is all."

"It doesn't make it okay."

"No, but it makes you human." He took another bite of his burger. "What was the catalyst?"

"Everyone thought Rita was a lesbian."

"Okay. I didn't see that coming. Since when is a person's sexuality an issue with you?"

"It isn't. I always knew Rita was different. If anything, I would've said she was bi. I remember her liking just as many boys as she did girls."

"Explains the marriage to Cullen."

Maggie nodded. "Her sexuality never bothered me, or got in the way. To be honest, most of the time, I didn't even think about it. We were just best friends, and our sexuality didn't matter. In fact, there was only one time that Rita's sexual orientation figured in our friendship."

"You guys kissed."

Maggie glanced around the barroom, feeling heat rise in her cheeks.

"Relax," Loomis said. "Teenagers experiment all the time. It's what they do. Hormones rage and kids do crazy stuff. Especially when alcohol is involved."

"Are you speaking from experience here as well?"

He looked amused by her comment.

"Anyway," she continued, "I was seventeen and impressionable. All I wanted was to fit in. It's different for girls than it is for boys. Girls can be cruel. Boys sort out their differences with their fists and move on. Girls engage in psychological warfare. And it can last a lifetime."

Loomis narrowed his eyes at her. "You didn't just push Rita away, though, did you?"

She shook her head, the heat refusing to leave her cheeks. "We started calling her Helga."

"You . . . Wait . . . What?"

"Kristen said it suited her better than Rita."

"You called her Helga?"

"It was stupid, I know. Childish. I don't know what I was thinking. Clearly, I wasn't using my brain at all." The lump was back in her throat, bigger than ever. "Can we get out of here?" she said.

"Sure." He peeled some notes from his wallet, tucking them under his empty glass. "Let's go."

Outside, the sun was low in the sky, dazzling, the air as hot as an oven. Orange-bottomed clouds peeking over the rooftops, and cars whizzing past on Sand Lake. Maggie felt a little light headed, a little too visible.

"You were scared of Kristen," Loomis said as they left the rock music behind. "That's why you went along with it."

Maggie hadn't made the connection at the time, or since, it seemed. But now that Loomis drew her attention to it, he was probably right. Without Maggie realizing it, Kristen had dominated her, turning Maggie into a reflection of herself. A bully. Maggie couldn't pinpoint exactly how Kristen had pulled it off, only that it had been an insidious takeover, a slow and steady indoctrination campaign designed to turn Maggie toward Kristen and away from Rita. And Maggie hadn't objected.

"It didn't end there," Maggie confessed as they began to stroll along the terrace of restaurants and boutique shops. "We totally embarrassed Rita at the lake."

The final nail in the coffin of their friendship.

It had been late September, just weeks before the house fire on Oak Street. A humid evening humming with insects. The air thick with conjoined lovebugs.

And a clandestine meeting underway.

What had started out as a low-key prank had swiftly escalated into a full-scale attack on Rita. That morning, and behind Maggie's back, Kristen had secreted a note to Rita, pretending to originate with Maggie. The note leaning heavily on Rita's and Maggie's one and only physical interaction—the kiss—and declaring Maggie's undying love for Rita, as well as her desire to take their kiss to the next step.

"I never should have confided in Kristen," Maggie said. "She used my secrets against me."

The note had acted as a lure, drawing Rita to the clearing after dark, ostensibly to rendezvous with Maggie.

But Kristen had had other plans.

Under the impression that they were going to hang out with friends at the lake, Maggie had accompanied Kristen to the clearing in the woods.

"There were a dozen kids from school already there," Maggie said. "And everyone except me was privy to what was about to happen."

A lookout had alerted them, and the teenagers had melted into the trees surrounding the clearing, whispering at each other to "be quiet." Kristen pulling Maggie into the underbrush, a finger pressed to her lips, indicating she should hush. Leaves getting in Maggie's face and tangled vines underfoot. And Maggie wondering what all the secrecy was about.

Then, to her surprise, Rita had wandered into the clearing, coming to a stop at the sandy middle, calling Maggie's name. Maggie had gone to respond, but Kristen had held her back, hushing her again and shaking her head defiantly. And that's when the deafening chant, "Dyke, dyke, dyke!" had erupted across the clearing, a barrage of eggs being hurled at Rita.

Rita had stood there, unmoving with shock, as the eggs had rained down on her.

Horrified, Maggie had yanked free of Kristen's grasp, clambering into the clearing, intent on rushing to defend Rita.

But Rita had just stared at her, a mixture of disbelief, loathing, and egg yolk on her face.

Then she'd spat out a single condemning word and fled the scene, leaving Maggie standing there alone, looking foolish, as the terrible chant had chased Rita from the woods.

"And that's why my skin was crawling Saturday evening," Maggie said. "I hadn't stepped foot on Devil's Landing since that fateful night."

Maggie had come to her senses, severing ties with everyone involved. But by that point, the damage had already been done, and she'd spent the following days and weeks reaching out to Rita, only for Rita to reject all her attempts to broker peace.

"I was going to call at her home that weekend," she said as they began to cross the parking lot. "Sit down with her and tell her how stupid I'd been and how sorry I was. But then . . ."

"The whole family supposedly burned to death in the house fire."

"Yes. And I've always partly blamed myself for what happened. As a child, Rita was fascinated with fire. She used to set things on fire all the time. Trees, fields, dead animals. Her biggest conquest was a derelict shack in the woods."

"Rita was a fire freak? I'm beginning to like her."

"Joking aside, she even mentioned burning down the family home once, after she'd fallen out with her dad."

"So when you heard about the blaze . . ."

"I thought the bullying had finally pushed her over the edge and she'd started the fire. All these years, I thought the whole family died because of something I did. Can't you see how that might have messed with my head? I've carried the guilt around ever since."

"No wonder you looked like you'd seen a ghost on Saturday night."

"Exactly."

They arrived at Steve's Tahoe.

"You know," Loomis said as Maggie popped the locks, "you could've told me all this. I am your partner. You can tell me anything." He didn't sound angry. He sounded wounded.

"It threw me," she said, knowing that she would feel equally stung had he kept his hurt from her. "Realizing it was Rita lying there burned to death brought everything crashing back. The emotions, the pain, the blame. I couldn't talk about it. Not until I'd gotten a handle on it myself."

Her phone rang. She took it out, glancing at the screen. "It's Nick," she said. "I need to take this."

"Have at it."

"Hey, Nick. What's up?"

"I just got off a difficult hour-long call with Casey," Nick said.

"I'm sorry."

"Don't sweat it. I suppose it had to happen at some point. The end result is, we've agreed to meet and talk things through."

"Nick, I'm thrilled for you."

"Well, it's a start."

"Was he able to . . . ?"

"Off the record, he confirmed the Grigoryans were offered witness protection in exchange for Big Bob turning state's evidence against the Moreno family."

"That's excellent news."

She saw Loomis mouth the word *WITSEC?* and she nodded.

"However," Nick said, "he couldn't say if the Grigoryans took up the offer, or where they may have gone if they did. But he was able to advise that exhuming their corpses would be an unnecessary waste of tax dollars."

"Thanks, Nick. I owe you."

"I've put it on your tab."

"So," Loomis said as Maggie hung up, "your hunch was right. The Grigoryans were in witness protection. Good call. Not sure how it helps our case, though."

"No, but this does. Take a look." Maggie showed him the photo on her phone of the wind chime sail she'd found at the crime scene, and then a shot she'd taken less than an hour ago of the wind chime itself hanging beside Kristen's front door.

"So *that's* what that little guy is," he said.

"Either Kristen gave it to Dana, or Dana took it herself. Either way, it connects Dana with Kristen, present day."

Loomis looked deep in thought. "And if your pops is right about Kristen stealing his revolver . . ."

"He's not often mistaken."

"It probably means . . ."

"You're about to come to the same conclusion I did."

Maggie had already visualized Dana and Kristen's encounter as she'd driven to the Whiskey, drawing up a loose time line in her head that started with Dana arguing with Cullen Saturday afternoon, followed by her storming out and going someplace to blow off steam. Her bumping into Kristen, and a whole fount of pent-up pain welling up inside her. All those immobilized emotions suddenly breaking loose and taking flight. Dana tailing Kristen back to the mobile home in Kissimmee. On her mind, revenge, in the form of verbal combat. Payback with words. A desperate Kristen reaching for the revolver she'd kept all these years. Her shooting Dana, perhaps in what she believed was an act of self-defense. A fatal mistake that had seen her transporting Dana's lifeless corpse to the clearing at the lake, intending to burn all evidence of the crime. Kristen planting the evidence at the Cullen house, then quitting her job and taking off.

"Kristen killed Dana," Loomis said. "Do we have any idea where Kristen is now?"

Maggie opened the driver's door and climbed inside. "Her neighbor said she hasn't been home since Saturday. And her place of work told me she quit this weekend."

"We need to put a BOLO out on her."

"Already did that on the way here."

"Countywide?"

"Statewide. All agencies."

"Any family in the area?"

"Not that I know of." She started the ignition, letting the vents blast cool air at her face. "Kristen is originally from Wisconsin. She came here with her dad, after her mom died. When we met up a few years ago, she told me he passed away. Right now, she could be anywhere."

Chapter Twenty-Seven

THE WITCHING HOUR

Something woke Maggie, jarring her from her sleep. Probably a noise outside, or the dull ache still pinching at her ribs where her attacker's sneaker had left its mark.

She cracked open her eyes, the familiar layout of her bedroom resolving out of the darkness. She was on her "good" side in her bed, facing the curtained window. The digital alarm clock on the nightstand reading three a.m.

Not for the first time in the last twenty years, she'd been dreaming of the cruel prank played on Rita at Devil's Landing. Not just reliving it, but actually *living* it in dream state. Instead of Rita standing in the middle of the clearing, being bombarded with eggs, it had been her, Maggie, stripped naked, dripping in gasoline. Demons cowering in the tangle of trees surrounding her, their eyes glowing blood red and their voices like breaking glass. Shredding laughter, and jeers of "Bully! Bully! Bully!" ringing through the woods.

It was like something Alice might have experienced through the looking glass, she thought.

Maggie let out a hot breath.

After parting ways with Loomis, she'd taken a roundabout route home, her thoughts queuing up and insisting to be dealt with. Like running, driving helped her zone out, to think things through without interference. She'd thought about the ongoing effort to locate Tyler and now Kristen, trying and failing to reconcile the two. It had been twilight by the time she had arrived at the house on Wineberry, a full moon rising behind scattered cloud.

After all the Halloween hubbub during the weekend, the cul-de-sac had been quiet. No leftover pumpkins going moldy on the doorsteps. No nosy neighbors peeping through their blinds, wondering if she ever brought her work home with her.

Maggie had parked the Tahoe alongside her Mustang in the driveway and come inside, switching on lights and heading straight to the kitchen. She'd found a bottle of Advil in a drawer and washed two down with cool water from the fridge dispenser. Then she'd made herself a cup of herbal tea, sitting at the firepit on her backyard patio, the flickering flames hypnotizing as her mind crawled over the cinders of the last forty-eight hours.

Had somebody told her, Saturday morning, that she'd be where she was now—emotionally and mentally—she would never have believed them.

For starters, she couldn't believe that Rita's first fiery death had been faked by the US Marshals Service. She couldn't believe that Rita had been alive all these years, only to die for real during the weekend, her body burned in the exact same place where she'd spoken her last ever word to Maggie.

Bitch.

She couldn't believe that Kristen had stolen her father's revolver when they were seventeen, and that she had entered the arena again after all these years, with the end result being Dana's death. She couldn't believe that Kristen had then gone on to frame Cullen for Dana's murder, and that it had all happened in her jurisdiction.

In a short span of time, her world had been upended, righted, flipped upside down again. The readout on the clock switched to 3:01 a.m.

Maggie sensed a weight pressing down on the mattress behind her. Is that why she'd woken?

She rolled over, thinking Steve had come back to her house instead of his, crept into the bed with her. It took her a second to realize his shape was all wrong. Stocky instead of streamlined. A clunky outline, picked out by the stray beams of streetlight leaking in around the curtains.

And Steve never smelled like a mechanic.

Tyler!

The realization hit her like a sledgehammer, punching hot adrenaline through her system.

She felt something hard and metallic press against the soft skin under her chin.

"Don't move," he said from out of the darkness, his stale breath on her cheek and in her mouth. "In fact," he said, "don't even breathe. Or I'll blow your brains out all over your nice clean sheets. You and me are going to have some fun."

Chapter Twenty-Eight

BAIT AND TACKLE

Maggie froze.

Despite the superheated adrenaline burning through her veins, she didn't even twitch. She clung to the fiery breath in her lungs, every sense straining and on high alert. Thoughts coming thick and fast. Instinct pleaded with her to physically react, to lash out, to fight for her life, to leap out of bed, to run, to do *something*, but any one of those knee-jerk reactions would be a deadly mistake.

Lose it, and she'd pay with her life.

Police training had programmed the panic out of her.

At first, when Maggie was a bright-eyed rookie, she'd labored to get the balance right. Putting herself in thought experiments, testing which options were likely to produce favorable results.

Controlling the genetic compulsion wasn't easy.

Instinct came as a fundamental requirement of her job. It helped save lives, enabled her to sniff out danger better than any bloodhound could. Right from the start, she'd been taught to listen to her gut, to trust it, to nurture it.

But some instinct was detrimental to an officer's own safety. This was the kind that resulted in poor decision-making and ultimately put the life of the officer and maybe others in jeopardy.

In real life-or-death situations, the natural human instinct was to fight or take flight. But police training had taught her that the choice wasn't limited to an either-or. A third option existed. One that could ensure an officer in the crosshairs survived long enough to pass beyond the panic stage and potentially come through the situation alive and in control.

The keyword here was *compliance.*

And the secret was knowing when to apply it.

Maggie didn't even breathe.

The hardness prodding under her chin was the unmistakable muzzle of a gun. Although she couldn't see it in the dark, she had no doubt about what it was. The cool metal, the taint of grease. One wrong move, one sudden shift in her position, and the gun might discharge, either on purpose or unintentionally.

Then what?

If she wanted to get through the next few minutes alive, she had to *comply* with Tyler's command.

But relinquishing control rubbed against her grain.

Right now, the dominant thought crashing through her mind was that, no matter how compliant she was, Tyler was here to kill her anyway.

She had to ignore it, move beyond it.

Trust her training.

Slowly, Tyler backed himself off the bed and to his feet, keeping the muzzle pressed against her throat the whole time.

Maggie's heartbeat was so loud she was sure he could hear it.

She sensed him reach out with his other hand, heard his fingers fumble at the bedside lamp. It came on, saturating the room in light.

Maggie didn't even blink.

Tyler loomed over her, clothed completely in black. A sweatshirt hoodie and cargo pants with big baggy saddlebag pockets on the sides.

The same outfit she'd seen on her attacker at the Cullen residence yesterday.

Fire raged inside her, but she kept her cool.

The fact that he was here now, in her bedroom, armed and dangerous, was proof positive that he had played a key role in Dana's murder.

"Get up," he said. "Slowly." He gestured with the gun. It looked like an antique Luger. His knuckles on both hands looked raw, dried blood caked in the skin.

Maggie forced the tension from her frame.

In high-stress situations, the adrenal glands flooded the bloodstream with epinephrine. A hormone, stimulating a spike in energy production that contracted blood vessels and increased heart rate. Consequently, it was an effort to get muscles to perform at any speed less than full throttle.

No choice.

Keeping her hands where he could see them, she slowly pulled the sheet back and then sat upright. The last thing she wanted was for him to mistake any of her actions as aggressive—until they were.

He waggled the pistol. "Good. Now. Toward me."

Maggie swung her legs around on the mattress and slid her feet to the floor. Then she stood with her arms dangling loosely at her sides, breathing deeply, heart blazing.

A smug smile creased Tyler's mouth as his gaze moved up and down her body.

Maggie slept in the nude. She always had, and it was nothing to do with the muggy Florida nights. She found any kind of nightwear restrictive.

She saw his hand move toward his crotch. "Don't even think about it," she said quietly.

His gaze shot up to hers. "No talking." He retreated a few steps, opening up a space between them. "Get dressed."

He had plans to kill her all right, but not here.

"Where are we going?"

He grabbed a handful of garments from the back of a chair and slung them at her. "I said get dressed."

Maggie pulled on a green OCSO T-shirt and jogging pants.

On the outside she must have looked completely calm, the epitome of placid. On the inside her mind was in overdrive, her senses stretching out to fill her environment, like sonar, returning billions of bits of information for analysis.

He gestured toward the doorway. "Move."

"I need footwear."

"No."

"If we're walking any kind of distance—"

"You don't need shoes at the lake." He snapped the words, as though stringing a sentence together was an imposition.

Devil's Landing.

Suddenly, Maggie's dream came hurtling back to her, the chants of "Bully! Bully! Bully!" igniting the flammable liquid, turning her into a human inferno. In the dream, Maggie was screaming as the firestorm vaporized her skin, bits of her rising on a swirling column of smoke.

Razor-edged fear sliced at her heart.

"Tyler," she said softly, "you need to think carefully about what you're doing right now. Just by being here you're opening up a whole world of trouble for yourself. Trust me. You don't want this. Please stop and think before you go too far. Killing a police officer comes with a mandatory death sentence." She sat down on the edge of the bed.

He waggled the Luger. "Move."

"No, Tyler. I won't let you do this."

She saw his jaw muscles clench.

"I said move!"

"And I said no. What would your grandfather say if he saw you right now, behaving like this in a woman's bedroom? I think you need to reassess what your aim is here, Tyler."

"I said no talking!"

Maggie patted the mattress next to her. "Come. Let's you and me both sit down and talk. Work something out before it's too late. Those anger issues of yours, they'll be the death of you. Come on. I won't bite. And I know you won't. Let's face it, Tyler, when it comes to women, you're not exactly the smartest chimp in the zoo, are you? You attacked Lindy and then you attacked me. I've got to wonder, is your temper trying to cover up the fact you're not particularly well endowed in the manhood department?" She pointed a finger at his crotch and curled her lip with disgust. "I mean, come on, who are we trying to kid here? No wonder Lindy gave you the cold shoulder. You're just a little boy."

He charged at her, suddenly, like a tormented bull. Head down, a low growl leaking from his lips.

And that was his first mistake—biting her bait.

Maggie had calculated it wouldn't take much to make Tyler explode; his fuse was short and his temper volatile. And physical interaction seemed to be his reaction of choice. She figured she stood a better chance of disarming him here, on her own turf and on her own terms, than in the dark at the lake, where any number of variables could cause her efforts to go disastrously wrong.

He came at her, snarling.

But Maggie was trained in hand-to-hand combat. Enough of a skill set at least to defend herself when she was given a fighting chance.

She saw him rush toward her, his free hand molding into a fist. If his intention was to cuff her on the mouth again, then drag her kicking and screaming to his car, he was sorely mistaken.

As he came within striking distance, Maggie tipped backward on the bed, raising her feet together in one fluid movement and planting her heels in the boy's stomach.

It was like something out of a high school gym routine.

Maggie's reverse motion coupled with his forward momentum lifted him cleanly off his feet. And the top-heavy teenager was too committed to do anything about it. Maggie straightened her legs, lifting them over her as she flattened herself to the mattress, the action hurling Tyler over the bed.

It seemed as though it all happened in slow motion.

Tyler flew over her, coming down heavily, headfirst in the gap between the bed frame and the window. Crashing against the wall and emitting a muffled yowl as he took a mouthful of carpet.

Maggie kept moving, twisting as she rolled, coming up on her knees on the mattress, ready to pounce.

Tyler was upturned, jammed in the tight space between the bed and the wall, hands scratching at the floor, trying to right himself. The red soles of his sneakers flashing like danger signals. The Luger on the carpet near the bathroom doorway.

Maggie jumped to her feet on the bed. With both hands, she grabbed hold of Tyler's ankles and pushed his legs higher into the air, straighter, preventing him from extricating himself from the predicament he'd landed in.

"Stop!" he cried.

Maggie didn't. She twisted his feet, feeling sinews straining. "Do not resist." She heard his ankles pop, gristle crunching.

Tyler howled.

"Stop!" he cried again. "Or she'll kill your dad!"

Chapter Twenty-Nine

TRIGGER

M aggie kept Tyler's feet hoisted in the air, the pressure on, repeating the move she'd used on him during the assault at Cullen's place. "What did you say?"

"I swear to God," he said, his voice muffled against the carpet. "They're together at the lake. That's why I'm taking you there. She said to tell you she'll kill him if we don't show up."

All at once, it felt like Maggie had been punched in the gut, the wind knocked out of her.

Kristen had her dad at the lake?

It didn't make any sense!

The shock of Tyler's statement relaxed her grip, just enough for him to take advantage.

He kicked out, and suddenly he was squirming out of her grasp and to his feet.

Maggie snapped out of her shock, realizing her error a second late. She saw him spot the Luger, and launched herself off the bed in the same moment that Tyler made a mad dash for the gun. She hit him from behind, allowing her full weight to bring him down, and they hit the carpet together, heavily, their hands scrabbling for the Luger. Tyler tried to land an elbow in her face. Maggie dodged it, finger punching him in his exposed armpit. Tyler yelped. Maggie pushed to her knees and scrambled over him, her hands reaching out, her fingers inches from the Luger. But just before she could snap it up, Tyler heaved to one side, throwing her off and into the wall. Pain crackled through her ribs, and suddenly the gun was in Tyler's hand.

"Stop!" he cried, waving it at her. "You're killing him."

Maggie's pulse was thumping hard enough to make her vision pulsate.

Tyler got to his feet.

"Don't do this," she said.

He gestured with the pistol. "Get up."

Maggie got to her feet. "You're making things worse for yourself, Tyler. Just give me the gun, and we can work something out."

"Go," he said, motioning her toward the bedroom doorway. "Or your dad dies."

Maggie moved through the darkened house, Tyler following a couple of yards behind.

Kristen had given the boy instructions to fetch Maggie to the lake, using her dad as bait.

For what reason? A final showdown?

Where was the logic in that?

When Maggie had run into Kristen a few years back, Kristen had given no indication of still being annoyed with Maggie for ending their friendship. In fact, it hadn't even come up in conversation. Instead, she'd been interested in catching up on Maggie's life, asking about Bryan and Nora, surprised to learn that her parents had divorced, and fascinated with the fact that Maggie had shunned the Novak family tradition of teaching in favor of law enforcement.

No longer had Kristen seemed to be the same manipulative and prejudicial person that Maggie remembered.

She'd come across as affable and genuinely nice.

Kristen had changed.

Yet, Maggie knew that one reliable constant in life was that people never truly changed. For good or bad they may try. Behavior could be adjusted, attitudes tweaked, and people might actually believe that positive change had occurred. Pragmatic psychiatrists like Steve believed that therapy could work wonders. And doctors the world over trusted medical intervention to neutralize rogue chemicals in the brain, preventing Mr. Hyde from taking over the asylum.

But when everything was stripped back, when a person was alone with their thoughts, change was an inconvenience, required to function in a society that would otherwise impose penalties.

According to Steve, everybody had triggers: a neighbor's dog continually barking, somebody cutting you off on the highway, a work colleague who stole your promotion.

Was Kristen's trigger her encountering Dana, a chance meeting that had unlocked repressed emotions, thrusting her back to a past of hatred and homophobia?

Is that why Kristen had killed Dana?

Did she have the same plan in mind for Maggie?

Outside, a dirt bike was parked at the head of the driveway, a red cycle helmet hooked on the handlebar.

Tyler pushed a bunch of keys in her hand. They were hers, taken from the dish in the hall. "The Mustang," he said. "You drive."

It was a warm night, insects chirruping. Bright moonlight peeping through cracks in the clouds. All she could think about was her father's welfare, and what she would do to both Tyler and Kristen if he got hurt because of them.

They got into Maggie's car, Tyler insisting they drive with the top down as he monitored her from the passenger seat.

Maggie started the engine and backed the Mustang slowly out of the driveway, reversing into the cul-de-sac. Then she hesitated before putting the car in drive.

"I need you to be honest with me here, Tyler," she said, "before we go any farther. Your knuckles are mashed up. Clearly, you've beaten somebody to a pulp tonight. I need to know my dad's okay." She stared at him. "Because I swear, Tyler, if you've so much as harmed a single hair on his head . . ."

"I didn't hurt him," he said. "Now drive."

Maggie switched on the headlights, pulling forward, then hitting the brake, sharply.

Nick Stavanger had appeared in the bright beams, standing in the middle of the street, both hands shielding his eyes. He had on a black Bruce Springsteen tour tee and plaid pajama pants. In flip-flops, he approached the driver's door.

Maggie heard Tyler release a quiet cuss. "Get rid of him." He let her see his finger on the trigger before hiding the Luger out of sight behind his thigh.

Nick leaned a hand on the doorframe, eyeing Tyler. "Everything aboveboard here, Detective?"

"Right as rain." Maggie flashed a broad grin to show that the opposite was true. "This is Tyler, by the way. Say hello, Tyler."

Tyler said a nervy, "Hey."

"Tyler, huh? Heard a lot about you, kid. You're Maggie's nephew, right?"

Tyler glanced sidelong at Maggie. "Uh, yeah. Right."

Maggie's cheeks were on fire. She was pleading silently with Nick to back off, painfully aware that if he pushed Tyler too hard, Tyler would push back, and with lethal force. The only trouble was, as a journalist, Nick couldn't help being pushy.

"You like pool parties, kid?" Nick said.

Tyler's mouth was a hard line.

"Your aunt Maggie here will attest to this. I throw them all the time. Loud music. Lots of girls. Beer on tap. Drive the neighbors nuts."

"Nick . . . ," Maggie began.

"Thing is," Nick said, ignoring her, "I've some pool furniture that needs moving. And my back isn't what it used to be. You look like a strong kid. I'll give you ten bucks if you lend me a hand. Only take a minute at the most."

Maggie sensed Tyler's nervousness move up a level, saw his hand twitch behind his leg. "Nick," she said, "I'm really sorry. But we need to go. I'll get Loomis to call you about the Devil's Landing gig."

For a second Nick looked down at her through buttonhole eyes. Then he leaned up off the door. "Oh, hey, I love that band. Okay. It's a deal. Listen, you guys drive safe now, you hear? Nice to meet you, Tyler."

Through the rearview mirror, Maggie saw Nick hopping back to his house as she drove up the street.

Chapter Thirty

BURNT OFFERINGS

Maggie pressed for information, but Tyler remained mostly uncommunicative on the fifteen-minute ride to the lake. Despite the breeze blustering through the car, he was sweating profusely, every now and then wiping a hand over his face.

She wanted to know what they had planned for her when they got there. She wanted to know the ins and outs of how they had abducted her father. She wanted to know the exact role that Tyler had played in both Dana's and Lindy's murders. She wanted to know why Tyler was doing this, and what was in it for him.

She appealed to any sense of morality and justice he had in him. She reminded him of the consequences of his actions, worsening the longer he held out.

Above all, she wanted assurance that her father was all right and that no harm would come to him if she submitted to their demands.

Finally, Tyler told her he wanted her to "shut the heck up," or he'd personally see to it that her father never saw sunrise.

Easy to be bold with a gun in your hand.

With the Luger pointed at her side, he instructed her to follow a circuitous route to the lake—Maggie suspected to avoid traffic cameras—and for her to observe the speed limits.

Maggie had no problem with complying. Even though she wanted to stand on the gas and race to her father's side, she deliberately took it easy, letting each red-lit intersection delay their journey just a little bit longer.

Tyler's eyes never moved off her the whole while. And each time she happened to glance at him, she saw a deadness in his gaze reminiscent of a death row inmate with only hours left to live.

Compliance and then confrontation.

Maggie had to play this by ear. And carefully. Use all her senses and years of experience to switch the game around in a way that minimized collateral damage. At some point Tyler's attention would become divided; he couldn't watch her indefinitely. And when that opportunity arose, she'd be ready to take control.

On Ocoee Parkway, near the high school, an old black Civic straddled the curb in the same spot that had been occupied by Tyler's red Charger on Saturday evening. Black as night, with moonlight glinting off its windshield.

Kristen's car.

Maggie pulled in behind it and cut the engine.

"You still have time to do the right thing," she told Tyler.

Tyler signaled with the pistol. "Out."

And they made their way off-road, on foot, downslope along the grassy trail, and into the dark woods. Warm sand under her feet, and only the seeping moonlight to light the way.

Although she wanted to, Maggie didn't rush. The lack of footwear wasn't a big deal on the fine soil, but the trail snaking through the trees was littered with brittle leaves and needling twigs. Several times she winced as debris stabbed her soles.

Tyler kept pace a yard behind, covering her with the Luger.

She wondered if it was even functional. It looked old. Probably an antique owned by his grandfather, never meant to be fired. Guns were Loomis's forte; she didn't even know if the ammo was still available for a Luger. For all she knew, the magazine could be empty.

Could she take the risk it wasn't?

Her head buzzed with counterstrike scenarios.

In her five years as a detective, Maggie could count on one hand how many times she'd found herself in a fix of this magnitude, when her own life was so clearly teetering in the balance.

None quite this personal.

Yet, it wasn't her own life she feared for right now. It was her father's. Her innocent dad who didn't deserve being dragged into a twenty-year-old feud, partly of her doing.

Try as she might, she still couldn't fathom why Kristen had chosen to involve him in the first place, or how Kristen had known where to find him.

It occurred to her that there might have been more to that brief encounter in the house the day of the party than he was letting on.

Did Kristen harbor a grudge against him all these years, and this was her chance to exact payback?

Other than the fact that his revolver had killed Dana, what else connected him to the homicides?

Was he involved?

The thought stung in her brain, and she swatted it away like an angry wasp.

Tyler's hand pushed between her shoulder blades, shoving her forward, and she stumbled onward in the dark.

Given the right distraction, she knew she could take the boy by surprise and disarm him. Turn the tables. Bring about a satisfactory conclusion to her abduction. Although Tyler seemed muscular, his bulk was all confined to his upper body. On balance, this inverted-triangle shape penalized him, giving Maggie the advantage when it came to agility. Literally, she could run rings around him while he lumbered to land a single blow.

Kick out his knees and he would go down like a felled tree.

But a successful self-defense relied on prior knowledge of all the variables. And right now, she was headed into a confrontation blind and uninformed.

Plus, she had her father to consider.

Bands of pale moonlight painted zebra stripes in the woods. Maggie edged her way through the spiky palmetto, following the sinuous trail to the lake.

She still couldn't figure out how Tyler had come to be in cahoots with Kristen.

At what point did their paths cross?

Why had he chosen to do her bidding?

Maggie rounded the last bend, the mawlike entrance to Devil's Landing coming into view. Yellowy light flickering through the trees.

"Keep moving," Tyler said from behind her.

She ducked into the clearing, expecting to see Kristen waiting for her. Kristen, with a tale to tell about killing Dana. Digging up the past and dumping all the hurt on Maggie. A flimsy excuse about homophobia that wouldn't wash with her. A game of blame and cowardice and deflection, constructed as a defense for her despicable behavior. Not enough. Maggie's analytical brain needed resolution. An answer to the one question that had been eating away at her after discovering Dana's true identity on Halloween.

Why?

But to her surprise, the clearing was empty.

The firelight, she realized, was coming from out on the water. Specifically, the small reed mound lying twenty feet offshore.

"Far enough," Tyler said as she came to the silt beach. Mud oozing between her toes.

The lake spread out before her, moonlight transmuting the flat water to quicksilver.

There were three people on the mud mound, two men sitting on either side of a lit garden torch that had been stabbed into the earth, its long flame licking at the breeze. A witch's broomstick on fire. Behind, in the reeds, Maggie could see a woman in clothes that matched Tyler's, her sweatshirt's hood pulled up, her face in shadow.

Both men had their wrists bound with silvery duct tape. One of them was Thomas Cullen, and the other was her father.

Maggie's heart leaped in her chest.

She took a step forward, squelching soft mud underfoot, but Tyler caught her by the arm, holding her back from the water's edge.

"Don't," he said, prodding the Luger in her sore side.

Pain flared, and Maggie's breathing quickened.

Her dad looked ancient, withered, his thinning hair plastered to his scalp, his sodden clothes hanging. But thankfully, no signs of damage.

The same couldn't be said for Cullen. His face was busted up and bloody, one eye swollen shut. Bloodstains on his shirt, a torn collar, and one shoe missing.

Tyler had beaten Cullen to a pulpy mess.

There was a distinct chemical odor in the air, and Maggie realized with horror that both men had been drenched in gasoline. One wrong move and they would burn alive.

Fear erupted through her vocal cords. "Dad!" Maggie strained against Tyler's grasp, but his grip resisted. "Dad! Are you okay?"

He lifted his chin, just enough to level his gaze on her, raising his tied hands at the same time to indicate he was in a predicament, but otherwise all right. He went to speak, but nothing came out.

Maggie had a lump of lead in her belly.

On the mud mound, the woman stepped forward into the flickering light, removing her hood at the same time. "Hello, Maggie," she called across the water.

Maggie felt her airway close, and she gaped, breathless, wordless.

It was all she could do.

The woman on the mound wasn't Kristen Falchuck.

Chapter Thirty-One

LOW CALORIFIC VALUE

Maggie's mind spun, her thoughts cartwheeling, unraveling. It was like she was on a carousel, seemingly stationary while the whole world orbited in a blur. Thoughts hurtling away at a hundred miles an hour.

Round and round, but then coming to a sudden jerking stop, centering on . . .

Dana Cullen?

Maggie felt dizzy, queasy.

How could this be?

It seemed impossible. But there she was: standing twenty feet away—the grown-up version of Maggie's childhood friend, in the flesh.

Dana Cullen.

Slightly heavier than the skinny girl of Maggie's memory. Older, for sure. Her pixie-faced youthfulness padded out, jowly. The shoulder-length hair that Maggie had seen in Dana's driver's license photo now cut short and bleached blonde. But definitely her. The sullen mask, those eternally hurting eyes—unmistakably Rita, even in moonlight.

She was alive!

It took Maggie a second to register the enormity of what her eyes were seeing, convinced at first that the gasoline fumes must be affecting her vision.

Everything she'd pieced together over the last two days, every murder clue and bit of evidence, every thread woven into the fabric of the case, insisted that Kristen should be the one standing here.

Not Dana.

Anyone but *Dana*.

Yet here she was.

Maggie's senses shrank back at the sight of her, tunneling her vision until Dana became the focus of everything, and Maggie was spellbound.

"You thought I was dead, didn't you?" Dana said before Maggie could summon up a response. "Well, tough luck. As you can see, I'm very much alive, and I intend to stay this way. Unfortunately, I can't promise the same for you."

In Maggie's seesawing mind, two trains of thought careered toward one another down the same length of track: her natural impulse to celebrate the fact that her childhood friend was alive, and her nurtured instinct to arrest her.

The first reaction would allow Maggie to apologize profusely for her bullying—something she wished she had been able to do for so very long. The second reaction would bring closure in a different kind of way. *Case* closure.

Maggie was torn, knowing that no matter which train she rode, a wreck was inevitable.

But she couldn't just stand here waiting for it to happen. Every second she wasted now was a second closer to that calamitous finale.

It could only mean one thing, the fact that Dana was standing here.

"You killed Kristen," Maggie said, breaking the spell. "And you faked your own death."

Her words carried over the calm water like a cloud of angry wasps, stinging every bit of flesh they touched.

It sounded extreme: Dana killing Kristen. Why would any sane person do such a thing? At what point did killing someone ever become the only viable option? When presented with the unfathomable, Maggie always asked herself, Why would anyone in their right mind choose murder over mediation?

Dana killed Kristen.

"It was Kristen, here, on Halloween," Maggie said, her mind working furiously. "You killed her and then you burned her. Made her unrecognizable. You planted your ID. And you cut off her finger so that I'd think it was you."

A slanted smile broke out on Dana's face. "Oh my," she said. "No wonder you're a detective, sweetheart. Look at how smart you got."

It was Rita's voice all right. Maybe an octave deeper than Maggie remembered, but undeniably hers.

As though a switch had been thrown, Dana's smile vanished. "But if you think this is the point where I make some tear-jerking woe-is-me speech about being a bullied teenager and the poor unloved wife of a cheating, scumbag husband, you've got another think coming. I didn't bring you here so that we could swap confessions, Maggie, or air our sins and be best friends all over again. That's never going to happen. I brought you here so that you could bear witness, and then die."

Dana uprooted the torch and, without the slightest hesitation, thrust it at her husband's face. His head burst into flame, his screams ringing out across the water like a death knell.

Chapter Thirty-Two

BAPTISM OF FIRE

Cullen's bloodcurdling screech hit Maggie like the concussion wave from an explosion, and she reacted on instinct, twisting her arm out of Tyler's grasp and plunging into the lake, splashing her way through the shallow water, focused solely on reaching Cullen and putting out the fire. No idea if Tyler was chasing after her.

Cullen writhed on the mud, his screams already dying. Like a flaming log, he rolled to the water's edge and became still. Skin crackling. Bits of charred clothing rising on the thermals. Within seconds, the fire had completely taken hold, turning him into a burning effigy of himself.

Soaked, Maggie waded out, then dropped to her buttocks on the mound. It was instinct to grab Cullen and haul him into the water. But she fought the impulse, knowing that it would mean reaching into the flames with her hands and possibly getting burned. Her feet were already wet, providing a little more protection from the flames. Pushing with both feet, Maggie rolled Cullen into the water.

Fire seared her skin, excruciating pain leaping up her legs.

But she didn't stop kicking until he was fully afloat.

Cullen's body hissed and spat as it flopped into the lake, floating facedown, a mixture of steam and smoke rising.

Maggie scrambled to her feet and followed him in, the water's relative coolness sucking the ferocious heat from her feet. Parts of Cullen's clothing were still ablaze, the gasoline feeding the fire. She manhandled him onto his back, splashing water over him, more steam hissing.

But her efforts to save him were all in vain.

Cullen's mashed-up face was a black crepe mask, blue smoke coiling from his mouth, the smell of scorched skin thick in her nose.

She swung her gaze at Dana, every nerve in her body electrified.

Dana was holding the flickering torch over Maggie's father. "It's your choice who dies next," she said.

Her slanted smile made a brief reappearance.

Dana was enjoying this.

Chapter Thirty-Three

HOSTAGE

Utter silence descended over water, an absence of sound like no other that Maggie had ever experienced, the only noise coming from the blood thundering through her brain. Cullen's screams had silenced all the insect activity in the vicinity, deadening the air.

Cullen's dead body floated at her feet, nightmarish, the stench of barbecued skin pungent.

"Let my dad go," Maggie said. "Take me instead."

"Trade places?"

"It's what you want, isn't it?" She stepped up onto the mound, the silt as sharp as broken glass underfoot. "He doesn't deserve any of this. Imagine if he was your own dad, sitting here, scared out of his wits, and you had the power to do the right thing. You'd let him go, wouldn't you?"

Maggie knew that if she could put some breathing space between the flame and her father that he would stand a much higher chance of surviving. As it was, a stray spark could ignite the gasoline at any moment, like a flash in a powder keg. Cullen had gone up in flames within seconds, dying horribly a moment later. She couldn't let that happen to her father.

"Let's be honest here," Maggie said, trying her best to keep her fear from creeping into her voice. "Your issue isn't with him. You got what you wanted. I'm here now. This is about you and me, Dana. And what I did to you. Focus on that. You need me to feel your pain and pay for what I did. This whole drama isn't about anyone but you and me. Don't turn this into something it's not."

Purposely, Maggie didn't mention the horror floating in the lake behind her. She avoided the subject of Dana murdering her husband, and the catalyst that had compelled her to slaughter him in cold blood. Crisis negotiation training had given Maggie the tools to defuse tense standoffs, but on-the-street experience had taught her never to confront killers on their motives in the heat of the moment, when tempers were still hot and the mood still volatile. Making potentially incendiary comments could kindle the crisis and blow up in her face. It was a surefire way to end things badly for all concerned. Cullen was beyond saving. Right now, her dad was her top priority. And Maggie was prepared to do anything to guarantee his safety.

Dana hadn't moved the torch away even a fraction of an inch from his head.

"But I went to all this trouble of bringing him here," Dana said, as though she'd done Maggie a favor and was now disappointed that her gratitude wasn't forthcoming. "It seems such an awful waste not to—"

"Dana!" Maggie's hands flew up in supplication. "Listen to me. You've waited years for this. Don't dilute the experience now. Your revenge is personal, like it was with Kristen. Remember how that felt? Remember the satisfaction that came from taking her life? That feeling of justice being served. It can be yours again, with me. But only if you let my dad go."

Still, Dana didn't move. She stared at Maggie, as though Maggie's proposal was the most ludicrous thing she'd ever heard. "What's stopping me from killing you both?"

"Nothing. But I know, deep down, you don't believe my dad deserves being treated like this. He was good to you. Remember? You both talked all the time. You liked my dad, and he liked you. What you're about to do, it's just not right."

Dana seemed to mull over Maggie's words. Then she relaxed her stance a little. "Okay," she said, swinging the torch away from his head. "Just don't make me regret conceding on this. Go ahead. Trade places."

Maggie didn't know whether to feel relief or fright. "Thank you."

Keeping her hands raised and her movements slow and deliberate, Maggie rounded the water's edge until she reached her father. Then she helped him stand. He stank of gasoline and fear.

"Dad, it'll be okay," she said, holding his tied hands. "I promise."

"I peed myself," he said, his voice low and wheezing.

Despite everything, his comment brought a smile to her lips. "What happened? Didn't Spartacus protect you?"

"Can you believe I was on the toilet when the kid forced his way in? As far as I know, the dog is still tied up on the dock." His hands trembled in hers. "Tell me, Magpie, you have this."

She squeezed his hands. "I do." Then she pecked him on the cheek and let him go.

He sloshed his way across the narrow strait, and once he was safely on the other side, albeit in Tyler's custody, Maggie turned to face Dana.

"On your knees," Dana commanded. "Or Tyler hurts your dad."

Maggie hesitated, long enough for Dana to strike her in the stomach with the blunt end of the torch. Pain tore through her midriff, and Maggie keeled over, gasping for breath. She dropped to her knees, fighting for air.

Dana reached into the reeds. "Be a sweetheart," she said, holding out a gasoline can to Maggie.

271

"Don't I get a last request?" Maggie gasped. It wasn't a unique response, but Maggie knew that every extra second of life she could buy delayed what could possibly be her last moments on earth. And she had no intention of making it easy for Dana.

Dana pushed the can into Maggie's hands. "No last requests. This isn't Hollywood." She flashed the flame across Maggie's face. "Now come on. Chop-chop."

Maggie unscrewed the lid, flinching at the smell. Every sense analyzing her surroundings. Every creative brain cell conjuring up escape scenarios and calculating the odds of coming out of this alive. "But don't you want to hear how sorry I am for what I did?" she said. She was, sincerely, and it came through in her voice, even though it wasn't her motive for asking the question.

But Dana didn't seem interested in taking Maggie's confession.

"Just get on with it," she said, her tone weary. "Don't force Tyler's hand. He's an impatient young man."

On the beach, Tyler had an arm looped around her father's shoulders, preventing him from moving, the Luger's muzzle rammed against his temple. Next to Tyler, her father looked small, weak.

Maggie's heart felt like it was being crushed in a fist.

She had to buy them time, she knew. Time to slow events down and to think. Time to give her father a fighting chance. Her own safety paled in comparison. This was all her fault; she couldn't let anyone else pay the price for her past mistake.

"If I do this," Maggie said slowly, "I need your word you'll let my dad go."

Dana waved the torch like a witch brandishing a magic scepter. "You're in no position to make demands! Now do the deed."

"Please. Rita. Think how you'd feel if it was your dad."

Maggie used the name deliberately, hoping that saying it out loud would ignite a spark of humanity in Dana, drive her childhood friend to the fore.

They'd once shared an emotional bond, seemingly unbreakable until Kristen had wormed her way between them. If any of Rita's feelings for Maggie still existed deep inside her . . .

But Dana's response was bereft of emotion.

"Rita's dead," she said. "You killed her, Maggie, the day you turned her into Helga."

The words smacked Maggie across the face, one at a time, sharp and stinging. She didn't try to duck them. She let them hit her full force, knowing that any kind of defense was not only inappropriate, but selfish.

After all, how could she argue with the truth?

For several months she'd made Rita's life a living hell, thinking nothing of the impact her name-calling had had on her. Sleeping well at night while Rita lay awake in her own bed, tears magnifying her eyes. Ostracizing Rita in school, indifferent to the air of awkwardness she cultivated. Her actions unforgivable, contemptible. Belittling her best friend, making fun of her, bullying her psychologically, chipping away at her confidence until the rebellious girl she knew and loved had been stripped bare and beaten, emotionally scarred.

Now there was nothing left of her.

Rita was gone.

Maggie had helped create a monster.

And any leftover feelings for Maggie had long since hardened into retribution.

Maggie hesitated, burning up precious seconds, the gas can poised over her head, knowing that each second saved added up to minutes, and each minute added to . . .

"Borrowed time," Dana said, as though reading her thoughts. She nudged the gas can with the blunt end of the torch. "Not so mighty now, are you?"

Maggie screwed up her eyes, clamping her mouth shut as gasoline drizzled over her, the liquid warm and hellish. It ran around her eyes, scalding the scuff on her chin. She wanted to gasp as fumes scratched at her nostrils. More than that, she wanted to run. Run for her life. But the thought of Tyler shooting her father kept her staked to the mud.

"Did you know," Dana said as the gasoline rained down, "that fire is the only way to purge a witch's soul?"

Chapter Thirty-Four

WHAT HAPPENS NEXT?

F aced with her imminent death, Maggie expected to be scared in a way that she had never been scared before.

Even as a small child she'd wondered what it might feel like to die, to let her last breath slip away, to go on to something better, or for her mind to cease eternally. Not necessarily the *when* or the *how* of the process, but rather the *act* itself. That fleeting moment separating life and death. The gap between heartbeats when the next heartbeat failed to come. That split-second transition from this world to the next, or to nothingness.

Would she notice a blip in her consciousness?

Or would everything just stop?

Although Maggie had been raised in a Christian household, she'd never been force-fed religion. Her family had attended church when they had to, and her father had kept a large leather-bound Bible in a prominent position on his desk in his home office, occasionally reading passages from it to himself and to anyone within earshot. As a family, they had never discussed religion, but despite her mother's adultery, the family had tried to observe Christian values. Where the subject of death was concerned, and the intricacies of what might happen *next*,

Maggie had been left to make up her own mind, to wonder whether some ethereal part of her would still exist after the corporeal part ceased.

The *death question* had stayed with her all her life, more so since becoming a Deathtective, as definitively unanswerable as it always had been.

Just the thought of it sent a shudder coursing through her.

Would she feel unquenchable pain as the flames stripped her skin from her flesh and her flesh from her bones? Or would her torment be momentary—instantly replaced with perpetual bliss or with absolute nihility?

Maybe the answer wasn't so much about eternal essence or endless oblivion, but rather how she coped with the act itself.

She held her breath, her eyes glued shut, waiting for the sudden unstoppable burst of intense heat that would signify her demise.

But it didn't come.

She heard a commotion rising around her instead. The sounds of distant splashing, and the sudden shouts of gruff voices carrying over the water.

"Police! Stay where you are! Do not move!"

She cracked open her eyes, blinking as the gasoline vapors hazed her vision. Through stinging tears, she saw Loomis and Deputy Ramos, together with several other uniforms, wading toward the mud mound from different directions, their flashlights and handguns trained on Dana.

Their sudden appearance must have taken Dana by surprise, because she had made no attempt to move, her face oddly emotionless. But then the reality of her predicament must have kicked in, because she dropped the torch and sprinted for the shore.

Maggie was on her feet in a flash.

She had no intention of letting Dana escape.

Maggie lunged for her as she ran past. Dana hit out, trying to prevent Maggie from grabbing her. But Maggie was committed. She threw her whole weight into the tackle, knocking Dana off-balance. Dana managed to make it to the water's edge before her legs gave out, and she went down with Maggie on top.

Tepid water swamped over Maggie, flooding into her ears and mouth. Dana thrashed under her. Maggie struggled to breathe. She grappled to keep hold of Dana, but Dana was hitting out and trying to break free. Maggie had the advantage of being on top. But it was fleeting. Dana bucked, throwing Maggie off to the side and pinning her underwater.

She saw Dana's silhouette loom over her, distorted by the disturbed water, her fingers reaching down to scratch out Maggie's eyes. Blunt fingernails scraping at Maggie's face.

Maggie's lungs screamed at her to *breathe*.

She reached up instead, her fingers finding Dana's throat. She wrapped her hands around her neck and squeezed as hard as she could. Dana tried to throw herself off, but Maggie clung on, pressing her fingers into Dana's flesh with every ounce of strength she had.

Fire raged in Maggie's chest.

Then Dana's struggles subsided, and she collapsed into the water next to Maggie.

Maggie broke the surface, gasping for air.

Loomis was standing over her, up to his knees in the lake.

"You cut that close," Maggie said.

"You wouldn't believe how bad the traffic is this time of night." He grabbed Dana by her hood and hauled her to her knees. She coughed and spluttered as he slapped handcuffs on her wrists.

Maggie staggered to her feet, her gaze swinging to the beach, her heart suddenly fearful for her father.

But he was alone on the sand, a stick figure in the moonlight.

"The coward fled," he called weakly. "Took off through the woods the second he saw things going south."

"Go after him," Loomis said to Ramos.

But Maggie was already one step ahead, instructing the deputy to stay with her dad as she splashed across the narrows.

Then she ran back through the woods as fast as she could in the dark, barefoot and wet through, clambering up the grassy incline and out onto the roadway as the wail from approaching EMS vehicles split the night.

Kristen's car was gone, and with it, Tyler as well.

Chapter Thirty-Five

THE DAY AFTER

With the notebook clutched to her chest, Maggie slid open the sliding glass doors. She stepped outside onto her patio, pulling the pashmina around her as she crossed to the firepit. It was late, stars speckling an inky sky. A pearlescent moon skimming the trees, and a chilly sixty-nine degrees to keep the crickets quiet. She placed the notebook on the patio table and then loaded kindling into the firepit. Satisfied there was enough tinder to get things started, she struck a match, her eyes narrowing at the sudden flash of incandescence.

A full day had passed since the fatal showdown at Devil's Landing. A madcap twenty-four hours in which Maggie had had hardly a moment to breathe, never mind gather her thoughts and evaluate her own emotional state.

Some things took longer to percolate.

The arrest and consequent processing of Dana Cullen had prompted a raft of paperwork and interviews, as well as airtime with a team of prosecutors from the State Attorney's Office—their job, to assess how best to proceed with a case of this complexity. Two perpetrators committing three homicides meant marrying up various time lines as well as confirming clear lines of communication between both parties in premeditation.

A confession only went so far.

At this stage, pretrial, it was vitally important to cover every base, and Maggie had provided detailed statements to that effect, describing the course of events that culminated in the face-off at the lake and the subsequent execution of Thomas J. Cullen. She'd sat through two back-to-back interviews of her own: Smits accompanying her on a step-by-step walk-through of her every movement since Saturday, and the state attorney's prosecutors combing through her statements to make certain there were no holes for Dana's public defendant to exploit, allowing Dana to slip through to freedom. Tomorrow, or the next day, Maggie would sit in front of the Professional Standards Section to review her professional conduct within the remit of the office of sheriff, both before and after her being taken off the case. This was just the beginning.

And Maggie was feeling worse for wear.

In one respect, being busy had kept her mind at bay, preventing her from overanalyzing every little detail to the nth degree. In and around conversations with Smits and Corrigan, she'd had no time to think about herself and the emotional impact the last few days had had on her. Self-criticism was inevitable, she knew, with sleepless nights to follow, filled with her agonizing over all the ways she might have acted differently to change the outcome.

The what-ifs that drove Steve mad.

That was one of his earliest observations about her—that she tended to overly dissect situations after the fact, when nothing could be undone. He called it *perceived control.*

Maggie wasn't big on labels. And besides, there was nothing she could do about how she was made.

So far, she hadn't divulged to him the details of her close encounter with death, not sure if she was ready for his kind of professional assessment just yet. She knew she'd get it even without asking for it. In his own soft-voiced way, he'd tell her all the things she already knew. Package them up in neat little parcels with pink bows. Not just about the guilt she carried—that barb in her brain—but also the responsibility she felt over Dana's murderous actions. He'd prescribe coping mechanisms to offset the trauma, and she'd most likely reject them. He'd tell her he had every right to express concern for her. And she'd tell him that she could live without her mistakes being highlighted and lectured on.

They'd argue, but they wouldn't fall out.

Steve would have his say, and she would do what she did best—throwing herself into her work.

Officially still removed from the case, Maggie had had to be satisfied with watching from the observation room while Loomis and one of their Homicide Squad colleagues, Detective Clayton Young, conducted the interview with Dana.

It had been a tough watch.

Maggie had thought Dana might clam up, say nothing, saving her verbal retribution for the courtroom, where she could express her twenty-year-old hurt to twelve strangers and the rest of the world. But to Maggie's surprise, Dana had held nothing back, answering Loomis's questions concisely and without leaving anything out; all the while her icy gaze had never moved an inch from Maggie.

Of course, Dana had had no way of knowing that Maggie was watching from the darkened observation room; she couldn't see Maggie standing with Smits behind the one-way mirror. Nevertheless, it hadn't stopped her from staring directly at her, and it hadn't stopped Maggie's skin from crawling.

Over the course of two hours, Dana had told Loomis everything.

Not once did she ask for a lawyer, even though one had been on standby. And neither did she stop talking the whole interview. It was as though the floodgates had opened and all the dark waters had come gushing out.

Maggie had listened to it all, wishing she could go back in time and change the past so that none of this ever would have happened.

But such thinking was folly, she knew.

Dana's plan to kill Kristen Falchuck, fake her own death, and then frame her husband for the murder had been a recent manifestation.

Contrary to Maggie's fears, Dana hadn't dwelled on their bullying. Thanks to WITSEC, her relocation to Arizona had given her an opportunity to start anew, to shed her old skin and emerge as Dana Burnside. Twenty years ago, she'd put their stupid teenage bullying behind her and forged ahead.

Infidelity, of all things, had triggered the recent reprisals.

Cullen's cheating had come to light during one of their heated arguments, and Dana had vowed to defend her nest to the death.

Apparently, in the summertime, Cullen had undertaken a small landscaping job for Kristen's landlord—at the mobile home adjacent to hers—and Cullen had met Kristen.

A chance meeting with devastating penalties.

Everything was innocent and aboveboard at first. But at some point, Cullen had shown Kristen photos of Dana on his phone, and that's when Kristen had realized his wife's true identity. Instead of backing off, Kristen had come on to Cullen—at least, according to him— increasingly over the days he was on site, until they'd ended up sleeping together during one of Dana's weekend walkouts.

Since Kristen was unable to answer for her actions, it was anyone's guess what had driven her to insert herself in Dana's life again. If Maggie were to hazard a guess, she'd opt for jealousy. Pure and simple.

With no idea that Kristen was *the* Kristen of her youth, Dana had gone to the mobile home in Kissimmee, intending only to scare her off. But then she'd met *the other woman* face-to-face, discovering the true depth of her husband's betrayal, and it had tipped her over the edge, sparking a fiery wrath.

Over the next few days, she'd devised a plan to make her husband and Kristen pay for their adultery. Dana had canceled her life insurance—so that her husband wouldn't benefit financially from her death—and she'd withdrawn most of her savings, intending to use them to start her life again elsewhere using Kristen's ID.

Rita had already switched identities once. She'd morphed from Rita into Dana, changing the habits of a lifetime to play the role. A simple haircut and a bottle of peroxide, and—at a glance—Dana wasn't a million miles away from the image of Kristen on Kristen's driver's license.

Dana would disappear, ostensibly dead, but secretly transformed into Kristen.

And so on Halloween, Dana had paid Kristen another visit at her home in Kissimmee, this time to murder her with the revolver that Dana had stolen from Maggie's house the afternoon of Nora's birthday party.

Dana, not Kristen.

It transpired that Maggie's initial thought on the gun thief's identity had been right.

In her interview, Dana had explained that she had accompanied Kristen to the bathroom that day, and that she'd shown Kristen the revolver to impress her, right before making sexual advances toward her, only for Kristen to push her away in the same way that Maggie had rebuffed Rita's advances at the lake. Rejected, Dana had taken the gun, mainly to be a "bad ass," she said, burying it wrapped in an oil cloth in a safe place near her home on Oak Street.

The revolver had remained hidden there for twenty years.

Meanwhile, in her role as school guidance counselor, Dana had come to know the intimate inner workings of Lindy Munson and Tyler Pruitt. In confidence, she'd learned of Lindy's deep hatred of Tyler and of his infatuation with killing her. But it was only in the wake of Dana confronting Kristen that Dana spied an opportunity to use the teenagers' antipathies for each other to her own advantage.

The cold sell was, if Tyler helped Dana rid the world of her philandering husband and his mistress, she would help him realize his fantasy of killing the most popular girl in school. To sweeten the deal, Dana had paid the $3,000 deposit on Tyler's beloved Charger and agreed to stand as guarantor on the car loan. Tyler had been putty in her hands.

The plan had two parts, beginning with Tyler bringing Lindy to the clearing at the lake early Saturday evening, together with a kill kit. Dana had held back from telling Tyler how she was going to persuade Lindy to meet up with him, only that she would. Lindy, meanwhile, had listened to Dana's story of her own embarrassing experience at Devil's Landing twenty years earlier, and how Lindy could ruin Tyler the same way if she followed Dana's lead.

That afternoon, Dana had spiked her husband's drink with sleeping pills, then driven to Kristen's home, forcing her to the lake at gunpoint. She'd killed Kristen in cold blood, putting her wedding band on Kristen's finger and snipping off her pinky with gardening shears taken from Cullen's toolshed. Then, wearing her husband's work boots, Dana had tossed her own purse out onto the mud mound before setting Kristen on fire.

Dana hadn't told either of the teenagers anything in advance about what they would find in the clearing that night.

She banked on them panicking and calling the police, knowing that this was Maggie's patch and that she would mistakenly identify the burned corpse as that of her childhood friend Rita Grigoryan.

Cullen would be found guilty of his wife's murder, and Dana would walk away scot-free.

A foolproof plan, if not for the loose ends.

To keep Tyler leashed in and Lindy from talking, Dana had abducted Lindy later the same evening, locking her up in the trunk of her car so that she could present the girl as a gift to Tyler the next day. Dana had told how they'd listened to Lindy screaming and choking as the trunk had filled with noxious smoke and unbearable heat.

It was all bordering on madness.

Later Sunday night, Dana had sent Tyler to recover cash from her home in Paradise Heights. The cash she'd forgotten after arguing with her husband on Saturday afternoon, and also in her haste to intercept Kristen before she set out to work. Dana's intention: to drive out west in Kristen's car on Monday, maybe home to Arizona, and begin again.

But Cullen's release after the weekend had thrown a wrench in the works. He'd turned up at the house while Dana and Tyler were there searching for her money, and Tyler had beaten him unconscious.

It was in that moment that Dana had realized the folly in her plan: Maggie.

She'd chosen to kill Kristen at Devil's Landing because she knew it would bring Maggie into the picture. But what she hadn't bargained on was Maggie pursuing every line of inquiry, including the possibility of an alternative killer. Maggie had turned out to be the fly in the ointment. And Dana had realized that if she wanted to get away with murder, then Maggie would have to die.

Maggie added more wood to the firepit, stoking the red-hot embers. Heat pressing against her face and shadows dancing around the yard.

She thought about her lucky escape from a fiery death, knowing that luck had played no part in it.

After their talk in the street, Nick had called Loomis, telling him that she was with some thuggish-looking kid called Tyler, heading out to some place called Devil's Landing. Alerted to her imminent danger, Loomis had called for backup, dropping everything to rush to the lake in advance of Maggie getting there. Yet, despite her taking her time on the ride over, Loomis and his deputy entourage had arrived a couple of minutes after her, too late to save Cullen as they'd splashed through the lake in a pincer movement.

Not for the first time, Maggie owed Loomis her life.

Her gaze settled on the notebook she'd placed on the patio table. It was jacketed in black faux leather, identical to Dana's, minus the

Disney stickers. But this notebook was Maggie's, given to her by Rita over twenty years ago.

She picked it up and opened it to the first page, reading the words penned by her own hand:

The Make-or-Break Year

Rita hadn't been the only one to pour out her heart and soul on paper. Throughout the twelfth grade, Maggie had logged her own thoughts on paper, too—starting on the first day of school and ending the night of the Oak Street house fire. Dozens of life experiences and personal reflections that now seemed woefully defunct and somehow worthless. The musings of a silly seventeen-year-old girl who thought the world was hers for the taking.

Maggie flicked through the pages, glimpsing scribbled reflections on her last year before college.

It all seemed such a long while ago.

In some ways, puerile.

Someone else's life.

Without hesitation, Maggie tossed the notebook in the firepit, watching as the flames burned up her past until all that was left was a flaky husk.

She sensed someone on the patio behind her. "How long have you been standing there?"

"Few minutes."

Slowly, Maggie turned around to face Tyler Pruitt.

He was standing near the sliding doors, hands stuffed in his hoodie's pockets. There was grime smeared on his cheeks, and his eyes were red raw. It looked like he'd been crying a bunch.

It seemed like every one of Maggie's muscles tensed. "What are you doing here, Tyler?"

"Nowhere else to go." He sounded stressed, on the verge of crying. "Dana and me, we were supposed to be in California by now. She told me she loved me." His hand emerged from the hoodie's pocket, holding the Luger. "She promised we'd be together. If I did everything she said, which I *did*. Once her husband and Lindy were out the way. She said we could start a new life. Together. Far away from here. She lied to me."

"If it's any consolation, she fooled us all. She convinced us she was dead. That takes some doing. Is that why you're upset, because she lied to you?"

He shook his head. "Not really. It's Lindy. I can't stop thinking about her." His eyes welled up, and a quake ran through him. "She's in my head. All the time. In my *brain*. She won't go away." He looked at her imploringly, tears rolling down his cheeks. "How do I make her go away?"

"You can't. It's called a conscience, Tyler. I'm guessing killing Lindy wasn't the kick you thought it'd be?"

He nodded, sniffed, and rubbed a hand over his damp cheeks. "I just can't stop thinking about what I did to her. I mean, who'd do something like that? What did I do?" He tapped the barrel of the gun against his chest. *"What did I do?"*

Maggie raised her hands a little. Her heart was skipping wildly in her chest, but she kept her composure cool and collected. In as much as crisis negotiation was about what words were said, it was also about what the body language didn't give away.

She edged a step closer to him. "Tyler. Listen to me. It's going to be okay. You've done the right thing coming here. It shows you want help, and that's a brave thing to do." She took another careful step. "How you're feeling right now, I can make a lot of that go away. I can get you the help you need. Start to heal your pain. Why don't you put the gun down and we'll get you that help?"

He turned the muzzle back on her.

Maggie halted her advance.

"Why should I trust you?"

"Because you're here, aren't you? Talking with me. That says something. You didn't just end up here by chance, Tyler. You came here because you know I can get you the help you need."

"What if I'm here to kill you?"

Maggie didn't move, not even to blink. "The reason you feel as bad as you do right now is because you took someone else's life. And that's hurt you. Killing me will only compound those feelings. Make you feel a hundred times worse. Believe me, Tyler, I've seen what happens to people who make those kinds of wrong decisions. Things go from bad to worse in a heartbeat." She raised her hands a little more. "I know you want to do the right thing. You've already made a start by coming here. We can fix all of this right now. Just put the gun down."

He looked at her as though she were crazy. "Don't you get it? Talking isn't going to fix this. *She's in my head and she won't go away!*" To emphasize his internal torture, he tapped the gun against his brow. "I just want her to leave me alone! I can't take any more!" He jammed the muzzle against his temple. "Tell Lindy's mom I'm sorry."

Fire flashed through Maggie's chest. "Tyler, wait! Listen to me—"

He pulled the trigger.

And Maggie froze, not even breathing. She heard the gun make a dull cracking sound as the firing mechanism engaged, expecting to see blood and brain matter hurtling from an exit wound in his skull. But he just stared at her, teary and mystified.

The Luger had misfired.

Maggie reacted, adrenaline catapulting her forward at breakneck speed, both arms outstretched. She crashed into the boy with the palms of both hands, flat on his chest, hard enough to knock him backward off his feet.

With a resounding *clunk*, Tyler's head smacked against the doorframe, and he slumped to the ground, out cold.

Maggie pried the Luger from his hand and only then did she start to breathe again.

Chapter Thirty-Six

LIFE BEFORE DEATH

It wasn't the funeral itself that reminded Maggie why she did this job. It was those in attendance, the mourners, in their raven-black attire and the stretch hearses, yearning to share one last smile, one last word, one last kiss with their loved one lost.

In her time, Maggie had attended more funeral services than she could remember. Sooner or later, every homicide victim had one, and although it wasn't expected, a police presence was standard procedure. Not only did it demonstrate the city's steadfast support for the family; it also formed an unspoken promise that justice would be sought and served, no matter how long it took.

"The dead can't talk," Smits had told Maggie at her first death scene five years ago. "You need to do it for them, Detective. They rely on you to shed light on their death, even if it takes you to some very dark places. You'll do good never to forget that dead bodies are still people, with family and friends and lives before they died. Let them speak through you."

Lindy Munson's funeral service at Woodlawn Cemetery had been over and done with in the blink of an eye. A handful of teary teenagers from Crown Pointe, a few stiff teachers and Principal Ellis, a bunch of habitual funeral-goers, and Ronda Munson with mascara streaking her cheeks, every bit a wraith in her skintight black dress. When the minister had asked Ronda to say a few words about her daughter and Ronda had promptly crumbled under the pressure, Maggie had stepped in, sharing something her father had told her a long time ago. A tale of how matter could never be destroyed, only converted into energy, and how Lindy lived on in the minds and hearts of those who knew her. Her words, though, had seemed to have little impact, and Maggie had come away from the interment feeling hollow and needful.

She'd spent the next few days at a loose end and trying Loomis's patience, especially when news had come through that Tyler had attempted to take his own life again, this time in county jail.

Finally, she'd asked Loomis to drive to Nora's house, stopping by Target on the way. And now here she was, at the doorstep, facing Nora and watching Whitney's eyes light up as she cuddled the plush unicorn toy that Maggie was hoping would make amends for Halloween.

"I believe it comes with magical powers," Maggie said. "Do you like it?"

Whitney beamed. "I love it! Thank you, Aunt Maggie!"

"My pleasure, sweet pea."

Whitney disappeared behind her mommy, running down the hall with the unicorn galloping in the air beside her.

Nora gave Maggie a reproving look. "You shouldn't have, sis."

Maggie made a face. "Look, Nora, I know you're pissed with me right now about what happened with Dad. And that's okay. I'd be pissed, too, if it was the other way around. But this is about Whitney . . ."

"No," Nora said. "You don't get to switch things around so they're more convenient for you. He could've been killed, sis. And it would've been your fault."

Her words cut Maggie to the bone, and she made no attempt to defend herself. Nora was right. Because of Maggie, their father had been abducted and bound, psychologically tortured, believing he was seconds from being burned alive. Luckily for Maggie, he'd come through the terrifying ordeal physically unscathed. A routine checkup at the hospital, with a prescription to take things easy, and he'd gone home the same night. But the experience had left him shaken, and Maggie suspected even frailer than before.

"He could've been *killed*," Nora repeated.

"Since when do you care either way?"

Now Nora gaped at her. And even though Maggie felt justified in saying it, she regretted her outburst instantly. A river of bad blood had flowed between her siblings and their father for years now, especially since their parents' divorce, but it didn't excuse her punching below the belt.

Nora looked like she was about to blow her top.

A car horn sounded.

Maggie glanced behind her at the sedan parked across the driveway. Loomis had the driver's window rolled down and was gazing over the top of his Wayfarers. He gestured at her to hurry things up.

Maggie turned back to Nora. "I have to go."

"No peace for the wicked," she said coolly.

Maggie bit her tongue, accepting Nora's retaliatory snipe for what it was. Now was not the time to *get into it* with her baby sister. The time would come; the emotional tension had been building up between them for quite some time now. Insults would be hurled, and feelings would get hurt. No avoiding it.

She saw Whitney hurrying back toward them down the hallway, the unicorn tucked under her arm.

"Aunt Maggie," she called. "Wait! You forgot your broomstick!" She pushed past her mommy, handing the toy broomstick to Maggie.

Maggie managed a smile. "Thanks, sweet pea. This will definitely help me clean up the streets." She looked back at Nora. "Maybe you could give him a call? Just this once. Make an exception."

"Maybe."

"I know he'd love to hear from you."

"I said *maybe*. Don't you need to be somewhere else, sis?"

"I guess so."

The right thing to do would be for the whole family to sit down and thrash things out. Show Bryan and Nora once and for all that underneath the gloomy picture their mother had painted of their father was a forgotten masterpiece waiting to be revealed. But Maggie feared any such engagement would only deteriorate into petty squabbles and punitive strikes, and things would end up worse than they were already.

She kissed Whitney on the head, then waved to her niece all the way back to the street.

"Nora giving you a hard time?" Loomis asked as she climbed inside the car.

"Just the usual family drama." She let out a long breath and put on her sunglasses. "Okay. What's the big emergency?"

"Lunchtime. My belly thinks my throat's been cut. Luckily, I know this great little doughnut shop . . ."

Maggie couldn't help smiling as they drove away.

There were two things in life that she could rely on with absolute certainty: her partner's innate ability to lighten the load and the fact that no matter how many killers she helped put behind bars, there would always be another waiting in the wings.

Author's note

Thank you for choosing to read my first Maggie Novak thriller. Your support is sincerely appreciated. I wrote this novel for *you*. I hope you enjoyed it. If you did, tell everyone!

To be the first to hear about my next Maggie Novak release and to enter into my exclusive competitions to win signed books, please join my growing Reader List at www.keithhoughton.com, where you are more than welcome to stop by and say hello.

If you look hard enough, you can also find me killing time on Facebook and Twitter at https://facebook.com/keithhoughtonbooks and https://twitter.com/keithhoughton.

Acknowledgments

First and foremost, I want to thank my wife, Lynn, for loving me unconditionally. It isn't easy living with a writer. At times, my characters distract, and my thoughts often inhabit a world from which she is excluded. It takes patience and tolerance to put up with me and my daydreaming, and I am truly blessed to have her support, guidance, and friendship—without which none of this would be possible.

Lynn, you are my rock, my muse, my soul mate. You define me. Thank you for being you.

I want to thank my family for their love and laughter. Our gorgeous daughters and sons-in-law: Gemma and Sam, and Rebecca and Ruben. Our beautiful granddaughters: Willow, Perry, Ava, and Bella. And our lovely parents: Lynn's mum, Lillian, and my mum and dad, June and Bill. Together, they are my world.

I want to thank Amazon Publishing and the Thomas & Mercer team for believing in me and my writing and for their support with my T&M books throughout the year. In particular, I want to thank Laura Deacon, editorial director, for trusting in my vision for Maggie Novak and for allowing me to turn my dream into reality yet again.

I want to thank Charlotte Herscher, my developmental editor, for opening my eyes for a fourth time around. Her insights always act like a microscope, revealing details I might have otherwise overlooked.

I want to thank my copyeditor and proofreaders. Your input has helped put a high polish on the final manuscript, and now it's gleaming. Great job, guys.

Last, but not least, I want to thank my reader fans and author friends for sticking around for as long as they have. Writing is a solitary process, and I depend on their interaction on social media to keep me sane.

About the Author

Keith Houghton spent too much of his childhood reading science fiction books, mostly by flashlight under the bedcovers, dreaming of becoming a full-time novelist. When he was thirteen, his English teacher—fed up with reading his space stories—told him he would never make it as a science fiction writer. Undeterred, Houghton went on to pen several sci-fi novels and three comedy stage plays while raising a family and holding down a more conventional job. But it wasn't until he started writing mystery thrillers that Houghton's dream finally became reality. Though his head is still full of space stories, he keeps his feet planted firmly on the ground, enjoying life and spending quality time with his grandchildren.

Houghton is the bestselling author of the three Gabe Quinn thrillers—*Killing Hope*, *Crossing Lines*, and *Taking Liberty*—as well as the stand-alone psychological thrillers *No Coming Back*, *Before You Leap*, and *Crash*. Please visit www.keithhoughton.com to learn more.